THE KING'S HOUNDS

MARTIN JENSEN

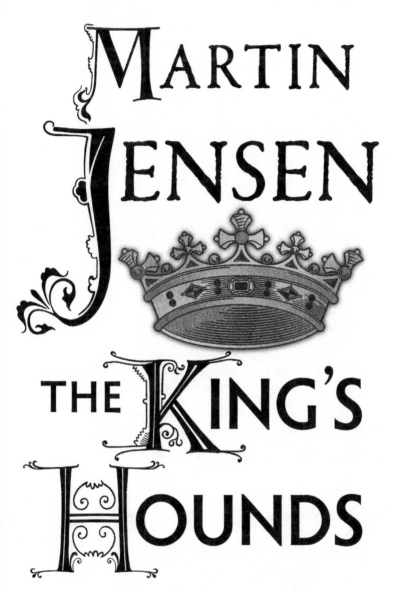

THE KING'S HOUNDS

Translated by Tara Chace

amazon crossing 🌐

Text copyright © 2010 by Martin Jensen and Forlaget Klim
English translation copyright © 2013 by Tara Chace

The King's Hounds was first published in 2010 as *Kongens Hunde*. Translated from Danish by Tara Chace. Published in English by AmazonCrossing in 2013.

Published by AmazonCrossing, Seattle

www.apub.com

ISBN-13: 9781477807262
ISBN-10: 1477807268
Library of Congress Control Number: 2013903047

Cover design by Edward Bettison
Front cover crown illustration created by Edward Bettison
Floral pattern—From THE ART OF ILLUMINATION—DOVER PICTURA Royalty-Free
Back cover illustration inspired by public domain images found in the British Library Catalogue of Illuminated Manuscripts, http://www.bl.uk/catalogues/ illuminatedmanuscripts/reuse.asp

England

SCOTLAND

NORTH
SEA

IRISH
SEA

IRELAND

NORTHUMBRIA

THE DANELAW

MERCIA   ELY
        ENGLAND   EAST ANGLIA
WALES   ASSANDUN
        OXFORD LONDON

WESSEX

FRANCE

North Sea Empire

NORWAY

SCOTLAND

DENMARK

IRISH KINGDOMS

ENGLAND

HOLY ROMAN EMPIRE

NORMANDY

Prologue

he prior had allowed Winston to have his way.

Winston's worktable was now pushed all the way up against the wall so the light from the window shone on his station from the left, just as he liked it.

Brother Theobald, with his white tonsure, had sulked for several days before giving in and instructing the other scribes to defer to Winston, even though he felt that Winston had stolen the seat that should rightly have belonged to him, the senior scribe, the brother who had been in charge of the scriptorium for as long as anyone could remember.

Winston didn't care about any of that. They had hired him to create a book, which the abbot and the prior had vigorously stressed was supposed to be unprecedented in quality—standing out even among the one-of-a-kind manuscripts routinely produced by the monastery—and Winston was therefore in a position to demand the very best working conditions, which included having the light fall just right on his worktable.

Although the idea for the book had originally been the abbot's, Prior Peter had been the one to send the messenger for Winston. The dark-haired prior with the chiseled face had handled all the contract negotiations, and Winston had only set eyes on the abbot once, on the day he arrived.

Winston had slid the contract across the table to the abbot and Prior Peter. He had scribbled the document a few evenings earlier over a tankard of ale in a tavern not far from Medeshamstede, in a village so small it was a wonder it even had a tavern. They had each read through it carefully and then, following a nod from his superior, the prior had simply signed it. They had given Winston everything he asked for.

The brethren valued high-quality work, and they were willing to pay for it. They also knew that they would need to meet Winston's terms if he was going to do his job to their satisfaction.

So, on top of his wages, they also agreed to pay for costly lapis lazuli, the best available grade of red lead, and the highest karat of gold leaf.

And when Winston rejected the first sample pages they showed him—the quality hadn't been anywhere near his standards—they also agreed to let him mark the lines on the vellum himself. Although Winston supposed laymen such as the abbot and the prior might consider the lines acceptable, to a trained eye, they were plainly crooked. Worse yet, the text was marred by spots where a scribe had obviously tried to correct his mistakes.

And as Winston pointed out to Brother Theobald and the prior—the former listening with his lips pursed—this was meant to be the most beautiful book the king would ever behold. So Winston crossed out a section of the contract and added a clause giving him the right to approve every individual page, even as Brother Theobald claimed through gritted teeth that that should be his right as the monastery's senior scribe.

As the scribes sat hunched, methodically moving their metalpoint styli over their manuscript pages, adding letter to letter, word to word, and line to line, Winston sketched out drafts of his illustrations on pieces of vellum of such poor quality that even Theobald would have thrown them away rather than wait for Winston to make that decision. Winston also spent his time browbeating the three scribes whom Brother Theobald considered talented enough to entrust with coloring the initial letters.

One of the scribes was actually skilled enough to task with outlining the initials using a graphite pencil, after which he would present them to Winston for approval. Then the scribe would ink over the outlines and hand them on to the other two brethren to apply the color—again, under Winston's strict, watchful eyes.

The abbot was deeply shocked to hear the news that Edmund had died and that Cnut Sweynsson now sat on the throne as the sole king of a unified England.

Although Ely Monastery had been established several centuries earlier, its coffers were limited. But like its founder, the current abbot dreamed of transforming Ely into one of the country's greatest and wealthiest monasteries.

Which was how the abbot had come up with the idea of commissioning a precious illuminated book. It would tell the story of their founder—Saint Audrey—in words and pictures, starting with her birth as an East Anglian princess more than three hundred years earlier. The book would feature her two husbands prominently, because there was no way she could have remained a virgin through two marriages without their consideration. Instead of forcing her to rule as queen of Northumbria, her second husband had even granted her leave to enter a convent run by an aunt, the abbess of Coldingham Abbey. The book would not mention that he had almost immediately come to regret this decision—and how his change of heart is what had driven Audrey to flee south to the Isle of Ely, which she had received as a dower gift from her first husband.

The abbey she founded on Ely grew under both her and her successors' leadership to become a rich, influential convent, which it remained right up until the Danes burned it to the ground a hundred and fifty years ago.

Now rebuilt, Ely was once again home to a religious community, this time a monastery of Benedictine monks whose abbot was commissioning this book. The abbot had planned to present the book to King Edmund Ironside as a gift and subtle reminder that the Isle of Ely had been donated to the Church for religious use and that it should continue to be used for that purpose in perpetuity.

But then a Danish king defeated Edmund in battle. And then Edmund died.

And now the brethren didn't know what to do.

Vikings had burned the monastery once before. And the English hero Byrhtnoth was buried here. True, he was not a saint—but many Englishmen still made pilgrimages to his grave, wishing to honor the loyal ealdorman who had suffered such a famous defeat after allowing the Viking army to cross the causeway at Maldon and gain enough of a foothold to vanquish the English. Byrhtnoth had lost his head for it.

Rumor had it that the abbot had even considered having the hero of the Battle of Maldon dug up to appease the country's new Viking king, but that he thought better of it after he dreamed he saw Byrhtnoth and Cnut piously kneeling before Audrey, each resting a hand in hers as she brought them together.

Yes, this book would be the perfect way to bridge the monastery's past and future, and Winston was the man to illuminate it. He was widely reputed to be the best painter and illuminator in all the land.

And what a timely dream, Winston had thought during the long winter months as he worked beneath that window in the scriptorium. If the hands of the English and Vikings could be joined, it would mean that the work he'd already done on this book, though originally meant for Edmund, wouldn't go to waste; it could be presented to Cnut instead.

Winston grew up in a monastery. He had been a pious novice until one day it dawned on him that his abbot always bent the Word of God to suit his own ends. Initially Winston kept this realization to himself, praying that God would allow him to accept that of course God would sooner speak to an abbot than to a novice. And Winston thanked the Lord for surrounding him with examples of the piety and pride that the other monks took in their work.

But the final straw came shortly before the end of Winston's novice period. One day, in the presence of witnesses, a freeman farmer said that his only sister should inherit his estate. But after the man's death the abbot lied, claiming that the farmer had changed his mind and on the following day said that his property should go to the monastery. The abbot won the inheritance case by reminding the man's sister of the Lord's own words—how it was easier for a camel to go through the eye of a needle than for a rich man to enter the kingdom of God—which meant that it was in her own best interest for the court to rule in favor of the monastery.

A huge argument had erupted between Winston and the abbot, which had resulted in Winston suddenly finding himself outside the monastery walls with nothing but the cowl on his back.

He prayed for God to smite the abbot with a bolt of vengeful lightening, but to no avail. God remained silent.

Winston resolved that very day to turn his back on a God who had sent his own Son to advocate for widows and the fatherless while allowing his holy Church to trample on the rights of those very same people.

Winston had not prayed, set foot in a church or chapel, or taken communion again since, and he had avoided the communal monastic prayer services wherever he worked. With an open heart and a straight back, Winston reassured God every morning that the day He allowed his wrath to rain down upon the abbot back home, Winston would once again dedicate himself to God's service.

Neither the abbot nor the Good Lord could take from him the things he had learned during his many years as a novice. He was an illuminator and painter, the best in the land—and not just in his own estimation but also that of the monasteries, noblemen, and bishops who sent for him.

His services were expensive. Very expensive. If you wanted the best, it would cost you. And the money was all his. That was one advantage of his having been ejected from the monastery.

The abbot tried to cause trouble, of course. He told everyone that Winston was a lapsed monk and that no one should work with him, but most people didn't care. A magnificent illumination was more important to them than a broken monastic vow. Especially when Winston told them it was a lie and that he had been kicked out of the monastery before taking his vows.

And then, many years ago now, the abbot died. Winston hurried home to find out how it had happened and was disappointed to hear that the less-than-pious father had passed away peacefully in bed. No wrathful lightening, no oozing boils, no painful, pus-filled sores. He hadn't even coughed up any blood.

Winston continued to paint, filling vellum after vellum with inspiring pictures and dazzling illuminations. And every morning he repeated his pledge to God. If the Almighty would shatter the abbot's headstone with lightening or cause his body to fly up out of the grave, blackened and infested with suppurating boils, Winston would once again dedicate himself to His service.

But as far as he knew, the brethren back at the monastery were still tending a tidy, unafflicted grave.

The light was fading outside, where the air smelled of spring, but Winston could still see well enough to paint.

He had begun coloring his masterwork ages ago. The image of Saint Audrey with King Cnut and the hero of Maldon kneeling before her filled more than half the page.

The text was unusually attractive, curling across the page above his ink-lined illumination. Not a single letter was wrong, each line was as straight as the ruler itself, and the initial letters, adorned with stags' heads, gleamed in blue and red. Under his hand, the painting in the middle grew day by day in fresh, radiant colors.

This was the last one. All of the other pages were ready. As soon as he was finished, the binders would take over. He would be out there in the spring air, on his way to a new job. He didn't know what it would be yet, but experience had taught him that some new opportunity always presented itself.

In a week at most, Winston would be able to retrieve his mule from the stables where he had been gorging himself full and glossy on the monastery's good oats. Together they would head off into the war-ravaged countryside, seeking shelter at the first hint of approaching danger. Winston mostly stuck to side roads and forest paths, far off the beaten track traveled by the soldiers, who wanted to get places quickly. After being shut up in this damp monastery for so many months, Winston was rather looking forward to drifting through the spring weather at a leisurely pace.

There was a sudden gust from the window as the door at the opposite end of the scriptorium opened. However, neither the draft, nor the sound of heavy footsteps crossing the floor—steps not made by sandal-clad monk's feet—distracted Winston from his work.

Winston only looked up when Prior Peter cleared his throat.

A redheaded Saxon warrior, well dressed and adorned with silver with clean skin and freshly washed braids, stood next to the prior.

"Winston, this is Alric. He has a message for you."

The illuminator picked up a rag from the edge of his table and carefully wiped off his marten-hair brush before turning his attention to the warrior. "For me?"

The warrior nodded. "The Lady Ælfgifu requests your services."

"Ælfgifu? The Mistress of Northampton?"

Another nod.

Ælfgifu was King Cnut's consort. This could prove to be a major assignment.

Chapter 1

uckily they didn't have any hounds with them.

From my perch lying on my belly on the branch, I could see them advancing through the woods, spread out in a line: grim-looking men bearing spears, swords girded at their sides, their eyes scanning the bluebells that blanketed the forest floor.

But they never looked up, not even once.

My brother, the ever-smiling Harding, had taught me that trick: men rarely look up when they're hunting. As a boy, I had followed him around loyally, the way a dog follows its master. When he and my father had gone off to fight for the king, Harding had promised to win me an estate.

Now his body was feeding the worms down in East Anglia, and I never did get that estate. Just the opposite—I lost the one my father had held. But I still remembered what Harding had taught me.

The leaves weren't as thick on the tree now as they would be in a few weeks, but it was old, with thick branches and plenty of twigs. As long as I kept my eyes hidden, I felt safe.

That was another thing Harding taught me: If you hide the gleam of your eyes, you hide yourself.

The branch I was on was so wide that no one would be able to see my body from below. So the moment I spotted the search party approaching, I calmly rolled over and stared up into the oak leaves above me.

I should have stopped at the bread. Even a Danish nobleman as tenacious as my pursed-lip pursuer down there wouldn't have bothered chasing down a bread thief. But this was the second day in a row that he and his men had been searching for me.

Oh, but the girl had been so pretty with her blonde braids, her wide, inviting mouth, and those curves beneath her dress, which she'd so willingly let me fondle.

Yes, *willingly*. I've never had to take a woman by force, and this girl had certainly been no exception.

I had made it out unhindered through the palisade that enclosed the estate.

The manor was large and prosperous, making it very clear that one of the Danish victors lived here. Someone who didn't fear his neighbors and who could afford to let anyone enter—tradesmen, wandering craftsmen, pilgrims, landless men in search of a place they could call their own, or even just a roof over their heads in exchange for some backbreaking toil for the lord of the manor.

There were warriors in the courtyard. Of course. This nobleman was confident, not stupid. The warriors were watching me, and I had made it halfway to the hall when three of them approached me.

I asked if there was any work to be had and got the same answer as everywhere else: a shake of the head. The victors were eager enough to expand their farmlands, but they had no use for a single man.

A man who showed up accompanied by a woman with a baby at her breast and several kids clinging to her skirts would receive a stick hut in exchange for the privilege of slaving away for the new master. A man with a family can be controlled. But no one has leverage over a single man.

One of the warriors—brawny, with a bare chest and ash-blond braids down to his belt—pointed silently back toward the gate. I turned around and took a few steps, then paused and went back.

This time I repeated my question in their language, instead of in English.

They stared at each other. Then they grabbed me, turned me back around so that I was facing the gate again, and shoved me on my way.

Idiots. Surely they could hear from my perfect Danish accent that I was not an Englishman. It's not like I'd painstakingly learned the language of the victors just to please them. My mother was Danish—so Danish was literally my mother tongue, and my father was Saxon, so I spoke both languages fluently.

I reached the gate just as an oxcart was rolling in. One glance over my shoulder told me that the warriors had already turned their attention elsewhere, so I ducked behind the cart and walked behind it, bending over as it rumbled past the Hall and came to a stop between two outbuildings.

No one had noticed me, not even the driver, and I didn't waste any time. I popped into the building next to the peat-covered outdoor oven—and luck was on my side. Several rows of bread were cooling on the long wooden racks mounted on the walls inside.

Without hesitating, I grabbed two wheat loaves—I could get rye or barley anytime. This was my chance to sink my teeth into sweet nobleman's food. I quickly tucked them inside my tattered coat, wincing as the still-hot loaves touched my belly. Just as I turned to slip back out the door, three women walked in.

The two in front were carrying a handbarrow between them filled with bread. The woman in back had blonde braids and soft, voluptuous lips. Her clothes betrayed her high social status—as did the fearlessness with which she looked me in the eye.

"What are you doing in here?" she said in Danish, clear and forthright, her head held high.

"They told me Asmund was in here," I said. I spoke without hesitation.

"Asmund?"

I nodded. There was bound to be at least one Asmund in any Danish manor.

"You mean Asmund the Shepherd?" said one of the servant girls, who also looked quite attractive under her gray shift dress.

"Who else? I don't know any other Asmund." You should always sound like you know what you're talking about.

"And just what would a shepherd be doing in the bake house?" This nobleman's lass wasn't dim.

I shrugged. "How should I know? They said he was here in the hut. I didn't even know it was the bakery until I walked in."

"Well, he's not here."

I grinned at her. "I can see that."

Cradling the loaves with my hand inside my coat so I wouldn't drop them, I headed for the door. I had just reached the threshold when her voice stopped me. "Well, don't you want to know where he is then?"

"That's all right. I'm sure I'll find him."

But it wasn't going to be that easy.

"Wait!" she called.

I looked across the courtyard. The three warriors hadn't noticed me yet, but they were bound to spot me once I got closer to the outer gate. So I waited while the three girls whispered together.

"He's grazing the animals in Cuckoo's Meadow today," she said, walking over to me. She smelled clean.

"Well, then I'll go find him there." The warriors glanced up at the sun, which was approaching its midday zenith.

"So you know where Cuckoo's Meadow is?" There was a hint of teasing in her voice.

I waved my hand vaguely toward the woods outside the palisade. The warriors were watching three of their colleagues, who were walking over to them from the other side of the courtyard.

And sure enough, once they were all together, my pals all headed straight for the Hall and their waiting dinners.

I nodded to the girl and strolled across the courtyard as if I owned the place, waving boldly at the new gate guards. I made it to the gate unimpeded. Although men entering a manor were stopped, anyone on his way out wasn't considered a threat.

The planting fields around the manor were a good arrowshot wide so no one would be able to approach me unseen.

As I set out toward the edge of the woods, following the dusty ruts worn deep into the dirt by years of carts and horsemen, I half expected her haughty voice to stop me again, but the girl had obviously believed me. No one stopped me from entering the woods.

I followed the wheel ruts for a while. Eventually I stopped and, hidden behind a tree, glanced back. I walked another few arrowshots before veering off between the trees, onto a narrow footpath, through a carpet of bluebells that led to a floral-scented clearing with a stream running through it.

Sitting against a beech trunk, I devoured the sweet wheat bread, noting my stomach's gratitude after several days without any food. Then I walked over to the stream and drank. I would have preferred ale, but after my run-in with those girls, it would have been tempting fate to search for the brewery as well.

My stomach was full, the day was warm, and my legs tired from several days of walking.

I woke up to someone kicking me in the side. Not hard, the way a warrior would have done, but not gently either.

I lay still without opening my eyes, but I didn't shut them tighter, either. I made sure my breathing didn't change. I know how important it is to control your body, so that you still look like you're asleep.

Another kick. I made a sleepy face, rolled over onto my stomach so that my right arm was just in front of the kicking foot, and continued to breathe deeply and evenly.

When the next kick struck me, I gave a good hard whack; the pain shot up my forearm as I hit the kicker's shinbone. I jumped to my feet with my knife out before the troublemaker had even hit the ground.

I dropped on top of the fallen kicker, straddling the offender's torso with a knee on either side and my knife under his jaw.

Fortunately, I recognized the person before I stuck the knife in.

Her eyes were dark with rage and her voice shrill, but there was nothing to suggest any fear in the girl's face. "What do you think you're doing?"

I grinned at her. The second time I had done so since I'd met her. "Right now? Nothing. A minute ago I was defending myself against an unknown assailant."

"Assailant?" she scoffed. "Get off me."

"Oh, don't worry, I'm not uncomfortable." My eyes slid down her body, then glanced back toward the path we'd both followed to get here.

"You lied," she accused me.

I nodded. "Not for the first time."

"You could have just asked for the bread."

"And a nobleman whose warriors had already kicked me out would have given it to me?"

She didn't say anything. "I would have . . . if you'd asked."

She might have been telling the truth. Or maybe—since I was still straddling her with a knife to her throat—she just thought a little white lie was in order.

"Who are you?" She didn't appear to be in any hurry for me to move.

I saw no reason not to tell her. "Halfdan."

"Halfdan. So your father . . . ?"

"Was Asulf of Oakthorpe. My mother, his second wife, was a Dane."

"Was?" She didn't look angry anymore, and was still not the least bit afraid.

"My mother died when I was very young. My father fell at Assandun."

"Oh." She still didn't show any signs of wanting me to get up. "A lot of good men died that day."

"Others survived. *Your* father, no doubt. As well as one person who should have fallen, but luckily *he* eventually got what he had coming to him." My voice oozed with bitterness.

"You mean . . . ?" She looked puzzled for a moment and then nodded as though she'd solved a riddle. "Eadric Streona." As a Danish speaker, she had trouble with the Saxon name.

"Yes. They call him Eadric the Grasper in your language." I spat on the ground. She didn't need to know any more than that. "And you are?" I asked.

"Tova, Ømund's daughter."

"Ømund?"

"Who fought with Cnut at Assandun."

A nobleman, in other words. A common warrior would not have fought *with* the Danish king, but *for* him.

"And now he owns that manor back there?" I guessed. Nothing like sitting astride the daughter of a Danish warrior who had surely taken many English lives.

"My father is King Cnut's thane and owns a great deal of land," she said, her voice laced with pride.

"For now," I said.

But she saw through me. "For now? So, you think the Anglo-Saxons are going to put together some kind of effective army?"

"No." I shook my head. She was right. The Danes ruled this land now. Well, the Danes and any Saxons who had made their peace with King Cnut. Eadric, that traitor, had paid with his head when Cnut discovered he had lied and switched sides. Other good men who had survived the Battle of Assandun were Cnut's men now, now that Edmund Ironside was dead. King Cnut and King Edmund had divided the country between them while they were both alive. Cnut would get everything north of the Thames, and Edmund all the land to the south. But whichever of them lived longer would inherit all of England.

So when Ironside died, Cnut got everything.

I looked at the girl. "Why did you follow me?"

"To see if you were lying."

"Hmm." I ran my finger over her cheek. "Why don't I believe you?"

Her eyes darkened, but I stopped her from answering by moving my finger over her lips and leaning forward. With my mouth right up to her ear, I whispered: "Where are the warriors?"

"There . . . there aren't any warriors." She couldn't ignore my weight on her body.

"A nobleman's daughter doesn't go out into the woods by herself to check if someone is lying."

"I . . . I . . ."

I let my hand fall over her breast, felt her nipple through her clothes. It was not immune to my caress. "You wanted to see what kind of man I was."

She shook her head and tried to break free.

When I brought my mouth to hers, she kept her lips clamped shut. At first. But I know how to caress a woman, and her mouth eventually opened to mine.

It wasn't rape. Although that might have been what she told her father afterward to try to avoid getting into trouble.

She was certainly no virgin. I was sure of that from the moment she first spoke to me. Her outspokenness wasn't just a consequence of her noble birth. No virgin would ever have spoken so cheekily to a strange man.

She was a young woman who knew how to enjoy lovemaking, and who finished me off with her mouth after letting me caress her to her own gasping delight.

She was too wise and experienced to let me enter her, but there was no way the man who came whistling down the footpath could have known that when he spotted us lying together, relaxed and naked, looking exactly like a pair of postcoital lovers.

The fleeting pause between his grin at spotting our intertwined bodies and his shudder when he recognized the girl is what saved me. I leapt up and forward, slammed my fist into his temple, and watched him fall like an ox under a butcher's ax.

"Who is he?"

Tova stared at him blankly. "One of my father's tenant farmers." Then she turned back to me and said, "That's some fist you've got."

"And I run fast, too," I said, grabbing my clothes. I gave her one last kiss and darted across the clearing. I didn't stop to put my clothes on until I was safely surrounded by tree trunks. The spring afternoon was still young, and I planned to be far away by nightfall.

Whatever story Tova made up for her father, it did not dispel his anger about a stranger bedding his daughter.

While resting under a tree that night, I was awakened by the sound of approaching warriors. That had been two days ago, and I'd been on the run ever since.

I considered climbing down from the tree and running in the opposite direction of the warriors, but I decided it wasn't worth the risk.

Instead I waited, my stomach complaining more and more vociferously. After evening had fallen, I was rewarded with the sight of the warriors, now retracing their steps dejectedly. With their spears over their shoulders and their swords sheathed, they were chatting casually among themselves and paying little attention to their surroundings. They didn't look up this time either, and soon disappeared back down the footpath.

I decided it would be foolish for me to go out on a limb now, so I stuck it out on my branch until morning, dozing in fits through the spring night filled with cuckoo calls, waking with a start each time I fell into a deep sleep, and eagerly awaiting the dawn as I muttered curses about my rumbling stomach.

As the sun began to warm the air, I weighed my options. I had to get down, but figured it would probably be wise to keep away from all the manors and villages until I was quite a bit farther from Ømund's estate. Tova had mentioned that he owned a great deal of land, and as Cnut's thane, he was quite a powerful man.

I might encounter another wayfarer like myself, one who would be willing to share his food. Or, more likely, as I accepted with a shrug, I would find a wayfarer who could be forced to share what he had.

And right then, just such a wayfarer came into view.

Chapter 2

he wayfarer was alone, which was the most important thing. He was a little stooped and leaned on his staff. His clothes were worn but clean, from his leather shoes to the felt hat he wore pulled down over his eyes, probably to keep out the sun.

Plodding along behind him was the oldest mule I've ever seen. Its mane was thinning and gray, as were the sparse, straggly strands of hair visible on its flanks between big bald patches. A packsaddle hung crookedly on its sharp spine, as though the man hadn't checked it since cinching it on earlier that morning.

Neither a halter or bridle hung from the animal's drooping head, but it followed right at the man's heels anyway. The man stopped at the foot of my tree, pressed his hands to his lower back, and straightened up. As he rubbed his back muscles, he looked ahead down the path, spat, and began rummaging among the many packs on the saddle. He pulled out a half-filled swine bladder, held it to his lips, drank, then spat again.

"Yes, yes, Atheling, old friend. We're getting there."

He spoke in a West Saxon dialect. His voice was gentle.

I pressed my body against my branch, craning to see back up the path, trying to figure out who he was talking to. There was no one in sight, and as I scanned back and forth, he put the water bladder away and gave his mule a gentle slap on the neck. "Well, Atheling. Let's go."

As they disappeared into the woods, I smiled at myself for not realizing he had been talking to his mule. After they were gone, I lay there for a while on my back, thinking.

I hadn't seen any weapons on the man, nor did he look like a warrior—though I knew he must have a knife hidden on him somewhere.

Not that that worried me. If I could just get close enough, surely my own knife would motivate him to share whatever he had with me.

But then there was his staff . . .

It came all the way up to his stooped shoulders and was as thick as my wrist. In the right hands it could definitely be a lethal weapon.

Whether his were the right hands, I didn't know, but I had no intention of letting the man's staff answer that question. Given its reach, if he was any good with it at all, my knife would be worthless.

Once I was sure he was far enough away not to hear me, I climbed down from my tree and tracked him silently through the woods, scanning my surroundings as I walked.

Birds chirped all around. Cuckoo calls mingled with the chaffinch's trills, the wren's warbling song, and the great tit's uniform *dee-dee, dee-dee*. The sun was stronger now, and sweat trickled down my neck despite the shade of the trees. I was thirsty after all that time up in the tree and kept an eye out for a stream.

Before long, I spotted a meandering brook in a meadow to my left. The water looked cold and refreshing. I squatted down and drank, scooping water up in my cupped hand so that I could keep my eyes on my surroundings at all times. But aside from a roe deer that suddenly appeared through the trees to stop and graze, there were no signs of life.

I saw a copse a ways downstream and headed toward it. I studied the slender oak saplings and supple ash trunks I passed on the way, and selected a straight oak—which could not have been very old as the trunk was no thicker than my forearm. Still, it took quite a while to cut it down with my knife and just as long to trim the branches and strip the bark. However, by the time I was done, I held a strong, supple staff in my hands.

I set out for the man again, hoping that he would provide me with sustenance for the day. I was careful not to make too much noise, and ready to hide at the faintest sound.

The man and his mule had a good head start, but they were obviously not in any rush, so it wasn't long before I heard him chattering away in English up ahead.

When I got close enough to see the mule's ass, I began eavesdropping on its owner's conversation, and determined that he was talking just to hear the sound of his own voice. Apparently he did not have anything very interesting to discuss with his old fart of a mule.

The sun had passed its zenith when the voice suddenly took on a firm tone, causing me to stop in my tracks.

"Now, Atheling, my noble friend," I could hear his words clearly and rolled my eyes at the pun in the pack animal's name—very funny, a prince's title for a lowly mule. "Here's a patch of grass for you, with shade for me. It even seems to be ant-free. Let's dine here, my noble friend."

I waited until I thought he'd had time to sit down. Then I snuck closer. I stopped, hidden behind a thicket, and peeked out, shading my eyes with my hand.

He was straight ahead of me, right where the path curved around a small knoll. He lay in the grass in the shade of the trees, gnawing on hunks of meat that he'd sliced off a leg of lamb with his knife. The knife, a short seax, lay to his right. My eyes immediately sought his walking stick, which was leaning against the packsaddle on the ground, well beyond his reach.

The mule was grazing noisily in the sun on the other side of the path, plagued by flies, judging by the way it kept shaking its head.

I couldn't have hoped for a better situation. I would be on him before he even realized what was happening, and could easily whack him on the side of the head with my staff. While he was reeling—or better yet unconscious—I would have plenty of time to rifle through his things. If he happened to come to, an extra blow would knock him out cold and give me time to make a run for it.

I smiled to myself as I checked that my knife was loose in its sheath. I was just standing up, clutching my staff, when I caught sight of something moving in the ferns up on the knoll above the man.

At first I thought it was an animal, maybe a fox, awakened from its sleep and only now realizing that there was a human being nearby. But then the sun reflected off *two* pairs of eyes.

I slid quickly back down onto my knees, relieved I was still in the thicket. Whoever those eyes belonged to, they clearly had evil intentions toward my intended target. I cursed to myself but decided to wait and see how things played out. If there were only two of them, as the eyes suggested, I might as well let them do the dirty work and hope to surprise them later.

I waited, my mouth watering from the scent of the roasted lamb that was filling my nostrils. Though there was still birdsong coming from the trees, the buzzing flies swarming around the mule's head were even louder.

A man's head popped up out of the ferns on the knoll. Judging from the wriggling I detected in the ferns, his companion started moving to the left, but then stopped and returned to his starting point. Then the companion's head appeared above the ferns and both men started moving forward slowly.

It seemed that my target hadn't noticed a thing. He kept chewing his meat and taking swigs from the bladder, which, judging from the way he delightedly smacked his lips after each slug, did not contain water, as I had first assumed.

The two men were on him so suddenly that I jumped even though I was braced for it.

With scraggly hair and ratty clothes, the filthy pair reminded me of my father's swineherd after the pre-Christmas slaughter. A blow to the stomach knocked the wind out of the eater. The next blow—to the back of his head—dropped him to the ground. The first bastard pounced on the leg of lamb while the second grabbed the bladder and put it to his lips.

It was clear from the way they attacked the food—gorging themselves on huge chunks of roasted meat once the bladder was drained—that they were even hungrier than I was.

Suddenly I thought: What if this was all the food the Saxon had? Then my painstaking pursuit of him would have been all for naught, while these two bastards would walk away with full bellies.

The victim groaned, but his attackers hardly gave him a second glance. His legs twitched slightly and then he went still again.

I gauged the distance between the thieves and myself. Five strides should do it. And my staff would probably make the last two steps unnecessary.

And I had the element of surprise on my side.

I quietly stood up again. Clutching the staff in my right hand, I burst out of the thicket, screaming.

That was another thing Harding taught me: "Scream like a pack of devils. You'll paralyze your enemies with your noise."

It worked. Their jaws dropped and half-chewed lamb tumbled out of their mouths as they gaped at me in terror.

One, two, three strides. I swung the staff and struck the closer one on the head. He fell over with a thud.

I pulled the staff back, then realized my mistake.

The second one now stood before me brandishing a sword in his left hand, and one look told me he knew how to use it. He swayed gently from side to side on firmly planted feet, his eyes locked on mine.

What a fool I had been not to notice his sword belt just because he wore the sheath on the wrong side.

He feinted at me. I jumped back, and tried to use the staff to my advantage, but he just knocked it aside and closed in on me so fast I didn't even have time to pull it back.

I smelled his foul breath and saw the triumph in his eyes and cursed the fact that I was about to die for the sake of a stupid hunk of mutton. I tensed my abdominal muscles for the blow I knew was coming.

He grinned, but then his eyes suddenly rolled back in their sockets, and he made a sound akin to that of air escaping from the stomach of a swine that was being slaughtered. He doubled over, moaning, and dropped his sword, which gave me a chance to swing my staff and strike him on the back of the head.

As the man collapsed, I spotted the Saxon sitting up on the ground with his own staff beside him. He had apparently drawn on his last reserves of strength to thwack the staff up into the bastard's balls.

"Thanks," I said. I surveyed the fallen men. The first bastard lay totally still, with blood and brain matter seeping out of his split skull. Although his companion lay face down, his moving chest revealed that he was still among the living.

I bent down and took his sword, noting how nicely balanced it was as I grabbed the hilt. Then I tied his hands behind his back with the man's own sword belt before turning to the Saxon, who was rubbing the back of his head.

"I'm the one who should be thanking you," he said, trying to stand up. He fell back on his ass and held his hand up to me.

I took hold of it and pulled him up, wondering whether now was the right time to hit him.

"You undoubtedly saved my pathetic life," the Saxon said, still rubbing his head but now standing. I noticed that he wasn't as old as I'd thought—forty at most. "What's mine is yours," he said.

In other words, I had found a wayfarer who would share with me willingly.

Chapter 3

t was good lamb, fatty and tender, and there *was* more than the one leg those bastards had sunk their teeth into.

From his mound of possessions, the wayfarer pulled a loaf of bread and another leg of lamb, brown and perfectly roasted, with rosemary rubbed into the fat. I hadn't tasted lamb like that since being forced off my estate.

He also pulled out a cask. The mead was sweet and not very refreshing, but I drank greedily until I noticed how strong it was and realized that my life might benefit from one less drunken night.

The Saxon watched me in silence as I devoured the meat and bread. His blue eyes were bright and fearless, his face tan, and his hair—both under his felt hat and in his curly beard—was as blond as my own. He had slender hands with long fingers and was more wiry than burly. Yet, he still seemed like a man who could look after himself.

As long as highwaymen weren't dropping down on him from the trees, that is.

When I had eaten enough, I wiped the lamb fat and cloying mead mustache from the corners of my mouth. Then I prodded our captive, who hadn't moved or made a sound since I had immobilized him.

"He's awake," the Saxon said, not making any move to put away all the food he had unpacked. "But he's good at playing dead."

"Not as good as his companion." I looked at the flies that had abandoned the mule for the blood on the dead man's head.

"I'm Winston," the Saxon announced.

Courtesy dictated that I announce my name as well. "I'm Halfdan."

I had felled his attackers, eaten his food, drunk his mead, and now we had learned each other's names. I gave up on my plan of attacking him.

"I'm on my way to Oxford. And you?"

I shrugged slightly. "Wherever the wind blows."

He raised his eyebrows. "You speak like a nobleman, but I've never met one of those who didn't know which way he was going."

I shrugged again, then leaned over the bound man. "Pisspots alive!" I exclaimed. "He reeks like a tannery."

Winston's eyebrows were still raised when I looked back at him. "A nobleman who doesn't like questions," he said.

Oh, what the hell. "I lost my father's estate to a Dane," I said.

"So you're saying you lost *your father's* estate? You mean, it wasn't even yours?"

I took a deep breath—why try to keep it secret when I'd already spilled half of it. "My father and brother died fighting the Danes at the Battle of Assandun. I was allowed to hold onto the estate as long as Ironside was alive."

"King Cnut claims he will recognize the existing land holdings of the English," Winston said.

I spat on the ground. "Kings claim a lot of things when it suits them. When Ironside died, English landowners were suddenly left in the lurch, without a champion. My men all abandoned me the first week, and a horde of Vikings descended upon me the next."

"And yet you're still alive?" Winston said, his eyebrows still raised.

"I was one man, alone. Well, aside from my thralls. At least I was familiar with the footpaths around my estate."

"You ran away," Winston surmised.

I glared at him. "I said I was only one man. Against a horde of Vikings."

Suddenly Winston smiled. "I'm not judging you. Far too many Saxons are rotting in the soil because they chose to die for honor rather than live for revenge. Is that what you're looking for? Revenge?"

"Revenge?" I replied. "Against whom? Cnut and the Danes, the victors who collected their spoils as they went? They fought valiantly and conquered this land fair and square. Or maybe revenge against a certain traitor? If anyone should bear the blame for the English loss at Assandun, it should be him, don't you think?"

"Oh," Winston said, his eyes widening. "You're one of those."

"Those?"

"Those who cheer the death of Eadric the Grasper."

I spat again. "Hard to think of a man who deserved his death more! May he burn in hell and be denied salvation."

Winston gave me a shrewd look and said, "So you have no bone to pick with King Cnut, even though he had Eadric—his own ealdorman and one of his most trusted counselors—assassinated?"

"I don't give a goat's fart about Cnut—or any other king. It is the right of kings to conquer. But Eadric's treachery—first he sides with Edmund, then Cnut, then back to Edmund, then Cnut again—was the reason Cnut won the Battle of Assandun. To betray your own is lower than anything." I stopped. I had not said so much to any man since I had fled.

Winston continued, "It's been almost two years since King Edmund died and you escaped the Danes on your estate. What on earth have you been living on?"

I didn't say anything. It was none of his business that I had stolen, robbed, and cheated to get food.

"You're a nobleman and yet you don't carry a sword?" Winston asked.

Would his questions never end?

I glared at him. "A sword can be lost," I said.

He fell silent and eyed me with uncertainty. Could he tell that I'd sold it one day after I hadn't eaten in a week? That its price had been dry bread and a half flitch of pork so salty I'd been parched all night because I was too hungry to soak the salt out of it before gobbling it up.

I could see from his eyes that he could tell even more than that.

"And you? Who are you?" I asked, trying to take the lead.

He chuckled. "Me? I'm no nobleman or warrior's son. I'm a peaceful il-luminator."

My ignorance must have shown on my face, because he explained: "I draw and paint."

He had to be joking. No one could live off of that. But he looked sincere when he asked me, "Can you read or write?"

Why in the world would I be able to do that?

"No," Winston said, shaking his head. "I don't suppose you can. But other men who can't read still value the importance of writing. Kings, bishops, and ealdormen are all eager to see their deeds written down so that their greatness—or whatever acts they undertook to honor God—will be known for posterity.

Now I understood what he was talking about. The local ealdorman once visited our estate on his way to the Witenagemot, the council of high-ranking nobles and bishops that the king convened periodically for advice. The ealdorman had shown my father a gift he was going to present to the king—this was during Ethelred's reign. It was an animal hide with something that looked like little, black spiders sprinkled all over it. A *book*, the ealdorman had called it, a story describing the deeds of Ethelred's father, Edgar. And I remember the picture painted on the top of the hide: King Edgar's face in vivid colors, a painting so lifelike I almost thought it would speak to me.

"Oh, so you write books." I wanted him to know I had understood.

"No," Winston said, shaking his head. "I leave the writing to other people. At one time I did, of course, but now I enhance the texts that other men write with my illuminations. Many people can write, but only a few of us understand the art of illumination."

The bound man could not hold still any longer. He whimpered and tried to raise his head.

"If you move, I'll stab you," Winston said casually, as though he were offering the brigand a sip of ale. The thief lay still.

"They caught me off guard," my new acquaintance continued, turning back to me. "Otherwise I'd have held my own."

I believed him. A man who spoke so casually of stabbing people was generally willing to do it.

"Why are you headed to Oxford?" I asked

"Ah," he said as he started packing up the food. "I have been summoned there by a lady who would like me to paint a picture of her husband in a book."

A lady? Well, I suppose he wasn't that old, and with his sinewy body and neatly trimmed beard, women might indeed find him desirable. But he'd said "lady" and not "woman," so did he mean a noblewoman? I gave him a questioning look.

He smiled fleetingly. "The finest lady in the land today, according to some. Of course, others say she has been outshined by her replacement."

I guess he could tell from my face that I had no idea who he was talking about, so he clarified: "Ælfgifu, the king's first wife, is in Oxford. Or on her way there, at least."

Ah, I understood. The replacement who outshines her must be Cnut's *second* wife—Queen Emma. I knew King Cnut had married his first wife, Ælfgifu of Northampton, a few years earlier when his father originally conquered England. She'd already borne him a couple of sons. Since Ælfgifu was a prominent landholder, it was a prudent match, and one that also gave Cnut an air of respectability. He couldn't be too much of a barbaric Viking marauder if he had an English wife and children, now could he?

I also knew that Cnut had recently married Ethelred's widow, Emma of Normandy. But what was news to me was that he had never actually divorced his first wife. So now he was apparently married to both of them, despite the outrage of certain members of the clergy. I reluctantly admired him for it—for being king enough to not give a dung heap about other people's outrage, not even the Church's.

"And what does the queen want with you?" I asked.

Winston narrowed his eyes. "Interesting that you say *queen*. I've heard that people call Ælfgifu Cnut's consort now, instead of queen. But in any case I've already answered your question. I'm going to paint King Cnut for her."

"So he will be remembered for posterity." I nodded.

Winston smiled again, fleetingly. "So the king will remember that it was Ælfgifu who paid tribute to his great deeds, in book form. Have you never seen two women competing for one man?"

Was he mocking me? There had, of course, been a time when I'd had my pick of the girls, so I nodded.

"And now," Winston continued as he began lifting his belongings back onto his mule, which had walked over to Winston as though he had read his mind. "It's time we got going."

"You call your animal Atheling and yet he is not the son of an English king, is he?" I asked.

He grinned. "Yes, a crown prince's title as the name of a mule. Whenever Danes hear it, they laugh out loud and immediately strike up a friendly conversation with me."

"And Saxons?" Not that I personally took any offense on behalf of a dead king.

"The Saxons who remember King Ethelred think he was such a bad king that his sons deserve to have a mule named after them and are favorably disposed toward me for expressing their feelings." Winston had finished securely strapping the packs on. "Shall we go?"

I looked at him in confusion. "We?"

"Well, I was thinking the wind seems to be blowing us in the same direction. Or would you rather live off what you can filch along your way?"

I was right. He knew far more than he let on.

"What about him?" I asked, kicking the bound man in the side.

Winston shrugged. "If you feel like dragging him to Oxford where he can be properly hanged, be my guest."

No thanks. I'd never have a moment's rest. But leave him here? I walked over to the prisoner. His eyes pleaded with me and he spluttered nonsensically as I thrust his own sword into him. Because, well, I didn't have a rope now, did I?

Chapter 4

lived better during the three days it took us to reach Oxford than I had for a long time.

The packs on Winston's mule were a seemingly inexhaustible larder from which he conjured forth meat, bread, cheese, and, yes, even butter—not to mention sweet, malty ale and several casks of mead. I ate my fill several times a day.

We spent two nights sleeping under trees so big they shielded us from the morning dew. Since the weather was warm and dry, we woke up to birdsong and the sunlight's elfin dance shimmering through the trees.

Winston was good company, actually. Not too chatty but not cross or glum, not even early in the morning, or at dusk as we dragged our weary feet through the grass.

He didn't ask any more questions about my previous life, which was fine by me. I was eager to gloss over any topics that would feed any of his lingering suspicions that I might rob him.

He, however, was quite forthcoming about himself, and during the first two days of our trip he told me his life story. His vivid and animated tales made the time pass more quickly as we walked along through the warm spring days.

I was right about his accent. He was born in Wessex more than forty years earlier, the son of a warrior who had served in King Edgar's fyrd and been granted a farm and land as a token of appreciation for bringing the body of the king's thane home for a Christian burial after a battle. Winston's father had gone on to wed his childhood sweetheart, Winston's mother. Though her father was quite anxious for her to marry a landowner, she had turned down several other good offers of marriage. But her fidelity paid off. When she married Winston's father, she became mistress of one of the loveliest farms in the village and mother to three strapping sons. Winston was the youngest.

The eldest of the three brothers had had to flee north of the Humber after being an accessory to the murder of King Edward the Martyr. Before it had even become clear that Ethelred would succeed him, Winston's family received word that his brother was dead. So Winston's middle brother took over the farm. He had been willing to share the farm with Winston, but Winston didn't want to spend his life trudging along behind a plough or find himself forever stooped from swinging a sickle under a burning autumn sun.

Instead, his brother had paid the nearby monastery to take Winston in as a novice. Winston's eyes lit up when he recounted his years with the monks, and he became very animated as he described the ornate books and scrolls he'd held in his hands. He even regaled me with a selection of the stories they contained.

"You weren't a monk, were you?" I asked.

That was the only time he'd gone quiet. His mumbled answer was so unintelligible that I still didn't quite understand why he had never taken his vows.

I fished for more details, of course. At first I assumed that he, like so many other young monks, had been tempted by carnal desires and that he'd incurred the wrath of some ossified abbot, but he firmly dismissed that.

He made no secret of his susceptibility to feminine temptations, but he said it wasn't until long after his days in the monastery that he first experienced the joys of resting upon a womanly bosom.

Then I suggested that maybe he'd been tempted by the monastic community's coffers—perhaps he'd been lining his cowl, so to speak—but that implication made him quite angry, and he said I should shut up about things I knew nothing about.

"I'd be happy to," I said, "but only if you tell me why you ran away from the monastery."

He grew vague again, and the closest he came to an explanation was that faith was very difficult to explain.

That didn't help me at all. After all, faith is very simple. We live, and then we die, and if we live the way the priests tell us to, we'll wake up in Paradise.

I said as much, but he dismissed me again, adding, "You have obviously never thought deeply about these issues."

Well, he was certainly right about that. He who thinks too much forgets to act, and he who does not act will be struck down by his opponent.

All right, I thought. *Everyone is entitled to their secrets.* I didn't ask him any more questions. Instead I listened as he explained how he had benefited from everything he had learned at the monastery.

While he was still within the confines of the cloister, it had become clear that he was a gifted artist. Whenever people looked at his drawings, they couldn't be sure whether they were looking at reality or just some reflection of it.

So, while he could undoubtedly have earned a comfortable living as a scribe copying texts, he earned much more from his painting, enough that he had never known hardship.

Bishops and abbots, earls and kings were willing to cross his palm with silver if he would illuminate the manuscripts meant to exalt and honor their names, decorate an altar, or enrich a monastery's library.

He preferred the word *illuminate.* Apparently "draw" wasn't fancy enough—though why he thought some fancy Latin term from across the sea was better than an English or Danish word was beyond me.

In any case, he had been living well for many years, and now—as he had already explained—he was on his way to Oxford at the behest of Lady Ælfgifu.

We continued to talk as we strolled along, with the mule following behind us. As I said, the weather was good, the days light and the nights warm. Although we encountered a fair number of other travelers, we didn't run into any trouble. Well—I did have one problem, but I didn't exactly "run into" it. Rather, it was following us: Atheling couldn't stand me.

That first night when I tried to help Winston unload the animal's packs, it scowled at me suspiciously. When I tried to run my hand along its flank to soothe it, it splayed its lips back and sank its stumpy teeth into my arm.

Those teeth may have been worn down some, but their bite was firm and hard. I ended up with deep tooth marks in my arm before the confounded beast relaxed its jaws. I swore and punched the animal on the forehead, to which it responded by stepping sideways onto my foot and scraping it bloody.

Winston, who was rolling out blankets on the grass, looked up at my enraged outburst. An amused smile spread over his lips, but after one look at my face, he sternly told the animal to behave.

I scoffed and pointed out that he was talking to a dumb animal, but Atheling took a step back, turned his back on me, and started haughtily munching grass.

From that moment on, the beast took every possible opportunity to irritate me.

I quickly learned to stay out of reach of those stumpy teeth, though it did me little good. The animal was neither small nor nimble but it had an uncanny talent for stealth—when it wanted to. Whenever I turned my back, I ended up taking a hoof to my ass.

When the path grew so narrow that we had to walk single file, I walked in front of Winston, because otherwise the mule would sneak up behind me and sink its teeth into my shoulder. Atheling would shake my shoulder and then let go before my yells drew his master's attention. I swear by Saint Wystan that by the time Winston turned to look, the animal would already have backed away. Winston simply shook his head sadly every time I claimed his beast had attacked me.

By the end of the second day, I had learned to keep an eye on the animal and keep enough space between us.

Soon the blue sky clouded over, and the swallows, whose twittering had followed us loudly all day from high up beneath the fluffy clouds, started swooping very low to the ground. Recognizing what this meant, Winston suggested that it would probably be wise for us to find some shelter for the night. Just as the first tentative drops of rain hit us, we saw smoke rising out of a clearing a few arrowshots ahead of us. As we started running toward it, Atheling brayed grouchily, objecting to our new pace.

It was raining hard and Atheling was a long ways behind us by the time we rushed through the palisade surrounding the hamlet, which consisted of three small farms and a few other buildings. As we huffed and puffed our way toward the biggest farmhouse, armed villagers stepped out of their doorways, and scrutinized us with wary eyes.

Winston stopped, gasping for breath, and held up his palms to the man he guessed was the hamlet's leader. Then he explained that we were peaceful travelers merely seeking shelter for the night.

The farmer, a short tree trunk of a man with big hands and fleshy jowls, eyed him skeptically. "Your companion is armed."

Before Winston had a chance to respond, a din of braying, hoof beats, and clanking erupted behind us. The farmers stepped forward, their eyes angry and their spears raised, but broke into smiles when the noise turned out to be Atheling finally catching up with us in a laughable approximation of a gallop.

As the farmers chuckled, Winston turned to me. Sure enough, I was wearing the dead robber's sword and sword belt. It was a good sword, one that had surely served the scoundrel well back in his pre-robber days, and I had taken it as well-deserved payment for having rid the world of two evildoers.

"Take the sword off!" Winston ordered.

I glared at him. I finally had a sword to display my rank as the son of a nobleman, and Winston was demanding that I take it off to pacify some flock of farmers?

My obvious rage did not deter Winston in the least. "Give them the sword, or spend the night out here in the rain."

It was pouring now, and judging from the brooding sky, it clearly wasn't going to let up before midnight. I looked at the hamlet leader, who had watched us in silence as I took orders from Winston—a man who was very obviously not my equal—but Winston showed no sign of backing down.

Fine! A couple of days ago, I hadn't had any sword at all, so I supposed I could do without it for one night. I frowned to make clear to everyone that I had decided to disarm *on my own* out of respect for my hosts, and was just about to unbuckle the belt when we heard voices calling to us from outside the palisade.

Everyone stiffened at the sight of five Viking warriors tramping toward us through the rain. The first three were dressed for battle in worn ring-mail byrnies, their shields slung over their backs. The last two wore only padded leather defensive jackets dotted with holes. Four were armed with swords, one with a long-handled ax that he swung menacingly in front of him. Five bedraggled warriors looking for some easy loot.

The ax-swinger came up alongside me, though he did not actually seem to notice me. The only reason he acknowledged us at all was that the hamlet leader stood his ground like a riverbank tree.

The Viking stopped in front of him, surprised to meet any resistance. "Move!"

He spoke like a Dane from north of the Humber.

I was not interested in giving up my lodgings for the night to a gaggle of bedraggled warriors, none of whom looked like they'd conquered anything more impressive than unarmed farmers lately. So I tapped the Viking's shoulder and stepped in front of him.

"Just a moment, there."

The Viking and his companions weren't the only ones whose eyes widened when they heard me speaking Danish. Winston, too, was astonished. He opened his mouth to speak, but one look from me made him shut it again.

"Are you talking to me, whelp?" the Viking said, evidently over his surprise.

"Here I stand, Halfdan of Oakthorpe, in the middle of one of my villages and, yes, I am speaking to you. And who are you?" I made no attempt to sound like anything other than the nobleman's pup that I had been two years earlier.

The corner of his mouth twitched nervously: I had guessed right. Here were five stray warriors on the lookout for easy plunder, but like all other underlings, they became insecure in the face of a superior.

"I'm Toste, my lord."

Good. He knew how to address me.

"And where are you headed?" I stared him down. Behind him I saw one of his companions start to move. It was all or nothing now.

"Uh, we're . . . we're going to London, my lord." Obviously a lie. He fiddled with the lead hammer pendant he wore on a leather thong around his neck.

"Then you're somewhat off course. Did you take a wrong turn after Derby?"

"Uh, Derby, my lord?" Good, I'd managed to confuse him.

That was yet another of Harding's lessons: If you want a man to respect your authority, you should do your best to confuse him by talking about anything other than what he expects or wants to talk about.

"Derby, yes. You're coming from the north. After Derby you should have turned southeast toward the paved road, Watling Street."

"Uh, well, no." He looked past me at his companions.

"Eyes on me!"

Harding was right about that, too. He'd said, "If you want respect, you need to act like you deserve respect." Toste's gaze returned to me.

"What do you mean *no*?"

"Uh, we were actually . . . We were just wondering if we could take shelter here."

"In my village? After you elbowed me? And called me a whelp?"

"I didn't elbow you, my lord." Now we were on the right track. I'd succeeded in making him make excuses for himself.

"And I suppose you didn't call me a whelp either?"

"Um, well yes, my lord." He looked almost remorseful.

"So you're a pack of soldiers from the north who think they can forcibly eat, drink, and fornicate in a village belonging to a thane from Kent? Who's your commander?"

"We fight under Thorkell the Tall, my lord."

"Thorkell is the Jarl of East Anglia. Are we in East Anglia now?" I said firmly. Winston moved next to me but froze when I flashed him a stern look.

"No, my lord. But Thorkell is on his way to Oxford."

"And you? Why aren't you with him?"

"We . . . we, uh . . ."

"You thought you would do a little plundering on your own, didn't you? Well, you've come to the wrong place. This is my village. I won it at Assandun. Were you there?"

He shook his head.

"Do you know what I would suggest?" Following yet another of Harding's tips, I made my voice cheerful now that I had the upper hand.

He shook his head.

"I suggest you get your asses out of here. And if I don't see you again before I reach Oxford, where I also happen to be headed, I vow not to mention this incident to Jarl Thorkell. How about that?"

He half turned to his companions, but stopped when I cleared my throat. I saw over his shoulder that the other four didn't have much to say. He was their spokesman and leader for good reason, and I'd cowed him.

"Uh, yes, that sounds fine, my lord."

"Good." I lowered my voice again. "Are you hungry?"

He nodded.

"Let no one say that I sent men out into the night hungry." I turned to the hamlet leader, who had followed the whole exchange in silence. "Give them some bread."

As I'd expected, he understood me. He turned and called out to a nearby building. A slave girl immediately appeared with five loaves of bread, which he handed out to the Vikings. They had already turned to leave when my voice stopped them in their tracks. "Toste!"

"Yes, my lord?" He was obviously struggling to keep from biting into the bread.

"If I see Jarl Thorkell, I'll tell him you're a sensible man."

His face lit up. "Thank you, my lord!"

Harding was right once again. Once men of low birth have recognized your authority, they're easy to satisfy. Perhaps he even thought I believed his story?

We stood there in the rain until they were out of sight. Then the hamlet leader gave a quiet order, and three peasants exited the gate to make sure the Vikings were really gone.

Winston walked up to me. "Halfdan of Oakthorpe in Kent?"

"My father's estate. It's so far away that I didn't think they'd know it belongs to a Dane now."

"You're Danish? I thought you were Saxon. You speak Saxon perfectly."

I grinned at him. Now that it was all over, I just wanted sit down. "I'm both, which, as you've just seen, can come in handy."

Chapter 5

he hamlet's leader provided us with lodging, food, and ale, and the villagers no longer insisted that I surrender my sword. Although we had hearty appetites, both they and we knew that if those rogue Vikings had had their way, it would have cost the hamlet a great deal more than a little meat, bread, and ale.

The rain let up overnight, and by morning, sunlight glittered in the dirt square, which the showers had failed to turn to mud. Winston announced that we planned to hit the road before the day got too warm, and no one tried to convince us to stay.

Gratitude has its limits, of course.

We walked briskly, Winston in the lead. As I rushed along behind, I kept one eye on Atheling, who only bit me once, when Winston stopped suddenly because a hare had leapt up right in front of him.

As I stopped to avoid crashing into him, I felt the mule sink his teeth through my shirt. I drew my sword and smacked the stupid animal's forehead with the pommel before it had a chance to react.

Atheling kept out of biting range after that.

After walking through the forest for a while, we reached the main road leading to Oxford. There was room for us all to walk side by side now, and more traffic than we had seen at any point in the last three days.

Peddlers struggled along under their heavy loads; farmers' wives carried baskets of eggs and vegetables in their arms with chickens tied together by their legs slung over their shoulders, on their way to town; freckled knaves were herding lambs to market; one lone, insolent, potbellied merchant astride a droopy-headed nag bawled orders for people to clear out of the way; and every once in a while we heard the shouts of marching soldiers— which quickly cleared the entire roadway ahead of them.

There were a surprising number of soldiers on the road. Imposing, well-armed, battle-hardened platoons, comprised of King Cnut's personal bodyguards and his housecarls, all marched in unison through the dust. Thanes draped in silver rode in front, each followed by their own retinue of housecarls. And on one occasion everyone had to scramble to the edges of the road for a splendidly dressed Saxon—undoubtedly some ealdorman—and his enormous entourage.

We didn't see any sign of our five Viking friends from the night before, which was fine by me since they might have had time to think things over and start wondering what a man claiming to be a Danish thane was doing in an apparently English hamlet without any Danish soldiers for support. I could only hope that they still believed me and had put some distance between themselves and Oxford to avoid my ratting them out to Jarl Thorkell.

The sun was getting hot. Dust caked our sweaty brows and lined our nostrils, but we walked on cheerfully, encouraged to be nearing Oxford and content in the knowledge that Winston was expected there.

Over our porridge that morning, which we ate at an inn, he had asked me what my plans were. He looked a little suspicious, as though he might be wondering whether I was planning to attack him. After studying him for a moment, I decided that he'd meant the question innocently enough, and so I replied that now that the wind had blown me to Oxford, I'd have to wait and see where it would take me next.

Winston spotted an earwig in his porridge and grimaced. Then he nodded at the girl who had been assigned to serve us and asked her to pour honey over it.

"You could stay with me," Winston said, sounding impulsive.

I looked at him, but he was peering down at his porridge.

"With you?" I asked.

He nodded. "It's not exactly safe to travel on one's own these days. I mean, you saw that for yourself the other day. You may not be the greatest of soldiers—among either the English or the Danes—but both then and last night you demonstrated your fearlessness. I'm going to be working in Oxford for a month or two, and after that I'll move on. I could use a man of courage. There has been hardly any law, order, or security in this land since the reign of blessed King Ethelred's father. And now, with an army of Viking conquerors roaming the land, conditions are unlikely to improve in the foreseeable future."

I mulled this over. As a destitute and landless man, I admittedly had little in the way of other options, aside from continuing to live as a thief. Although I was a skilled swordsman, there were thousands of those, all of whom were applying to serve in the king's army now. And even if I should be accepted into his ranks, I didn't really have my heart set on that.

Though Edmund's very convenient death shortly after the Battle of Assandun had made Cnut ruler of all Britons, there was no hiding the fact that Cnut was merely a boy, victorious perhaps, but objectively speaking, untested both in war and on the throne.

However, it was true that he had demonstrated kingly mettle last year when he made short work not just of that lout, Eadric the Grasper, but also of other members of the Saxon nobility—even those of royal descent—who might pose a threat to him. And his hasty marriage to Emma of Normandy had further secured his safety.

By taking a Mercian princess, Ælfgifu, as his consort, Cnut had bound the Mercian nobles to his cause. And by marrying Emma, the widow of Ethelred the Unready, Cnut had gained a powerful ally in her brother Richard, the Duke of Normandy.

Still, the current peace was by no means secure, and I did not relish the thought of having to fight and die for Cnut—the man who was ultimately to blame for the deaths of both my father and my brother.

Winston's offer was definitely worthy of consideration.

"You'll pay me?"

He used his finger to wipe up the remainder of his porridge, sucked it clean, and looked up at me. "I'll feed you."

"I don't eat enough for that to make sense," I said. "My food, plus four pennies a month."

Winston spat a fly out onto the floor. "And you pay for your own clothes and weapons."

I thought for a moment and then nodded.

"Agreed." He got up, spit into his palm, and held it out.

As we shook hands, I wondered if I'd been too quick to agree.

For the first time since my family had died, I would no longer have to live hand to mouth. I could look forward to eating my fill every day, sleeping under a roof, and, at the end of each month, putting little silver coins into a coin purse, which was the first thing I planned to buy on payday.

As we were approached town, we saw plumes of smoke rising in the distance ahead of us. We were soon crossing the river at the ford that gave Oxford its name.

The actual ford was plenty wide, but so many travelers were crossing at once that it was mayhem. Some kept starting and stopping as they sought the crossing point that would keep them driest, while others had horses, donkeys, or mules that refused to step into the water at all. And still others were looking for ancient stones along the river's edge with which to say a prayer or make an offering to the river god, as the river was sacred to those with the old beliefs. And a last batch was looking for the ale stand that some enterprising townswomen would inevitably have set up.

The crossing didn't get any easier with troop after troop of soldiers and noblemen demanding the right of way and cutting ahead of everyone else.

So we had to wait awhile—time that I spent shooting Atheling menacing looks and patting my sword hilt, which caused him to bray defiantly back at me. Finally there was a gap, and we were able to cross.

As we walked into town, I saw that it had recovered from the fire that had razed it ten years earlier. The buildings and farmsteads looked well maintained. The fences around the yards and vegetable gardens were in good repair, there were no holes in the thatched roofs, and I saw no drooping doors or window shutters; the overall condition of the streets and buildings suggested a wealthy town. This impression was reinforced by the new church, which, like its precursor, was dedicated to Saint Frideswide.

Beyond the church, we spied a green branch over an open door, the mark of an inn. After Winston had tied Atheling to the designated post outside, we ducked through the doorway into a dark tavern filled with three long tables surrounded by low benches.

Six soldiers were seated at one table. Well-armed and burly, the men wore ring-mail byrnies with gold-hilted weapons and metal bands around their biceps. They had taken their helmets off since they were indoors, but kept them on the table next to their ale. These warriors were always on guard—even when they were drinking.

Winston glanced at them, mumbled a hello, then turned to me. I nodded to show that I understood what kind of men they were. King Cnut's personal housecarls accepted only the best warriors—and only those who owned swords with gold-inlaid hilts.

In front of an opening in the far wall stood two sawhorses with a plank laid on top of them. A woman got up from a stool behind the plank and asked what she could do for us.

She was not bad looking. A little old for my taste—probably around thirty—but well preserved and not badly dressed, in a linen blouse (which did nothing to hide her ample bosom) and a gray wool skirt dyed with green stripes. Her dark blonde, almost red, hair fell below her shoulders.

I couldn't help but give her an appreciative look—despite her age—to which she responded with a sarcastic grin before turning her full attention to Winston, who asked if she had a room available.

She studied him for a long time, and then looked me up and down. I flashed her my best smile.

"For how long?" she asked.

"A month, I should think. At least." Winston scratched his beard.

"Paid in advance. Board not included."

The room was behind the tavern, off a little hallway. There were four doors along the hallway, which led to the host couple's room, our chamber, and one other room that they probably also rented out. The last door led out to the alleyway behind the building, the hostess explained.

Our room was barely big enough to turn around in once we had brought our things in, but the bed was wide enough that we wouldn't be right on top of each other, and a window opened on to the narrow alleyway in back, so it wouldn't get too stuffy at night.

It took a while to haul all of Winston's things in through the tavern. In addition to everything I'd already seen, which included his various foodstuffs, he also had a lot of small parcels in his possession. There were little clay pots, bark boxes, triangular bags twisted out of worn parchment, neatly tied-up cloth and leather sacks, tins made of thin metal, and a bunch of parchment rolls—in addition to two duffel bags and a few rolls of fine cloth wrapped in canvas.

As I carried each load in, Winston stacked everything carefully in the room. After we were done, Winston pulled Atheling over to a stable that our hostess had recommended.

While he was gone, I took a seat in the tavern, which was now empty aside from our hostess, who was washing drinking bowls and tankards in a bucket she kept on a stand in the corner.

She glanced over at me, but continued her washing. She set the clean dishes up on a board that hung below the ceiling and tossed the water out the doorway. She didn't come over to the table where I was sitting until she was done.

"Yes?" She regarded me with almost total indifference.

"Ale, thanks," I requested.

She set a tankard in front of me and held out her hand.

"Uh . . . I . . ." I stammered, but Winston walked in the door just then. "And one for my friend, too."

When she set the second tankard on the table I nodded to indicate that Winston would pay.

The hostess accepted the coins, and Winston shot me an annoyed look, to which I replied, "Food was included. That was the deal."

"Hmm." He wrinkled his brow. "As long as you're not planning to live on ale."

I chuckled at him to put his mind at ease, then smiled at the hostess, who was back on her stool behind the counter. My smile had no effect on her.

The ale was good—malted and sweet—and we were both thirsty. Winston was soon peering sadly down at the bottom of his empty tankard. He turned to the woman and ordered two more. When she brought them, he held out his hand. "I'm Winston, and this is Halfdan."

The woman nodded at him. "I'm Alfilda."

"You're the alewife who runs this place?"

"Yes. And I'm the *owner*."

So, she was single. A shame she wasn't a little younger.

Chapter 6

inston asked the hostess to bring another couple of tankards, plus one for herself.

I could tell from her eyes that Winston shouldn't assume she was available for the price of a tankard of ale. Although he probably needed a woman, I thought he was moving a bit too fast. Even women who are getting on in years like to be flirted with a bit before being wooed in earnest.

But perhaps I had misjudged Winston's motives. When Alfilda returned to the table with our ales and a small cup of mead for herself, Winston didn't start showing off his tail feathers.

Instead he glanced around the empty tavern, took a slug of ale, carefully wiped his beard, and leaned over the table. "The town is full of soldiers and noblemen," he said.

She seemed surprised. "Of course."

"I'm sorry?" Winston looked confused. "Why do you say *of course*?"

"The king has convened a meeting of the traditional Saxon witan to meet here along with all his own Danish advisers."

"Here in Oxford?"

Winston looked at me, but I just shook my head. It was news to me, too—although it did explain why Ælfgifu had summoned Winston to Oxford.

"Where better?" Alfilda said, suddenly looking somber, as though troubled by a bad memory. "Everyone knows Cnut hates Oxford even more than London. London because the city opposed him. Us because of Saint Brice's day."

This time I nodded at Winston. I knew the story, though I had been merely a lad of five when it happened.

King Ethelred the Unready had truly deserved his reputation for acting on bad advice. That is, unless he'd come up with all his failed policies on his own, as some claimed. But frankly, I simply cannot believe that one man could have been so unwise. I can only think that someone advised him to have all the Danes already living in England massacred on Saint Brice's day.

My father had received the order as well, but he just rolled his eyes and ignored it. I mean, what was he going to do? Kill his own wife and son?

Many people thought the way my father did and simply ignored the king's command. But many others took the order as a welcome opportunity to do away with any ethnically Danish neighbors whose land they had been coveting.

In Oxford, the residents wrought a bloodbath at the order of the shire reeve. Oxford's Danes sought refuge in Saint Frideswide's Church, but to no avail. The English mob, whipped into a bloodthirsty frenzy, set fire to the church and many—far too many—Danes perished in the flames, King Cnut's aunt among them. People said that Cnut's father, Sweyn, swore to both Christ and his older, bloodier gods that his revenge would be terrible.

Years later, when the two Viking kings, Sweyn and his son Cnut, landed in our kingdom to conquer it, they attacked us with fire and swords, but nowhere were they as vicious as Oxford. They burned the town to the ground, and only after most of its residents were dead did King Sweyn permit the survivors to purchase his mercy.

Sweyn forced Oxford's survivors into their church—which the residents had rebuilt in the intervening years and which the Vikings had spared in the attack—and there, on the very site where his sister, Princess Gunhild, had met her death in the massacre, the people of Oxford were forced to prostrate themselves and beg for the king's mercy.

My eyes fixed on Alfilda. "Cnut summoned all the Saxon ealdormen, thanes, and senior clergy here for a meeting of the Witenagemot so that the Danes could kill them in revenge for the massacre?" I asked.

Alfilda shook her head. "No," she said. "Where have you been?"

I muttered "here and there," while Winston informed her that he had been hard at work within the secluded walls of various monasteries and that he'd been out wandering the peaceful roads for several weeks since then. Of course, if you asked me there was some debate about how *peaceful* those roads had been . . .

"So you haven't heard anything?" Alfilda asked skeptically.

"Not a damned thing," I said. Winston frowned sharply at me, probably to signal that I should let him do the talking since he was paying me. I frowned right back at him. Was I not the son of a nobleman?

Alfilda eyed both of us. Though she pretended otherwise, this innkeeper lady was quick on the uptake. She ignored our frowns and forthrightly explained that King Cnut had summoned simultaneous meetings of the Saxon Witenagemot and the Danish Thing in Oxford in order to broker a peace between the English and the Danish and unify the kingdom.

"After his victory, Cnut imposed the heregeld on all landowners—an army tax of 72,000 pounds of silver, which doesn't even include an additional 10,500 pounds he's demanded from London alone, because of that town's unmatched hatred of him. Now he's summoned everyone to Oxford to pay up, because his soldiers want to be paid for conquering England for him. So the nobility and clergy are flooding into Oxford from every corner of the land, with their mules and packhorses practically on their knees from their heavy loads of silver. Once the heregeld has been paid, Cnut will release the hostages he took to ensure that the payments would be made as promised. Only then will the entire kingdom truly be his."

"Amazing," I said, ignoring Winston's look. "But why hold the meeting in Oxford?"

Alfilda bit her lip. "Cnut is a tough devil—a lesson we paid far too dearly to learn. But I think he's also a wise man, because he says this meeting of a combined Witenagemot and Thing will mark a new beginning. He wants to sow the seeds of a single unified kingdom here, one where all his peoples—Saxons, Angles, and Danes—will live bound by the same laws and with the same rights and obligations."

"And Oxford is a better place to achieve that end than any other," Winston said, leaning across the table.

"Yes," Alfilda said, nodding. "Oxford has been the flashpoint of the hatred between the English and Danes. By making it the birthplace of a new national peace, Cnut is demonstrating that he means what he says."

"Hmm," Winston said, tugging on his beard. "That explains why Ælfgifu asked me to come here. Do you know where I can find the Lady of Northampton?"

Alfilda shook her head. "The king has been here for a few days, but I haven't seen or heard anything of either Lady Ælfgifu or Queen Emma."

"Well, I'll find her easily enough. Any Danish soldier is bound to know where she is." Then something occurred to Winston. "The town is full of people, and yet you still have a room available for us?"

"Yes, yes." The alewife ran a hand through her hair, shaking it so that a cascade of gold streamed over her shoulders. She certainly was pretty. "The king's shire reeve has a hall in town that Cnut has taken over. He ordered everyone else to pitch camp north of town. He ordered them all to camp together, with the Angles', Danes', and Saxons' tents all mixed up side by side. Only the king's housecarls and noblemen with special leave from the king are permitted to take rooms in town."

It was clear that she considered this to have been a wise move on the part of the king, and I was inclined to agree with her. First, it kept all the soldiers apart from his own bodyguards out of town. Second, it ensured that there were no enclaves within the camp where single ethnic groups could gather and hatch plots.

Winston stood up. "Then I know where I can find Lady Ælfgifu."

I stood up as well, raising a curious eyebrow at him.

"The shire reeve's Hall, of course. Come on."

It wasn't hard to find.

We ran into a platoon of housecarls the moment we stepped out of the inn. Since we figured we had a fifty-fifty chance—they were either on their way to the king's Hall or coming from it—we followed them, keeping about ten paces behind.

The streets and lanes were even more crowded now, so we moved closer, until we were right behind the soldiers we were tailing. Since the crowds parted for them the way a school of perch parts for a pike, we were able to get through before the crowd closed back in again.

The king might have ordered that only his housecarls could stay within the town limits, but no man of importance, be he Saxon or Dane, would dream of going anywhere without his retinue, so there was no lack of soldiers following behind their masters, all eyes vigilant. Cnut's personal housecarls lined the major streets, standing a few feet apart, warily watching the crowd. Not a single one of these battle-hardened men was slouching or even resting on his spear shaft.

After walking for a while through the lattice of narrow lanes, which were lined with the kitchen gardens and fences that surrounded the bigger houses, we came to a large square with a log building at its center. The Hall was half a spear-throw long and wider than two townhouses. The roof was freshly thatched, and the smoke rising from the smokehole was white from proper, dry firewood.

Three guards stood at the front entrance, which was wide enough for four men to enter abreast, with two more to either side of it. A platoon of housecarls lined the square in front, each with his spear butt resting at his feet and loins girded with heavy swords.

Winston walked up to the door without hesitation and stopped politely when the three guards in mail shirts positioned themselves in his way. He looked at them questioningly.

As I stood there in my shabby clothes with the highwayman's sword at my waist, one of them gave me a look that conveyed just enough scorn to make me feel that I had been sized up and found wanting.

A second housecarl, who wore a gold band around his arm that looked slightly heavier than those of his buddies, looked Winston up and down. Then in the guttural Danish spoken by men from the homeland—as opposed to the smoother Danish spoken in the Danelaw here in England—he asked, "What is your business here?"

"I have been summoned by Ælfgifu, the Lady of Northampton." Winston's voice was polite and unafraid. *That's when I discovered that the man could keep a secret!* He spoke Danish better than most Saxons. I stared at him wide-eyed, but his eyes stayed focused on the guard.

"So?" The Viking guard didn't move.

"So if you would take me to her or let her know that I'm here," Winston said, sounding somewhat less courteous. "I'm Winston the Illuminator, and this is my man, Halfdan."

The Northman looked at me blankly. "And you want to see the Lady of Northampton?"

"Who summoned me."

"*Summoned* you?" The guard flashed his buddies a jocular look, which they responded to by grunting, which I suppose was their version of laughter.

"Summoned me, yes. To perform a task."

"So our Danish king's consort is *summoning* Saxons now?" The Viking spat between Winston's feet. "Well, maybe that's how the king wants things."

"And you have a problem with that, Ragnar?"

None of us had noticed the man step into the doorway. He looked like he was the same age as me, but he was taller and broad shouldered, with a prominent, hooked nose and a narrow gold crown set on his dark blond hair. He was dressed in a leather tunic, with a blue doublet over it, and red trousers tucked into soft-leather ankle boots. A heavy sword hung from his gold-embroidered belt.

As Winston bowed, he shot me a look, but he needn't have worried. I wasn't dumb enough not to bow before the man who had just conquered the country.

However, the king paid no attention to the back of our bowed heads. He was instead glaring at his guard with a look that bordered on rage. The guard in question closed his gaping mouth and saluted by raising a hand to his chest.

"Well, do you, Ragnar?" The king's voice was quiet, but insistent.

The guard shook his head.

"Do you, Ragnar?" the king repeated, now in a voice that sliced through the air.

"No, my lord."

"Good." Cnut glanced at me and then at Winston. "You're looking for the Lady of Northampton?"

"She summoned me, my lord."

"So you said. To perform 'a task'?"

"She wants me to illustrate a manuscript."

"I see," the king said. A hint of amusement flickered across his blue eyes. "With any specific illustration?"

"With a portrait of my lord."

"Aha." Now the king was smiling. "Ah, women. Yes well, unfortunately it will be difficult to—" He stopped midsentence and looked out into the square.

We heard the guards cry out from somewhere behind us and instinctively turned to look.

The housecarls in the middle of the square had lowered their spears to hold a man back. Though dressed like a nobleman and carrying a sword, he lacked a retinue. He looked somewhat older than Winston and appeared to be wealthy, but his clothes weren't showy, apart from the blue cape over his shoulders, which was trimmed in expensive fur. The face beneath his graying hair was red, but I couldn't tell whether from anger or exertion.

"Not now, Osfrid," the king ordered in a hard voice.

"Not now, not yesterday, not last month, not tomorrow. Maybe never?" the man said. He could speak the language of the Danes, but there was no mistaking his Saxon accent.

"When it suits me." King Cnut nodded to the guards, who pushed the nobleman back with the tips of their spears. Though the man tried to force his way through, the housecarls dealt with him swiftly, spinning him around and nudging his coat-clad back out of the square.

The king had already turned his attention back to Winston. "As I was saying, it will be difficult to take you to Lady Ælfgifu. She's not here, you see."

"Oh . . ." Winston said, puzzled and disappointed. "She led me to believe that she would be."

"I decided otherwise." The king obviously didn't think his reason for this decision was any of our business. He turned, paused, and then turned back to us. "Have you traveled across the country?"

Winston nodded. "I spent several months working at Ely Monastery. The lady's message reached me there, and I've been walking for several weeks now to get here."

"And you?" the king asked me.

I looked the king in the eyes. "I have been on the move a bit longer than that."

Cnut's lips curled at the sound of my accent. "A nobleman?"

"I was. Until my father was killed."

Cnut correctly surmised that my father had opposed him, and gave me such an uncomfortable stare that it was hard not to look away. "Your father fought against me," he stated.

He was quite astute! If my father had been on Cnut's side, I would *still* be a nobleman.

"And he paid the price." I held my head high. I might have been face-to-face with my king, but I was still a free Dane, wasn't I? Well, a half-Dane at least.

The king was quiet. Then he nodded. "Did *you* fight against me?"

I shook my head.

"Good," he said. "Hand over your sword and follow me, both of you."

Winston and I looked at each other in surprise but did as he commanded.

A large fire was burning in the middle of the floor in the Hall. The walls were lined with bodyguards, and men were seated on benches between them. Judging from the men's clothing, I surmised that they belonged to the uppermost echelons of the king's entourage. There were several Christian clergymen, one of whom wore the white wool collar of an archbishop around his neck. He looked old, and I guessed it was Wulfstan of York himself.

None of them looked up or paid any attention to us as we followed the king across the Hall to a wide, carved chair. After sitting down himself, he gestured for us to sit on two stools that two attendants scurried over with.

"Now," the king said once we were seated. "Tell me how you intend to draw me."

The king listened as Winston spoke at length of illustrations he had seen. The king nodded occasionally, as though he remembered having seen them at one time. Winston also spoke of his own work, describing scrolls, manuscripts, monasteries, and churches I had never heard of. The king watched him attentively all the while. He nodded once when Winston mentioned a picture he had painted in a manuscript ordered by Queen Emma while she was still the late Ethelred's queen.

When Winston was done speaking, the king asked him several questions. First about Winston's work, then about his travels and the various monasteries and churches. Then about the abbots and bishops he had met, the towns he had lived in, and men he had met along the way.

Each question was carefully crafted in such a way that it was easily answered but left room for an attentive listener to infer a great deal more than what was said. I could see in Winston's face that he was fully aware of the king's intentions, but apparently he didn't mind.

Finally the king asked Winston about his trip from Ely to Oxford. Winston recounted what had happened to him day by day, the roads he had traveled, and the people he had met. He reported how he had met me, and the king snorted in disdain at the account of how the two highwaymen had met their ends. Winston then went on to describe our experience in the hamlet the evening before, though I tried to stay his tongue with my eyes.

When Winston had finished, the king turned and looked at me.

"And what about you, Halfdan of Oakthorpe, scarer of Vikings?" His voice was firm, but I heard a touch of indulgence in it.

"I have little to say. My father and my brother fell at Assandun, and my estate was taken from me."

"And you blame me for that?" Cnut's eyes darkened.

I shook my head. "No more than a horse, running around riderless after the battle, blames the Viking who grabs its reins. Soldiers fight, and they win or lose. My relatives lost."

"Hmm." Cnut studied me for a long time. "But there is one person you hate."

I took a deep breath. "The dishonorable ealdorman who betrayed his own men and switched sides midbattle to fight for you."

"Him, yes. He is now rotting with London's garbage," Cnut stated.

I nodded. "And yet my hatred for him lives on."

"Hate is wasted on a dead man. Grow up and learn to use your hatred instead of wasting it on the dead," the king said, pausing to nod at a servant, who rushed over to offer us tankards of ale.

The ale was better than any I had drunk in a long time. I emptied mine, but Winston took only a sip.

"Have I given my lord what you wanted?" Winston asked.

The king's lips curled. "You have confirmed many things I already knew, and that's a good thing. I may have need of you, so your trip here won't have been in vain. And of you, as well," he added, snapping his fingers at me.

Just then a commotion erupted by the door. People were shouting in both Saxon and Danish, and we heard steel striking steel. A guard toppled backward through the doorway, and was followed by a screaming figure whose arms were spinning like mill wheels.

The king showed no reaction, but housecarls rushed forward from all sides with their spears lowered. The interloper was soon standing in the center of a circle of spear tips, which, however, had no effect on the screaming.

I looked at Winston, whose face shared my surprise at a woman bursting into the king's Hall. Before either of us could open our mouths, however, the woman pointed an accusing finger at the king, unleashing a scream that reverberated through the Hall: "Damn you who call yourself king but are no more than a common murderer!"

Judging from the woman's Saxon accent and appearance, I guessed that she was a nobleman's wife in her mid-thirties, but it was hard to tell, since her silhouette was dark, backlit against the bright doorway. The king nevertheless seemed to recognize her.

"You're not making any sense, Tonild. Go back to your husband and ask him to teach you how to behave."

"My husband! My husband?" Tonild screamed. "Whom you've had murdered and tossed like some dog in a common alleyway?"

The king stood up so abruptly that he tipped his chair over. "What is this nonsense? I saw Osfrid healthy and alive just a short time ago."

"I suppose you've been sitting here surrounded by witnesses while you had one of your Danish dogs stab him," the woman spat, frantic with despair.

"Godskalk!" The king took a step forward and bellowed the name again. An opulently dressed housecarl rushed over. "What is this woman talking about?"

"I don't know, my lord, but I have men waiting outside."

"Good. Let's go."

No one stopped us from following closely on Cnut's heels—which we did both out of curiosity and because the king hadn't finished talking to us yet. He hustled out the door with three housecarls in front of him and Godskalk at his side. Outside, three men were lying dead on the ground. Though the housecarls and Saxon soldiers alike were breathing heavily at each other, all their weapons were now lowered since the Saxons were clearly outnumbered and the presence of the king held the housecarls in check. Three housecarls escorted the woman out of the Hall and paused as the king brusquely ordered her to take him to her husband. "To his body," he said, correcting himself. "Your men will stay here."

We walked across the square, down a narrow street, where people stepped well out of our way, and took a sharp right into an even narrower alley. The woman stopped before a small group of people clustered outside the open door of a shed. The king had his housecarls clear everyone out of the way so that he could step up to the doorway. Winston and I followed behind him unimpeded, and we all peered together into the shed. The man we had seen earlier lay on a white-scoured floor, his unseeing eyes staring straight up into the air and blood congealing on his stomach. A faint scent of horse manure emanated from the room.

The king whistled as he inhaled deeply, and then he turned to the gawkers behind us. "Did anyone see anything?"

The people backed away in horror, not wanting to get involved in such a serious matter. People might have a certain natural curiosity about a killing, but one that had drawn an obviously irate king to the scene of the crime was beyond dangerous.

I watched in amazement as Winston walked into the shed, sniffing. Then he bent down over the body and slowly inhaled through his nose.

The king noticed him as well. "Just what in the name of all the saints do you think you're doing?"

Winston looked calmly at Cnut. "It might be easier to find this man's killer than one might think."

"What do you mean?" The king stared at him, not understanding.

"I'm almost certain he wasn't killed here. I think he was killed somewhere else and then dragged to the shed. A murderer who strikes in a back alley may do so unseen. Someone who carries his victim around afterward will have a harder time."

Cnut shook his head. "Explain yourself, man."

Winston looked over the king's head at the woman, who had finally fallen silent. "I'm sorry for your loss, my lady. I wonder if you could tell me, did Osfrid visit the stables often?"

"The stables?" Tonild looked at Winston as though he were a raving lunatic. "My husband was a thane. He had men for that."

The king shot an irritated look at Winston. "I said explain yourself."

Winston ignored Cnut and looked at me. "Did you notice Osfrid's cape earlier when he was leaving the square?"

"It was blue."

"And dirty?"

I shook my head, because it hadn't been dirty. It had looked fairly opulent, actually.

"And yet this place stinks of horse shit." Winston looked at the king. "If I'm right, my lord, the cape beneath the body is smeared with horse manure. And if that's the case, he was killed somewhere other than here."

At a nod from Cnut, Godskalk walked over and took hold of the dead man. With some effort, he turned the corpse over, and we all stared at his cape. It was indeed caked with blood and horse manure.

The king inhaled, whistling again, and looked at Winston. "I see that you can think. I have a job for you." Cnut glanced at me. "For both of you. Follow me."

Chapter 7

he king's back was straight as a spear shaft, his footsteps heavy, and the back of his neck flushed with anger as we followed him back to the Hall. Alert housecarls marched on all sides of us. Godskalk, his eyes vigilant and his hand on the hilt of his sword, walked on the king's left.

When we reached the front door of the Hall, Cnut strode through, his footsteps reverberating through the floorboards. A guard stepped up to challenge Winston and me, but one look from Godskalk stopped him, and we were able to follow the king inside. The king settled back into his chair, which seemed to serve as a sort of simple throne, his long legs stretched out before him and his face looking up at the smoke-blackened rafters.

The men sitting on the benches had stopped speaking the moment the king entered. Once Cnut was seated, two of them stood and approached him. One was the man I thought must be Archbishop Wulfstan of York, the king's main adviser, and the other was a tall Viking with a chiseled jaw and iron-gray hair. The Viking wore gray breeches but, unlike the king, his tunic was largely covered by a thin, finely worked ring-mail byrnie. Hanging from his sturdy, silver-laden belt was a heavy sword, whose hilt was adorned with elaborately intertwined dragons curling down the blade, clearly the hallmark of a talented blacksmith.

Though Cnut glared at the two men, they looked him calmly in the eye. When the king spoke, he confirmed the clergyman's identity.

"You're right, Wulfstan," Cnut began. "Without laws, my land will be squandered and drowned in blood. Odin himself is sending us discord where I wish to create peace."

The archbishop's face remained impassive, despite Cnut's flagrant reference to the pagan god. Wulfstan undoubtedly remembered, as we all did, that Cnut had been baptized only a few years before. Wulfstan surely understood that even true Christian aspirants were still in the habit of ascribing power to the old gods.

"Thorkell—did you order Osfrid killed?" the king asked, looking from Wulfstan to the Viking.

Ah, so this was Thorkell the Tall. I was curious to see this man who may have cinched Cnut's victory by agreeing to fight at his side. If anyone was responsible for the conquest of my country, it was this man.

"No," Thorkell said in the deep and booming voice of a man who was used to making himself heard over the din of battle and winds of the North Sea.

"You heard Jarl Thorkell," the king said, looking back at Winston. "And what I said earlier. Neither I nor my men ordered this killing."

Winston didn't respond. His eyes had taken on a contemplative look.

"And now that you know this," the king continued, "you can begin the task I am about to assign you."

"I am an illuminator," Winston said matter-of-factly.

Cnut nodded. "Who came here to serve at the behest of my Lady Ælfgifu," he began. "But the lady is not available at the moment. Would you prefer for your trip to have been in vain, or would you like to take on the job I'm offering you—not only to gain your king's favor but also to earn some money? What was the lady going to pay you to paint me?"

"We had not yet agreed on a price," Winston said, scratching his thigh absentmindedly. I wondered if he was really as accustomed to spending time with earls and kings as his nonchalant demeanor suggested.

No. I saw a vein throbbing below his eye. It had never done that before in all the days I had known him.

Jarl Thorkell cleared his throat. Cnut looked at him and nodded, inviting him to speak.

"Perhaps, my lord," the Viking jarl grumbled, "you would consider informing the rest of us of your plans?"

The king summed up what we had discovered in the shed and Winston's theory.

Thorkell studied Winston, who appeared not to notice this scrutiny.

"And Osfrid's widow is blaming you for the murder?" Thorkell asked.

The king nodded.

"Well, I suppose that was to be expected," the archbishop said, speaking for the first time. His voice crackled in the way that old men's voices often do, but he sounded firm and authoritative. Though Wulfstan was slightly stooped with age, his head heavy, and his neck and wrists gaunt, his eyes suggested that he was still quite lucid. Cnut glanced at Wulfstan but did not speak for a moment as he considered the archbishop's statement.

"Yes, I suppose it was," Cnut said with a nod, and turned back to Winston.

"My lord," Winston began. "You have earls, ealdormen, and reeves who do this kind of work for you all the time. Why do you want *me* to investigate this matter?" Winston sounded genuinely curious.

"Not just you," Cnut said, waving a hand at me. "*Both* of you."

I looked from Cnut to Winston, aghast. Winston was the one who had been showing off out in that shed. I had simply stood beside him and answered the questions posed to me.

Cnut must have sensed my surprise as he raised a hand in a gesture that Godskalk—still standing just behind the king's chair—apparently understood, because he barked an order to everyone in the Hall. Servants instantly came running over with chairs, which they placed behind Winston, Jarl Thorkell, Archbishop Wulfstan, and myself. The jarl and the archbishop quickly took their seats. Winston followed suit. I realized I had no choice and hurriedly sat down.

The king straightened himself in his chair, leaned forward, and rested his hands on his knees. "Many men believe I am being disingenuous when I say that I want peace to prevail throughout my kingdom," he said. "Peace between you and us, between Angles, Jutes, Saxons, Danes who have been living here for generations, and more recent Viking arrivals. They will claim I am looking out only for my own interests and that I will show my true colors once I have received the heregeld's many thousands of pounds of silver.

"Well, they *will* see my true colors," Cnut continued, "because those people are wrong. The silver is mine—there is no debating that. It was won honestly in battle, and in exchange for payment, my army will refrain from fighting, both during the collection period and after the heregeld has been paid.

"In a few days' time, once we have received the silver and duly weighed it, it is my intention that the Witenagemot and Thing will meet jointly to decide how this country should be ruled as we move forward," Cnut said. "Ruled so that Jutes, Saxons, Angles, Danes, and Vikings will enjoy the same rights and obligations and can live side by side and farm their lands in peace.

"As you may know," the king continued, "Archbishop Wulfstan is a legal expert. It will be his job to ensure that everyone, be they English or Danish, will be bound by the same laws. As soon as the heregeld has been paid, this will be made clear to one and all." The king paused.

"It is vital that the Witenagemot and the Thing meet in peace, with a spirit of mutual trust. But now a man has been murdered, a man you all knew was my enemy. Not killed honorably in battle but murdered in secret and dumped in a back-alley shed like an old dog. Do you think the men who are supposed to meet and secure the peace in England can trust one another as long as this murder remains unresolved? How many people will think I was behind it?

"I swear to my innocence. Countless others will swear with me. But if I invoke my right to compurgation and swear I am innocent, will that change anyone's mind? Even if I bring the requisite number of compurgators to testify to my character, the law only requires that I be absolved of *guilt*— not of *suspicion*.

"Which is why I need the murderer found.

"I have reeves, you say. Yes, Saxon reeves and Danish reeves. If I ask a Saxon to investigate the murder, his fellow Saxons might be satisfied with his findings, but what if he concludes that the killer was a Dane? How many Danes would believe that his investigation was unbiased? And vice versa: If a Danish reeve were to determine the guilty party was a Saxon or an Angle, how many Englishmen would believe him?"

The king finally stopped speaking and looked at Winston and me. I could have sworn there was a twinkle in his eye. "But now I have been sent the two of you," he continued. "One Saxon and one Dane. And one of you has demonstrated that he can think.

"Find the killer, and I will reward you well," the king said with a nod.

I cleared my throat and spoke. "I'm only *half* Danish."

Cnut waved his hand dismissively. "You are a Dane. You speak Danish, you act like a Dane. People needn't know any more than that."

And, you know, he was right. There wasn't a soul who wouldn't believe me if I said I was a Dane. And my name did not reveal whether my father or my mother was the Dane.

I didn't say a word and looked at Winston, who was biting his lip. "I could have simply made a lucky guess out there in the shed," Winston admitted.

The king brushed Winston's concern aside. "Perhaps. But my announcement alone—that I've assigned a Saxon and a Dane to investigate the murder together—will be effective. Men will see that I want to know the truth."

Winston looked from the king to the archbishop, who nodded his heavy head. Jarl Thorkell initially furrowed his brow, but after a moment he, too, nodded his approval.

"All right, my lord. I accept the job," Winston announced.

I felt a tingle of outrage and cleared my throat loudly. Everyone looked at me in surprise. "*We* accept the job," Winston said, correcting himself.

"Now we'll see if *you* can think, half-Dane," Jarl Thorkell teased me, suppressing a smile.

"Good." The king slapped his hands on his thighs and stood up. "Then we've reached an agreement."

Thorkell and the archbishop immediately stood. Thorkell raised his eyebrows at me sternly, and I obediently stood as well. Winston, however, remained seated.

"You're not going to find the killer by just sitting there," Cnut said, annoyed.

"I'm going to *begin* to find the killer by sitting here," Winston said calmly. "With you, my lord."

The king's eyes darkened.

"I have other business to attend to."

Winston nodded. "But if you want this murder solved, you'll give me a little of your time."

"I don't know any more than you do," the king said sharply. "We went to the shed together."

"All the same, my lord. I need to know who this Osfrid was. And why you and he were enemies." Winston calmly observed the king, who bit his lip but sat back down despite being clearly annoyed.

Cnut gripped his thighs for a moment before looking up.

"Osfrid was a South Saxon thane, who owned a great deal of land on the plain between the southern uplands," Cnut began. "He fought with Edmund at Assandun and accompanied him when he retreated. When Edmund the atheling and I divided the country at our meeting"—I noticed Cnut avoided referring to Edmund as king, instead using the term *atheling,* essentially the heir apparent—"Osfrid was among those who offered his own son as a hostage to ensure that they would abide by the agreement.

"Oslaf, his son, was ten summers old, a rather wild blond boy. He came with me as I ordered, but he was always getting into trouble. He wanted to ride the wildest horses and picked fights with the housecarls—who were twice as old as he was and weighed three times as much. If we were camped by a river and someone reported his boat missing, we knew Oslaf had *borrowed* it—as he liked to put it—and that we would find him out splashing in the river somewhere.

"Eventually he got himself into real trouble. He saddled one of Jarl Thorkell's stallions without permission and swung himself up on his back. You know how it is with a stallion; he won't tolerate just anyone on his back. Also, this stallion was being trained for horse fighting. As soon as Oslaf rode him out of the stall, he lost control.

"There were several breeding horses in an enclosure not far from the stall, including a number of stud-crazed brood mares, and as soon as the stallion caught a whiff of them, he threw the boy and raced down to the enclosure.

"Now, we can say many things about Oslaf, but he *was* a brave boy, and he ran after that stallion, grabbed its reins, and tried to hold on. But as I'm sure you know, it is as hard to lead a stallion away from willing brood mares as it is to stem the tide.

"Several men there saw what was going on and rushed over, but in vain. The boy had been trampled to death before they could reach him. I had the boy's body sent back to his father with my apologies, but that wasn't enough for Osfrid.

"In his eyes—and he was not shy about telling me this—I owed him wergeld for the boy, since he died in my custody. Naturally I refused, since the boy died because he tried to take a pleasure ride on another man's stallion without permission."

The king stood. "There, now you know. So, go solve the murder."

I stepped up to Cnut, who raised his eyebrows at me.

"My sword, my lord."

The corner of his mouth twitched. "Of course."

I accepted my belt and sword from a housecarl and put them on.

"My lord," Winston said, now also standing. "I am a Saxon illuminator, unknown to anyone. Halfdan is an equally unknown Dane. What right do we have to question thanes, warriors, and other people?"

Cnut looked over at Godskalk and said, "Make it known that Winston and Halfdan are acting in our name."

Godskalk bowed and walked through the Hall to the door. Shortly thereafter, we heard him issuing orders to the housecarls in the square out front.

Cnut, Wulfstan, and Thorkell had left us before Godskalk even made it to the door. Thorkell smiled at us on his way out. Though he may have intended it to be encouraging, it came across as condescending.

I looked at Winston, wondering what we had just gotten ourselves into. He just shook his head at me as if to say he had had no choice.

"A man would have to be bigger than we are to say no to King Cnut," he said quietly.

"Maybe he means it when he says he will reward us," I said, nodding. "Where do we start?"

Winston bit his lip. "With the body. Maybe it can tell us more than we noticed the first time."

Chapter 8

omeone had removed the body, which came as no great surprise. Tonild, the dead man's widow, hadn't wanted her deceased husband lying in plain sight in a shed, so she had him taken back to the camp north of town, where he now lay in their tent, surrounded by his own men.

Someone—presumably Godskalk, because I hadn't noticed the king give any such order—had stationed a housecarl in front of the shed and he willingly told us that when Tonild had brought Osfrid's men by to retrieve the body, she swore her husband's murder would not go unavenged.

"Well," Winston said, scratching his chin and carefully studying the doorway. "But the murderer must be found, first."

He ducked into the shed. I followed him and looked around. It wasn't a big shed. Five paces long by three wide. The unfinished floorboards were scoured white, as I had noticed earlier, and a bloodstain marked where the body had lain.

Winston looked over at me. "They must have turned the body over."

What did he mean? Then I understood. "Unless he was stabbed all the way through," I pointed out.

"Hmm," Winston said. Now it was his turn to stop and think. "I can't remember if he was . . . Let's hope the widow will let us examine the body."

He walked over to the back wall, which was constructed of horizontal boards but looked older than the floor. "Who owns this shed?"

I shrugged. How in the world would I know that? "I guess we'll have to ask," I said. "Does it matter?"

"Maybe." Winston was standing in the doorway now and placed his hand on the rough-hewn door. He stepped outside and closed it. Suddenly I was in the dark.

"Can you see any light in there anywhere?" Winston asked, his voice quiet through the door planks.

When he swung the door back open, I shook my head.

"The walls and door don't let any light in," he said. "What does that tell us?"

I had no idea where Winston was going with this, and I said as much.

"I'm just wondering whether we'll find that this shed belongs to a merchant," he said, his blue eyes twinkling. I got the feeling he was teasing me. I just blinked back at him, so he added, "It's recently been converted into a mouseproof storage space." Then he turned to the guard. "Who owns this shed?"

The housecarl shrugged but then looked thoughtful for a moment. "Alfred the Merchant, I think."

"And does this Alfred also own stables nearby?"

This time the guard was certain of the answer. "That building down there," he said, pointing to a long building on the corner where the alley met a narrow cross street.

"Aha," Winston said, rubbing his hands together. "This whole complex wouldn't happen to be Alfred's, would it?"

The guard nodded.

And with that, Winston was off. By the time I caught up to him, he was standing in front of the door to the stable, peering in at three horses, a donkey, and a mule. In addition, there were four empty stalls. The stable's packed-dirt floor had several damp patches on it.

I was about to follow Winston—who was already walking calmly through each of the stalls with his head tilted down—but he turned around and told me to stay where I was.

Once he'd examined the whole floor twice, he looked up with a satisfied smile.

"There!" He pointed to a flattened pile of horse dung. "There are drops of blood in the manure."

Then he pointed toward me in the doorway. "And there's a wide swath where the surface of the packed soil has been disturbed. The swath shows where the murderer dragged Osfrid's lifeless body across the floor. Go follow it, would you? See if it continues all the way to the shed."

I did as he asked, and walked back down the alley to the shed, scanning the dirt alley for marks.

"Can you see the drag marks?" Winston called to me from the stable.

"No," I said, shaking my head. "Too many people must have walked through here already. There was certainly no shortage of curious bystanders earlier."

Winston walked back to the shed with me, cocked his head to the side, and asked, "Did you notice anything strange by the door up there?"

Again I shook my head.

"There was no lock . . ." Winston began.

"What's so strange about that?" I asked.

He gave me a quizzical look. "Don't you find it strange that someone spent money to convert this shed into a secure storeroom but didn't bother putting a lock on the door?"

"Nope." I was pleased with myself for knowing the answer for once, though I tried not to sound too smug. "I mean, the shed was empty, right?"

Winston blinked at me for a moment, then broke into a smile. "Good point. Let's return to the important question now."

"Why someone would kill Osfrid?" I asked.

"No, it's too soon for that question. We'll likely know who killed him by the time we figure that out. I was thinking instead about why the body had to be moved at all."

Once again I tried to keep my voice from sounding smug. "The killer needed to hide the body," I said.

"Of course," Winston said, slapping his leg. "People come and go from stables all the time. The killer hoped that with a little luck, the body wouldn't be found for several days in the shed."

He paused and stood for a long time, lost in thought. Finally he asked, "Who found the body, anyway?"

I shrugged. "Tonild obviously already knew he'd been found when she burst into the king's Hall."

"With her retinue of armed men, yes. Someone must have found the body and notified Tonild, who then assembled her men and set off to accuse the king," Winston said. He stopped to think again. "Strange, though. Wouldn't she have gone to see her dead husband first? Why didn't she attend to the body before approaching the king?"

The answer was obvious. "She wanted revenge."

"Maybe. Maybe she's a noblewoman first and a widow second? I mean that's how it is with nobles, right?" Winston said with a wink, as though those of us born into noble families were somehow less than human.

I didn't dignify that with a response.

"So," Winston said with a look of satisfaction on his face. "Whom should we go see first: the widow or the merchant?"

Before I could respond, a homunculus dressed in gray turned into the alley and headed straight for us. He stopped short a couple of paces away and curtly asked what we were doing there.

"Are you Alfred?"

He ignored Winston's question. "I said *what are you doing here?*"

"We are here on the king's business," I said, casually moving my hand to the hilt of my sword.

"There's nothing else for you to take here. My lord has already paid his outrageous share of the heregeld," the gnarled man said in a whiny, outraged voice.

"So you're saying you're not Alfred," Winston confirmed.

The gnome looked crossly at Winston. "I'm Wigstan, Alfred's servant."

"And Alfred? Where is he?" Winston asked.

"In his market stall."

"To which perhaps you would be so kind as to take us," Winston said, flashing an encouraging smile at the homunculus, who turned on his heels without a word and walked to the corner, where he turned left from the alley onto a larger street. We hurriedly followed. He stopped in front of a canvas awning beneath which was a wooden table, which served as a counter.

Behind it stood a fat, bald man with bushy eyebrows and hair sprouting from his ears. The man was meticulously dressed in immaculate clothes. Behind him, a door led into a house.

"Is this Alfred?" Winston asked.

The gnome nodded and got the merchant's attention with a loud cough.

"How may I help you?" the merchant asked in a syrupy, fawning voice, assuming we were customers.

"You can tell us who the last person to enter your stable was, and when that was," Winston said.

Alfred looked in surprise from me to Winston. "What the . . . ?" he began.

Winston repeated his question.

"I . . . I heard you the first time . . . Wigstan?" Alfred said.

The gnome shrugged. "I was in there this morning to feed the animals and muck it out."

"And I haven't been in there since . . . the day before yesterday," Fat Alfred squeaked.

"So you don't routinely keep an eye on the stable?" Winston asked.

Alfred shook his head. "Why should I?"

"People do steal animals," Winston said.

"In the middle of town? With the king here and his housecarls teeming everywhere like ants?" Alfred scoffed, his fat face breaking into a grin. "Though law and order do usually prevail here in Oxford, even without royal visits."

"So neither of you was in there during the day today?" Winston asked.

They both shook their heads.

Winston eyed the little one. "And yet you were just on your way in there," Winston pointed out.

"I was on an errand, and then I saw you two standing in the doorway to the stable when I returned," Wigstan said.

"I see," Winston said. "And Osfrid?"

"Osfrid?" Alfred asked with a glare.

"The South Saxon thane. When did he shop here?"

The merchant's eyes widened. "I have no idea who you're talking about."

"A nobleman who talked the way they do down in Sussex didn't buy anything here today?" Winston asked.

"Not for many days," Alfred said.

"And you didn't hear any sounds coming from the stable?" Winston asked.

The two men shook their heads again.

"Thank you," Winston said. He turned and walked away, and I followed him. I hadn't even opened my mouth.

"Hey! What is this all about?" the merchant asked, his voice even higher pitched than before, if that were possible.

He received no answer, as Winston had already turned the corner. I didn't know if it was part of Winston's plan to tell Alfred that the murdered man had been killed in his stables—though I was surprised that Alfred hadn't wondered about that himself.

"Tonild wishes to pray in peace beside her departed husband's body," the priest said gently but firmly. I saw several gruff-looking soldiers eyeing us from behind him.

It had taken us awhile to find the right tent.

The camp where the king had ordered all visiting noblemen to stay occupied most of the meadow, stretching from the edge of the forest to the shacks at the outskirts of town—a distance of two arrowshots by more than three arrowshots.

There was no organization to the camp aside from the king's specification that the various ethnic groups should be intermixed, and it was debatable whether you could call that "organization," since it meant that no one knew where anyone else was.

Whenever I inquired about the South Saxon's tent, the Danes stared at me blankly, the West Saxons shrugged, the East Anglians said they had never heard of Osfrid, and the Viking chieftains stared down their noses at me and claimed that all the various English tribes looked the same to them. A thane from Mercia thought he had heard about a South Saxon whose tent was six sites down from his, but when we got there, it turned out to belong to a Northumbrian nobleman, who was insulted at having been mistaken for a Saxon.

Along the way, we bumped into soldiers, bodyguards, slaves, precariously laden peddlers, ale sellers, bread hawkers, messengers, town criers, street performers, jugglers, and pompous thanes—who were endlessly having their men clear paths through the crowds for them.

In addition, there were a fair number of young women openly displaying both their fores and their afts. A couple of them batted their eyes at me . . . but unfortunately I had to rush along after Winston, who was walking from tent to tent asking for Osfrid, and didn't have time to pay attention to the surrounding crowds. Besides, I didn't have so much as a penny, and these were not the sorts of girls who frolicked with men for free.

Our efforts eventually paid off. A friendly-looking thane, who spoke the guttural version of Saxon mastered only by residents of the area along the Welsh border, directed us to a tent with a pointed top ahead of us. When we reached it, the guard confirmed we had found the right place.

But he also refused point-blank to admit us. It wasn't until Winston threatened to call in a platoon of housecarls that he agreed to convey a message into the tent, which almost immediately resulted in the aforementioned priest sticking his head out to report that Tonild did not want to talk to us.

Winston, however, refused to budge, and I remained at his side. With a sigh, the clergyman emerged fully to talk to us. Meanwhile, the guard stepped over to chat with a few of his buddies, continuing to give us the evil eye all the while.

"I understand that Tonild wants to honor her husband. But I'm sure she'd also like his murderer found and punished," Winston said loudly, possibly hoping that his words would be heard through the tent canvas.

"I believe Lady Tonild already knows who did it," the priest replied harshly.

"So I gathered," Winston said, nodding, "but the king is willing to swear to his innocence and has asked us to investigate the matter."

The priest shot us a look that suggested he didn't put much stock in us.

"Would you kindly ask Tonild to meet with us? Just very briefly," Winston asked.

"No," the priest said. "I have been expressly instructed not to admit any-one into the tent today." He spoke with the soft accent of the South Saxons.

"Would you ask her to meet with us tomorrow, then?" Winston inquired.

"I will ask her, yes, after you've left," the priest said.

Winston pursed his lips, then took a deep breath and said, "I would also very much like to inspect the body."

The priest shook his head. "That's out of the question!"

Winston's face flared with anger again, then relaxed. "You've seen it?"

"Yes."

"So, tell me this," Winston said. "Did the stab wound go all the way through?"

The clergyman stared at him, not understanding the question.

"Was there blood or a wound on his back?"

The priest responded with a nod.

"Thank you. We'll be back tomorrow." Winston turned on his heel, and we started walking back through the encampment.

A short while later, I grabbed Winston's sleeve. "I'm starving."

The afternoon was more than half over and we hadn't eaten anything since our porridge that morning.

Winston stopped and nodded. "You're right. I could stand to eat, too."

We were soon seated back in the tavern at the inn, which was empty apart from two less-than-rich-looking Saxons, who I guessed had been spitting in their ales for a long time, judging by the disgruntled looks Alfilda was giv-ing them.

We each got a roll with salted ham and a tankard of ale. Our hostess hadn't finished getting ready for dinner yet, so that was the best she could offer.

Chewing the bread satisfied the worst of my hunger, and by my second ale I was starting to feel like a person again. I watched Winston, who was picking his teeth with a splinter of wood he'd pulled from the edge of the tabletop.

"Do you think we're going to be able to solve this murder?" I asked.

Winston looked up. "What do I know? It beats sitting around with noth-ing to do."

"Well, the best thing would have been if Ælfgifu had met with you as she'd promised."

"Of course, but the king wanted something else. At least this way we'll be paid."

"If we succeed," I reminded him.

Winston smiled to himself. "Which is certainly reasonable," he said. "Who wants to pay for a job not done?"

He was quiet and sat leaning over the table for a moment.

"You know," he said reluctantly, searching for the best way to phrase his thought. "This is a little like being a painter, all this."

I had no idea what he meant, and I said so.

"Ah, no. You can't read, can you?"

I'd already answered that one.

"You see," he continued slowly. "I draw or paint a single thing. Maybe the first letter in a long text, maybe a picture in the middle of the text. You know what I mean?"

I shook my head.

"Well, I focus on a single detail taken out of the bigger picture," Winston began. "Like when you read, you see. Or perhaps you don't. Try to imagine how someone actually reads. First you see the letters, then you string them together into words, and then you string the words into lines, the lines into a text—and suddenly you see the whole. Which is then made richer by the illustrations. The details of the pictures illuminate the bigger picture.

"This investigation works the same way," he continued. "We find a detail: horse manure on a cape, no lock on the door, a merchant unaware of a murder in his stable, a widow initially ravenous for revenge but who later prefers prayer over helping the people trying to find her husband's killer.

"At some point," he said, "we'll have filled in enough details that we'll be able to see the bigger picture. And then we'll have our killer."

It sounded strange to my ears—but what did *I* know about reading and other scholarly things? I nodded all the same because I had noticed something about Winston as he spoke: He seemed to be enjoying himself.

Chapter 9

inston turned to look through the window in the tavern wall behind him. The springtime sun had not yet set, and it was still light out.

"So what do we do now?"

I shrugged. I figured we had to wait until the next morning and hope the widow would talk to us then.

But Winston had other ideas. He rose from his chair and caught our hostess's eye. "Would you mind joining us for a moment?"

Alfilda nodded and walked over to us, casting the Saxons—who were still bent over their presumably empty mugs—a disgruntled look. I admired her graceful movements. The rocking of her skirted hips did not escape my notice any less than the swaying of her breasts beneath her linen top.

She was smiling to herself as she sat down, which meant she had noticed my attention. When I batted my eyelashes at her, she responded with a look of distaste—somewhat to my surprise.

So be it. If she thought I was so skirt-crazed that I would waste any more time on her when the town was teeming with young maidens . . . well, it was her loss.

Winston leaned across the table. "Did you hear about the murder this morning?"

Alfilda nodded. "That's all people have been talking about, in fact. This is a tavern," she explained, "so things like that are good for business—even those two over there were all worked up about it when they came in." She lit up in a grin. "Of course you'd never know it to look at them now that they've had a tankard or two. I suppose it makes sense that they're the last ones here—everyone else came in for ale and some gossip and then left because they had something to do."

The three of us looked over at them. Sitting there clutching their tankards in their hands, they looked asleep. Maybe they were each waiting for the other to buy the next round.

"But did the day's gossip also include the fact that Halfdan and I have been hired to find the killer?" Winston asked.

Alfilda shook her head. "Who asked you to do that?"

"King Cnut himself," Winston said, raising his mug in triumph as Alfilda looked at him in surprise.

"Wasn't Ælfgifu the one you were asking about?" she asked.

"Yes, but she isn't in Oxford apparently. I had an audience with the king instead," Winston said, and briefly related our conversation with Cnut, Tonild's accusations, and the outcome of the whole episode while I fished a fly out of my ale.

Alfilda listened in silence. Winston finished by describing how I'd gotten my sword back, and then nodded at me to pick up the story where he'd left off. Which I did not do.

But then something else seemed to occurr to Winston, because suddenly he asked Alfilda, "Did any of your customers say anything about who found the body?"

"Oh, sure," Alfilda said, suspecting she hadn't heard the whole story yet.

Winston smiled almost imperceptibly. "And do you think you might be willing to share that information with us?"

"Why not?" she said, adjusting her linen top so her breasts heaved. "You'll find him at Alfred the Merchant's place. He's a tiny little guy, works for Alfred."

I saw my own astonishment reflected in Winston's eyes as we both exclaimed, "Wigstan?"

"You know him?" she asked.

Winston nodded. "We spoke to him, yes. And I suppose we'll be speaking to him again." He pushed his tankard away. "What else are people saying?"

"About the murder?" Alfilda asked. "Oh, everyone knows there was bad blood between the victim and the king, of course."

"So people think Cnut had Osfrid assassinated?"

"Yes."

"But the king is willing to swear that he is innocent," I said, thinking it only right that I should contribute something to the conversation.

Alfilda snorted and said, "Kings and noblemen, yes, yes. They never seem to have any trouble finding compurgators to swear they're telling the truth, do they?"

Winston nodded. "And we know the king isn't shy about having his enemies taken out. Either openly, as with Eadric the Grasper, or secretly, as with many of his opponents last year."

"Not to mention old king Ethelred's sons," Alfilda said.

Winston shook his head at Alfilda, who looked back at him, puzzled.

"No, they're still alive," Winston said.

Alfilda snorted again. "Thanks to their mother, Queen Emma, who had the foresight to ship them off to her brother, the Duke of Normandy, before she married Cnut. She knows all too well what happens to fatherless athelings."

"You think Cnut would have his stepsons assassinated?" Winston asked skeptically.

"Doesn't a young cuckoo push all the other eggs and hatchlings out of the nest?" Alfilda said.

I looked at Winston, who nodded to himself. "They say Emma has now borne Cnut a son."

"Lady Ælfgifu has borne him one as well. The king is young and eager to prove his manhood," Alfilda said, turning to smirk at me. As if my manhood needed proving!

"Or to make sure he has heirs," I replied annoyed.

Winston scowled at us both. "We were talking about whether or not Cnut could have been behind Osfrid's murder," he said.

"He wouldn't have asked us to solve the murder if he did it," I said, shaking my head.

"Oh, sure he would," Winston said, leaning back against the wall. "Maybe he thinks we won't be able to prove that he ordered the killing. And how better to convince everyone that he genuinely wants the crime solved than to make it known that he's paying for the investigation?"

I thought about it. "Do you believe that's what happened?"

"Well," Winston said, standing up. "Let's just say we shall consider every possible option."

I stood as well. "Where to?"

"I wonder if we shouldn't go have another chat with Wigstan," Winston said, nodding at Alfilda. "Thank you for your help."

Alfred shot us a grumpy look. He and a Viking were standing behind the counter of his market stall, talking. The Viking had a deep voice and hardly deigned to glance at us when we stepped politely up to the counter across from them. I looked over his merchandise.

There was some fabric at the far end of the counter and a few covered wooden crates stacked on the ground underneath. A selection of silver hammers and crosses, along with a number of silver chains, was laid out on the counter in front of Alfred. He had little to sell, but it was possible that he had several stalls around town—otherwise it was hard to see how he could own such a large house.

I couldn't hear what he and the Viking were discussing, but given that Alfred seemed to keep trying to get the Viking to shake hands—and that the Viking kept pulling his hand back to avoid the handshake—they seemed to be concluding a deal. This impression was confirmed when the merchant finally succeeded in grasping the Viking's palm and shaking it vigorously.

"It'll be delivered by tonight," Alfred said. The Viking emerged from behind the counter and walked away down the street without another word or so much as a glance at us.

"Did you get a good deal?" Winston asked, smiling politely over the crosses and hammers.

"Maybe," the merchant said, obviously disinclined to be chummy. "I don't suppose you're here to buy something."

Winston shook his still-smiling head. "We're here to talk to Wigstan."

"I pay him to get things done, not to talk to you." Alfred rehoisted his paunch up over the belt that held his breeches up.

"I appreciate that," Winston said. "All the same, he will have to set his work aside for a moment." Winston no longer had a smile on his lips.

"Oh, he will, huh?" the merchant scoffed. "He will do no such thing. I'm actually the one who decides that."

"Halfdan, would you go call a couple of housecarls?"

I turned and started walking toward the street but was stopped by Alfred's squeaky voice. "Housecarls? You have housecarls?"

Winston smiled again, but this time in a cold way. "We're asking questions on behalf of the king. His housecarls handle anyone who doesn't want to answer our questions and anyone who stands in our way."

The merchant turned his plump body toward the door behind him. "Wigstan!" he called.

A moment later, the little man stuck his head out.

"These . . . men would like to speak to you again."

The little stump scuttled out from under the awning, spit on the ground, and then looked from me to Winston. "Yeah?"

"There's one thing that's puzzling me," Winston said, gazing up at the canvas awning over Wigstan. "A man finds a dead body, but he doesn't consider it worth mentioning when two strangers later question his master and him about it." Winston returned his gaze to Wigstan. "Don't you find that odd?"

The gnome spit again. "No. I don't even see how those two things are connected."

"Maybe they're not," Winston said. "Do you find murdered men often?" Winston watched expectantly as Wigstan shrugged.

"Happily, no."

"You found him in the shed that belongs to Alfred?"

The little man nodded.

"And what business did you have in there?"

"Business? It's Alfred's shed. I work for him."

Winston nodded. "We know. But what *business* did you have in there?"

Wigstan looked around. He seemed to be trying to make eye contact with Alfred. "I had something to attend to."

"And what was that?" Winston asked, smug as a cat.

"Uh, I don't remember."

Winston's face suddenly went blank. He gave his nose a tug and stared down at his feet, his right hand opening and closing as if of its own accord. He suddenly turned to me. "Halfdan," he said.

I stepped forward.

"Ask the merchant to take off his shoes and hand them to you."

I stared at Winston in bewilderment for a moment but then walked behind the counter to Alfred, who backed away a couple of steps. "You heard the man," I said to him.

"I . . . you have no . . . I don't want to," he stammered.

Without a word, I held out my left hand. My right was resting firmly on my sword grip. Even so, the merchant made no move to obey.

"Do I need to take them off for you?" I asked. I thought I knew why Winston wanted to see the shoes.

Alfred tried to take another step back from me, but he bumped into the wall of his house behind him.

"Well?" Continuing to hold out my left hand, I drew my sword out halfway before allowing it to slide back into the sheath with a chilling clang. Finally accepting defeat, Alfred sat down on the stone step in front of his door and removed each of his leather shoes in turn. After he handed them to me, I walked back around the counter to show the soles to Winston.

He nodded. "Just as I thought," Winston said. "You said you hadn't been in the stable since the day before yesterday. And yet there's horseshit on the bottoms of your shoes."

"I forgot to clean them," the merchant said in a high-pitched voice.

Winston shook his head with a smile. "A man like you? Who parades around town in fancy clothes like a maiden on her way to a dance? You're lying."

He turned to Wigstan. "As are you. The truth is that you found the body in the stable, and you both dragged it to the shed together. Isn't that so?"

The homunculus was practically blown backwards when Winston roared once more, "Isn't that so?"

"Well then," Winston said, turning back to Alfred. "Maybe I should summon the housecarls after all?"

The merchant shook his head, his fleshy jowls wobbling like jelly.

"All right," Winston said, nodding at me. "But if you want to avoid getting them involved, then you're going to need to tell us the truth."

Chapter 10

lfred admitted everything. Perched on his doorstep, he conceded that he and Wigstan had moved the body from the stable.

Wigstan leaned against the wall next to his master, his arms crossed. Though he was trying to act tough—the corner of his mouth twitched every time I glanced at him—he looked even more cowed than Alfred, if that was possible. Winston stood before them, firm but relaxed while I sat on the counter, my belt stretched taut and my sword sheath resting over my thighs.

Their story was that Wigstan had gone into the stable to muck it out and had practically tripped over the body. Terrified about what might happen if word got out that a strange nobleman had been murdered in his stable, Alfred had devised a plan to get rid of the body. They had been lucky that no one was in the alley when they dragged the dead man up to the shed, and no curious onlookers had walked by as they were washing the blood off the stable floor.

Winston studied little Wigstan, who held his head up, trying to look defiant. "Where was the body lying?" Winston asked.

"Lying? Uh, on the ground," Wigstan said.

"Yes, I realize that," Winston said. "In what position? Face down, or on his back, or on his side?"

"Um, well kind of curled up, on his side."

"Was there a lot of blood?"

"Yes."

"In a pool?"

The little guy thought about it. "No, sort of more all over the floor."

"Hmm." Winston thought for a moment. "Did it look as though someone had rummaged through his clothes and pockets?"

"How would I know?" Wigstan said with a shrug.

Winston glanced at me and said, "If a man is stuck through with a sword, he falls toward the blow, does he not?"

"Unless the killer puts his foot up and pushes back on the body to pull his sword back out," I said. "How do we know we're dealing with a sword?"

"Was there a wound on the man's back?" Winston asked, looking over at Alfred.

Alfred looked uncertain and glanced at Wigstan, who hiccuped a "yes."

Winston looked back at me knowingly. I nodded. Osfrid must have been stabbed in the stomach.

If the murderer had aimed for Osfrid's chest, he would have had a tougher time. It takes luck to stab a man right between the ribs—and more strength than most people possess to force a sword through the rib cage.

An experienced swordsman will go for the soft belly but aim diagonally up from beneath the ribs to try to pierce the heart. If the victim isn't wearing ring mail, which Osfrid wasn't, there's nothing to stop the tip of the sword from penetrating all the way through the body as long as you stay clear of the spine, which isn't hard to do.

And because swords are so long, they often slice cleanly through the victim's body, leaving an exit wound on the back.

"Why move the body to your own shed if you were afraid of what might happen to you if he were found in your stables?" I asked, looking at Alfred.

"There weren't . . . there weren't any other options," Alfred said, his feet fidgeting nervously.

"And you knew the shed was empty," Winston said, scratching his beard. Alfred nodded.

I had a thought and said, "And with a little luck, the body might have stayed there for quite a while before anyone discovered it."

Another nod. But then Alfred stared in terror at Winston, who suddenly all but shouted, "Then why in the devil's name did Wigstan go and 'find' the body?"

The two men looked at each other uncertainly. The gnome frowned, while the merchant bit his lower lip.

"We forgot to lock the door to the shed," Alfred said, shrugging in resignation.

"Because you don't keep a lock on it, because the shed is usually empty?" Winston asked them, nodding approvingly at me since I had correctly figured that one out.

They nodded.

Alfred held up his arms in a gesture of helplessness and explained, "When we'd finished cleaning the stable floor and came back out, we looked up the alleyway and saw that the shed door was swinging open on its hinges. A gust of wind must have blown it open. Wigstan hurried up there, but . . ." Alfred said but stopped to look at his assistant, who petulantly reported that by the time he reached the shed, some people were walking down the alley. Winston's face lit up in understanding.

"So you realized that your only option was to 'discover' the body?" Winston asked.

Wigstan nodded, still petulant. He evidently hadn't noticed the change in Winston's facial expression.

"But . . ." I said, scanning the merchant's sparse selection of merchandise. "You're not exactly drowning in goods here. Why did you have the shed converted into such a secure storeroom in the first place?"

"My business prospects looked very different a couple of weeks ago, but this new . . . *Danish* king . . . is going to be the ruin of me," Alfred said, his lips pulled back in an embittered sneer.

Winston whistled quietly. "The heregeld?" he asked.

Alfred nodded. "Oxford's share of the army tax is far too great. And when the high reeve came to collect, he didn't even stop once my coffers were drained of coin."

"He took your goods as well?" Winston asked.

Alfred flung up his hands in frustration. "What you see here is all I have left after paying the heregeld and the town's new fire tax."

"What made you suddenly realize how it all fit together?" I asked Winston.

After having spent a good deal of time at the merchant's stall, we were once again seated in the tavern.

Winston smiled slightly. "I should have seen it ages ago," he said. "What got me thinking was Wigstan's reluctance to divulge his business in the shed. That fool should have realized that someone would eventually be asking that question and he should have been ready with some made-up story. If he'd visited the shed a week ago, that would've been one thing. But did he really think I would fall for his claim that he couldn't remember why he'd gone to the shed a few hours earlier?"

"Yes, but . . ." I began. Ever since Winston's shoe inspection and the merchant's subsequent admission, it had been bugging me that I hadn't been able to see through Alfred and Wigstan's lies the way Winston had. "You seemed so sure when you accused them of lying."

"Yes, because I remembered what we'd seen in the stable," Winston said.

"You mean the blood we noticed in the horse shit?" I asked.

"No, that just showed us where the murder took place," Winston said with a mischievous glint in his eye. "The damp patches on the floor. We should both have noticed those and guessed what they meant."

"Of course," I said, suddenly feeling really dumb. "They must have washed the blood off the dirt floor!"

Winston nodded. "But they overlooked that small pile of blood-spattered manure."

So it *was* as simple as that: All you had to do was remember the details and put them together to see the bigger picture.

Several of the tables in the tavern were occupied now.

Some of the noblemen preferred to eat at the tavern rather than bring their own cooks and kitchen staff to the camp. There were also three clergymen silently gulping down Alfilda's wonderful stew, four men who might have been anything from peddlers to merchant soldiers looking for a new master, and a drooping, thin-haired man who, judging from his clothes, was on a pilgrimage, perhaps to the shrine of Saint Frideswide, Oxford's own saint.

I was hungry. The bread that afternoon had only taken the edge off my hunger, and I dug with relish into the rabbit stew, which was seasoned with onion and thyme.

Winston was also devouring his portion. He seemed very satisfied following our chat at Alfred's stall, as though the confirmation of his hunch had given him renewed faith that we could get this job done for the king.

Finally he wiped his mouth and beard with the back of his hand, belched behind that same hand, and stretched his legs out under the table.

"Not a bad day's work," Winston said.

Something had been puzzling me. "Why did you think to ask whether someone had rummaged through Osfrid's pockets?" I asked. He gave me a nod of approval, as though he were pleased with my question.

"Well, first of all, it's not such a surprising question, is it?" Winston said. "Osfrid must have been murdered for *some* reason. Maybe he was in possession of something that someone wanted. But there was also another reason. As you pointed out earlier, left to his own devices, a man who's been stabbed in the stomach will grab for the sword and thus fall forward. A killer, however, will do everything he can to pull his sword free and, as you said, will push the victim backward in order to do so.

"So, the body should either end up on its back or its stomach. But according to Wigstan, Osfrid's body was lying on its *side*," Winston continued. "There wasn't a pool of blood. It was—how did he put it?—'sort of more all over the floor.'"

Winston looked at me expectantly, waiting to see if I could explain that.

"Because Osfrid tried to get away?" I suggested.

"Exactly," Winston said. "He lived long enough to drag himself across the floor."

"That means . . ." I hesitated, still uncertain. Winston nodded encouragingly. "That means that he didn't die right away," I said.

"Unless someone was searching the body and dragged it across the floor while they were doing so," Winston said, nodding.

"But . . ." I said, hesitating again. "What does that tell us?"

"How should I know?" Winston shrugged. "But it *is* a detail."

I grinned. "And at some point we'll see the big picture. Oh, and one more thing," I said. Winston cocked his head, eager to hear what I had to say.

"I noticed that Osfrid's hands were all cut up, as though he'd grabbed at the sword to keep it from going in," I said.

"So he tried to defend himself, you mean?" Winston said, tugging on his nose.

But I had realized there was another possibility. "Or because he still had the strength to grab the sword *after* he'd been stabbed."

"Which wouldn't be all that unusual," Winston said. "A man in a great deal of pain will try to remove the source of it. So you're right: Maybe he actually helped his murderer pull the weapon back out."

"That doesn't really help us though," I said and sighed. "Now what?"

Winston stood. "I'm going to go look after Atheling," he said.

But before we reached the door, the king's housecarl Godskalk entered the tavern. When he spotted us, he said, "The king summons you two to an audience with him."

This time the king's guards didn't ask me to hand over my sword before allowing me to enter the Hall.

Cnut sat at a table that was positioned in the center of the room to the left of the fire. Thorkell and Wulfstan sat with him, with silver chalices and empty food platters before them. Cnut's platter was covered with bones—pork ribs, it looked like—that had been picked clean. The silver chalice in front of him was quite a bit larger than the others.

At a gesture from the king, servants rushed over with chairs. He nodded at us to sit down at the table. Wooden drinking bowls were placed before us, and before Cnut opened his mouth, he raised his own chalice and drank to us.

The wine was sweeter than the one my father used to drink.

"Do you have any news?" Cnut asked.

Winston eyed the king. "I'm afraid not much, my lord, though we have figured out where Osfrid was killed."

"Let's hear it." Cnut reached forward and took a bone from his platter. Two large dogs immediately rose. The king tossed the bone to one and then threw one to the second dog.

Winston brought the king up to date on our investigation.

"Excellent," Cnut said.

I cast a sidelong glance at the king. Why did he seem so pleased? It wasn't as though we were any closer to figuring out who had killed the thane.

"Do you think this Alfred fellow can afford to pay the wergeld for Osfrid's life?" the king asked.

My surprise turned to bewilderment.

Winston shook his head and clarified, "I don't think he's the murderer."

Cnut was incredulous. "You don't think he is? He admits to moving the body. He's the only one we know who had any contact with the body, he and his assistant that is. Obviously he is the killer."

Winston looked at the king for a long moment. When Winston finally spoke, his tone was tinged with anger. "My lord, if all you want is a murderer who will satisfy everyone, then you're right: You should simply lock Alfred up until he can pay the wergeld or until Osfrid's family exacts its revenge and be done with the matter. But if you want to catch the *actual* killer, you should let me finish the job you have asked me to do."

"How can you be so sure this man isn't the murderer?" the king asked, his voice skeptical.

"I'm afraid I can't be sure—not yet. No more than I can say for a fact that he *is* the murderer. You gave me a job to do, my lord. Was that not because you wanted me to actually do it?"

The king looked angrily from Winston to me. "I am convening the Witenagemot in three days. Can you have the actual murderer in irons before then?"

"Perhaps," Winston replied.

"Perhaps isn't good enough," Cnut said. "Three days, Saxon. Otherwise, this merchant *will* be accused of the murder before the entire assembled nobility of England." The king turned away from us. We took the hint and made our exit.

As we reached the door, I glanced back into the Hall. Jarl Thorkell was holding his chalice, and the archbishop was leaning over the table speaking to the king, who seemed distracted.

Once we were back outside, I turned to Winston. "'A murderer who will satisfy everyone'?" I asked.

"Ideally a Saxon, but not a nobleman," Winston explained. "That would make the murder just a one-time event—not the result of a feud or any sort of treachery. The crime would be resolved, and no one would be obligated to take further action. Beyond that, it would be quite convenient if the murderer were from Oxford, a town Cnut hates. What could be better? I don't think Alfred is as poor as he pretends to be—so he has the added advantage of being a man who can actually pay the wergeld on Osfrid's life." Winston paused. "But one thing's bothering me."

I turned to look at him.

"I'm certain Alfred's innocent. And now I have only three days to prove it."

Chapter 11

hat night I learned that Winston's snoring could wake the dead.

The bed was wide and there was plenty of room for both of us, so I had no trouble falling asleep—especially since Alfilda had given us a tankard of her strongest ale before bed.

The room was already half-lit from the first light of the late spring dawn when I woke up. The room was reverberating with a deep rumbling noise, which I had a hard time placing at first. I thought it might be coming from outside the window until I noticed that the bed was shaking. I sat up and stared through the semidarkness at my bedmate, who was flat on his back with his mouth wide open, puffing away like a workhorse.

My bladder was full from the late-night ale, so I got out of bed and staggered into the hallway. I fumbled my way to the back door and into the alleyway, where I pulled down my breeches and relieved myself. As I did so, I listened to the swifts, which had already begun their shrill hunt for flies high over the town.

When I returned to bed, Winston's snoring was even louder than before. I pulled my side of the blanket all the way up over my ears, but couldn't block out the noise.

I slept in fits and starts for the rest of the night, awoken intermittently by extra-loud snores from my bedmate. By the time Alfilda started clanking around in the kitchen, I was quite groggy.

Winston, however, sat up bright-eyed and wished me a good morning. I answered with a surly grunt.

He looked over at me and asked what was wrong.

After my crabby reply, he looked sheepish.

"Oh," he said. "I should have told you just to kick me."

I mumbled that I would keep that in mind in the future, then stumbled out through the tavern to the well that I'd spotted four buildings down from the inn. I hoisted a bucket of water, dumped it over my head and upper body, and gasped myself the rest of the way awake, though my head did not feel any lighter nor my body less tired for the effort.

There was honey to go with our bread, the ale was malted and sweet, and I ate and drank with a growing appetite, only half listening to Winston and Alfilda, who were chatting away like old friends.

Finally Winston wiped his mouth, drained the last little gulp from his tankard, and stood up. "Time to go have a chat with the widow."

On our way, he insisted that we stop by his mule's stable. We found Atheling in the company of several mounts and pack animals, his muzzle buried in a sack of oats that probably rightly belonged to the horse next to him, but neither Atheling nor Winston seemed interested in doing anything about that.

The animal snorted at Winston, causing the chaff to fly up around its ears. Atheling then gave me a disdainful glance and returned to his gluttony with a scowl at the animal next to him, which meekly started munching chaff. Bite marks on the shoulder of the neighboring horse suggested that Atheling had bullied it into submission.

With Winston reassured that his animal was not suffering any hardship, we left the stables and walked through the narrow, twisting streets out toward the meadow of noblemen's tents, which we found every bit as busy as an anthill someone had poked a stick into.

The bustle was even greater than the day before. More tents had been erected and a great many more men were scurrying around pretending they knew what they were doing—which I very much doubted.

We headed straight to Tonild's tent, which we found ringed by men armed with spears and swords and watchful eyes. One of them stepped forward and gruffly asked us what business we had here.

Winston calmly stroked his beard and said, "We have an appointment to speak to the lady."

Curtly instructing us to wait, the guard walked over to the tent, cleared his throat, and flung open the flap after a muffled response from inside. He disappeared for a few seconds, then came back out and returned to his post without glancing at us. He resumed his position with his legs firmly planted, his hand on his spear, and the hilt of his sword pulled up clear of its sheath.

I glared at him and began to walk over to the opening in the tent, but Winston's hand on my arm held me back.

"Have you forgotten the ways of the nobility?" Winston asked me quietly. "Keep the riffraff waiting until *you* feel like talking to them. Let's just play by Tonild's rules for now."

"But . . ."

"If we barge in, we risk her refusing to speak to us at all," Winston said calmly. "Patience, my friend."

So we waited. Though the camp hubbub continued all around us, Tonild's guards remained perfectly still. A long while later, the tent flap slid to the side, and the same clergyman from the day before waved us in.

Tonild was standing by her husband's bier.

The manure-smeared cape and the other clothes he had been wearing when we found his body had been removed, and he was now dressed in a clean outfit. Wearing soft buckskin boots, delicately woven scarlet breeches, a white linen shirt embroidered across the chest, and a cornflower blue cloak, his outfit was obviously quite expensive and even a bit ostentatious.

The dead man's hands were folded around his bare sword, the hilt resting in the middle of his chest.

He was a warrior who had gone to God.

I hadn't been able to see Tonild all that well the day before. When she burst into the king's Hall, she was backlit in the bright doorway, and later I'd been preoccupied by Winston's observations about where the murder had taken place. I looked at her closely now.

She was younger than I'd thought—based on her voice I'd guessed she was in her mid-thirties, but now I realized that there was no way she could be any more than twenty-five. She was buxom and tall and blonde, judging from the few strands of hair poking out from under her wimple. She was dressed in a floor-length, pigeon-blue dress with a silver chain around her waist. The pin at her bosom that held her dress together was made of gem-inlaid gold: she was a warrior's wife, who looked more like a woman seeking revenge than a widow in mourning.

She looked us in the eye. Her eyes were gray, her mouth small, and her cheekbones high. Her skin was smooth and healthy, and only the fine lines around her eyes and her headdress revealed that she was a woman and not a young maiden.

There were no children in sight. Either Osfrid's dead son had been their only child, or the children had stayed at home so that the king wouldn't be tempted to take yet another hostage from their family.

Winston bowed slightly. "I'm sorry for your loss, my lady."

She remained silent while I, too, expressed my condolences.

"Did you know that the king has asked us to investigate your husband's killing?" Winston asked casually, as though he were asking if she'd been out riding recently.

She responded with a snort.

"Yes, I know," Winston said with an audible sigh. "You think the king is responsible for the murder."

"I *know* he is," Tonild said, her words striking like the lash of a whip.

"If you're right, perhaps we can count on your help in proving it?" Winston asked.

Tonild's eyes widened a little. "Proving that the king is guilty?"

Winston nodded and explained, "The king has asked me . . . us . . . to solve the murder. I will not hesitate to name the man I determine to be guilty."

Tonild shook her head skeptically and replied, "And I'm supposed to believe that?"

Winston nodded.

"You would accuse the king himself?" Tonild said, a note of derision in her voice.

"If I find evidence of his guilt, yes, my lady, I will present that evidence. To you, to him, and to the Witenagemot."

Now she sneered openly and retorted, "So he can just swear his innocence before all the noblemen in England, conveniently already gathered here in the same place."

Winston nodded again. "That possibility does exist. But you're forgetting one thing, my lady."

She looked at him with eyebrows raised.

"The compurgation defense entitles Cnut to swear that he is innocent," Winston continued. "All he needs to do is enlist twelve compurgators to swear that they believe him. And, yes, I agree with what you haven't said yet, namely, that the king won't have any trouble finding twelve people to swear they believe him."

"There. You see?" Tonild said, sounding downright scornful.

"And yet I see what you do not," Winston said with a twinkle in his eye. "If I present evidence that the king is to blame for your husband's death, no oath will exonerate him. He would not have to pay any penalties or fines, but do you seriously think the Witenagemot would still accept him as king?"

Tonild bit her lip and glanced from Winston to me. I looked her in the eye—which was no hardship, truth be told. She was a fine-looking woman, and I would have been happy to gaze into those eyes for a good long while.

"Cnut's well-armed housecarls will be attending the meeting in force," Tonild pointed out. "They will make sure everyone at the Witenagemot understands that Cnut will remain king whether they accept him or not."

"Cnut has convened a joint meeting of the Thing and the Witenagemot for only one reason," Winston said. "As I'm sure you know, my lady, the king wants the Saxons, Angles, Danes, and all the other peoples of England to choose unity—and for everyone to abide by the same laws. If I present evidence when they meet that the king is guilty of Osfrid's murder, and Cnut decides to swear he is innocent anyway, how many of the assembled witan, noblemen, and clergymen will give him what he wants—namely, a single, unified kingdom?"

Tonild looked at us. I had difficulty not staring at her breasts and her tiny feet, whose tips were just peeking out from below the hem of her dress, but I forced my gaze to remain on her gray eyes.

But then she suddenly looked away and turned to her priest. "What do you say, Father Egbert?"

With dark hair and a flat face, he looked to be about Winston's age and had a nose that protruded like a juniper bush in a moor. His voice was gentle, but his words were neither tentative nor uncertain. "What do you have to lose by taking them at their word?" he asked Tonild.

Tonild obviously wasn't one to follow advice simply because she had asked for it. She sat quietly for a long while looking at Egbert, who gazed calmly back at her. Finally she nodded.

"Fine," she said looking over at Winston. "I choose to believe you."

"That's enough for me," Winston said with an almost imperceptible smile.

"So what do you want to know?" Tonild asked.

"I would like you to tell me about yourself, your son, and your husband," Winston said gently.

Tonild wiped her eyes. "Well, I think you'd better sit down then."

She clapped her hands, and a servant stuck his head in through the tent opening. "Bring chairs!" she ordered. "And a flagon of wine and cups."

He bowed and disappeared, and Tonild held out her palms in a welcoming gesture. "Be my guests."

Noblemen's wives always remember their manners in the end.

Chapter 12

onild's father, a thane by the name of Wighelm, owned land in several different shires. Once the trusted man of King Ethelred the Unready, Wighelm had sworn fealty to Edmund Ironside after Ethelred's death. Wighelm survived the Battle of Assandun and was loyal to Edmund for the six months his short reign lasted. When Edmund died and Cnut became king of all England, Wighelm had refused to swear allegiance to Cnut.

Tonild had been very calm up to that point, but now she stopped and slumped down, her eyes blazing with anger.

"And then what?" Winston asked, although it was clear from his voice that he had already guessed what she was going to say next.

"Cnut decided to clear the most powerful of his enemies out of the way," Tonild said, her voicing trembling with rage.

"So when Cnut culled the ranks of Saxon noblemen who did not want to swear allegiance to him, he ordered your father killed, but your husband Osfrid survived?" Winston asked.

Tonild raised her cup and drank. As her breasts rose and fell, I had a hard time keeping my eyes off them. "My husband and I were introduced while Osfrid was serving King Edmund, just like my father," she continued. "We were married the very day Cnut and Edmund signed their agreement to divide the kingdom between them and rule as coregents. When Edmund died, my husband decided to give Cnut his full support—something my father refused to do. Osfrid was a law-abiding man, and a man of his word. He said it would be wrong not to respect the agreement that both the kings had made."

I looked up from her bosom, and my eyes met Winston's. "So Oslaf wasn't your son?" I asked.

Tonild shook her head. She was breathing more calmly now. "Oslaf was the son of Osfrid's first wife, Everild."

"Who?" Winston asked, sipping his drink for the first time and peering into the cup appreciatively before setting it down.

"Her name was Everild," Tonild said. "She died in childbirth with a second son for Osfrid."

"And that baby?" Winston asked.

Tonild's eyes glazed over. "Once Osfrid realized he might lose both the baby and his wife, he ordered that his son's life should be saved, so the midwife sent for a doctor from the monastery that my husband supported financially." Tonild paused and looked down at the floor.

"Where is this son now, then?" Winston asked.

I followed his example and tasted my own drink. The wine was sweet and good. I shook my head at Winston, to warn him that this was a sensitive topic.

Winston saw me and turned to Tonild. "The doctor failed," he surmised.

She nodded. "They both died." No one spoke for a moment.

"And you don't have any children of your own?" Winston asked, breaking the silence.

"No."

I saw Father Egbert lean forward and rest a hand on the widow's arm. She gave him a strange look and moved her arm away.

A childless widow only slightly older than myself, who had probably inherited a large South Saxon estate. It *was* fertile between those hills down there. Suddenly it wasn't only her breasts I was thinking about.

"Who is Osfrid's heir?" I asked.

All three of them looked at me in astonishment, so I hurried to add that we *were* investigating a murder.

"You're right. That might be important," Winston said, nodding. He looked to Tonild for an answer, but it was Father Egbert who answered. "Apart from the money Osfrid set aside in his will to establish a monastery following his son's death, everything else goes to her ladyship."

I immediately corrected my posture, hoping to make a better impression on her, and suddenly regretted that I was still in my tattered clothes. At least they were freshly washed.

Winston rolled his eyes at my efforts and then looked back to the widow. "So you're a rich woman all of a sudden," he said.

Tonild's eyes widened.

"Are you suggesting that I had my husband murdered in order to become a wealthy widow?" she said. Winston shook his head and held up a hand to ward off any further objections.

"Not at all," he said. "I saw you stand up to the king yesterday, and I have no doubt you were a good wife to your husband. But you should think of yourself now," Winston said. "I mean, the Danes' law is the same as ours—a widow has full right of ownership to her land and property until she remarries. Yesterday you were your husband's wife. Today you're a much-coveted, childless widow of childbearing age. Perhaps you should consider approaching the king and asking him to help find you a new husband in order to avoid dealing with a long line of suitors trying for your hand."

"Approach the king?" Tonild scoffed. "Never. Besides, my husband is lying right there." She stretched her quivering hand out toward his bier. Winston nodded.

"Of course you'll hold onto your property for the requisite year of mourning," he said. "But bear in mind that men will pursue you even during that period. It would also be wise to bear in mind that, in three days' time, Cnut will no longer be merely the conqueror of our country. He will have been crowned the country's sole, anointed king, and he will govern in harmony with the Witenagemot. A young widow would certainly be wise to avoid open displays of hatred for the new king."

"Did you forget that you promised me evidence that Cnut had my husband assassinated?" Tonild scoffed.

Winston shook his head and clarified. "I promised you that *if* I found evidence that he was behind the killing, I would present it to both the Witenagemot and the Thing," he said. "But if you're asking whether I think that's likely, I have to admit I do not."

Tonild leapt up. "Then you lied to me!"

"By no means," Winston objected. "I said I would find evidence if I could. I have never hidden the fact that I doubt such evidence exists."

Tonild sat down again, her eyes still blazing. I smiled at her.

"I do not plan to approach the king," she said, spitting out each word.

"That is your choice, my lady," Winston said. He leaned back in his chair and asked, "Whom did your husband meet yesterday?"

Tonild looked every bit as surprised as I felt at Winston's abrupt change of topic. "Meet?" she repeated, looking over at the priest. Father Egbert cleared his throat.

"The, uh, thane did not mention his plans," the priest said.

"He didn't?" Winston said, raising his eyebrows. "He just walked out?"

Father Egbert and Tonild looked at each other.

I opened my mouth to speak but stopped when Winston raised his finger to his lips.

"My husband . . ." Tonild said hesitantly. "My husband knew a great many people, and most of them are here in Oxford right now."

"Of course," Winston said, raising his glass to take another sip. "All of the noblemen in the kingdom are present or on their way. So, which of them was he meeting yesterday?"

The widow's voice turned sharp. "Didn't we just tell you we don't know?" Winston glanced quickly at me and then smiled.

"Yes, my lady," he said. I leaned forward.

"Who accompanied him?" I asked.

Tonild and the priest exchanged looks again. "I . . . I don't know . . . ," Tonild said, trailing off.

"Osfrid left by himself," Father Egbert said with a courteous smile, but his smile faded when he saw the expression on my face.

"You're lying," I said without raising my voice.

Tonild stood up abruptly with an insulted look on her face. "My husband left *by himself*," she repeated. I smiled affably.

"That's hard for me to believe," I said. I do have some manners after all. I know better than to accuse a Saxon nobleman's widow of lying. Sadly, however, her face told me that any hope I had had of winning her hand was now dead.

"My lady," I said, my voice deliberately courteous. "Osfrid was a thane. Show me a thane who walks around without a retinue. Besides, he was an enemy of the king. He wasn't stupid, was he?"

Her eyes again flamed with rage. "Certainly not," she exclaimed.

"I thought not," I continued. "Only a stupid man would walk around without a retinue amidst all his enemies' housecarls. So, I'm asking you, whom did he go with?"

"Horik," Tonild admitted, her voice scarcely audible.

"And Horik is . . ." I said, fishing.

"Horik is Osfrid's trusted man and the leader of his retinue," Father Egbert said, standing up and glaring at me. "I presume you'll want to speak to him next?"

I nodded. We waited in silence while the priest flung the tent flap aside and walked out. Winston looked down at the floor. I allowed my eyes to focus on the place they seemed most drawn, but Tonild did not seem to notice my fascination with her breasts.

A few moments later the priest returned alone. "Horik is not here," Father Egbert said.

Winston looked at me and I nodded. The devious father had had just enough time to send Horik out of the camp. Winston's voice nevertheless remained calm.

"Where is he?" Winston demanded.

Father Egbert shrugged and replied calmly, "Soldiers do not routinely keep me apprised of their plans."

"What does this Horik look like?" Winston still sounded quite calm.

"Look like?" Father Egbert asked, obviously trying to catch Tonild's eye. "He's very tall and has red hair that he wears in two braids."

If we had a look at the many tall Saxon soldiers around camp, we might be able to pick Horik out based on his hair color.

"And you'll tell him we want to talk to him when you see him?" Winston asked politely.

The priest nodded.

"Thank you," Winston said and turned to the widow. "When will Osfrid be buried?"

Tonild looked up, her eyes suddenly full of tears. Perhaps her anger had been suppressing her grief, of which she was suddenly reminded. "This afternoon I expect," she said. "His brother is on his way."

Winston raised an eyebrow.

"I sent men out to meet Osfrid's brother Osmund last night," Tonild said. "We heard he was spending the night in Ramsbury."

I instinctively took a step forward—it was news to me that Osfrid had a brother. But Winston quickly turned to Father Egbert and asked, "You said Lady Tonild inherits everything?"

Father Egbert nodded and explained, "That is the truth. The thane's will was quite clear."

"Hmm." Winston rubbed his chin. "Are there any other relatives?"

"Just two brothers-in-law from his first marriage," Egbert said.

"And where are they?" Winston asked.

"Here in Oxford. They both swore fealty to Cnut a long time ago," Father Egbert said.

Winston closed his eyes for a moment. When he opened them again, he gestured for me to follow. "Thank you for your assistance," he said to Tonild and Father Egbert. He bowed to Tonild, stepped up to the tent's opening, and flipped the flap aside.

I took a sudden step back, blinded by the sunlight shimmering over the camp. Father Egbert was so close on my heels that I stepped on his feet. To protect himself, he pushed me in the back so that I toppled forward onto Winston.

We both fell out of the tent. I could tell from the guards' smarmy grins that they were glad to see us go.

Winston walked through the camp without uttering a word. He was tugging on his nose and chewing his lip, clearly lost in thought. I didn't interrupt, and instead kept an eye out for a soldier with red braids. No luck, of course. Horik was long gone.

Winston and I sat down opposite each other at a rough, unfinished wooden table outside an ale tent on the outskirts of the camp. There was so much commotion all around us that we could only hear each other by leaning way over the table. Our heads were practically touching, but this meant that we could speak freely without any risk of being overheard, which suited us just fine. As we debriefed about the investigation, Winston agreed with me on one point.

"You're right," Winston said after a freckly, flat-chested wench had brought us our drinks. "Egbert told Horik to scram."

We raised our tankards to each other and took a sip. "Ah," Winston said, setting his tankard back down. "I must admit that I do prefer malted ale to sweet wine. But now the real question is, why is this Horik supposed to steer clear of you and me?"

"In other words," I said, "who was Osfrid meeting with yesterday?"

"Exactly," Winston began tugging on his nose again. "Tonild doesn't seem to want us to find that out, but that's exactly what we're going to do. Any guesses?"

I thought it over. "Another woman?"

Winston shook his head. "No, Tonild inherited the estate. As long as the estate remained hers, why would she care whether Osfrid had a woman on the side?"

"But the estate wouldn't be hers anymore if the other woman had a child," I said.

Winston considered that for a moment. "I suppose," he said. "But Tonild could have found men to swear that Osfrid hadn't fathered the child. No, I think there's some other reason why they're not talking."

I cocked my head, puzzled.

"Like *fear*," he suggested.

I shook my head. "Who would they be afraid of?"

He taunted me with a mocking smile. He sat there in silence while I thought so hard that smoke practically came out of my ears. I finally figured it out. "*The king!*" I exclaimed in a hushed voice.

"Yes, the king. I'll wager that when we find this Horik, he'll confirm that there are Saxons in the camp who are doing everything in their power to keep the Witenagemot from proclaiming Cnut king. That's the only way they have even the slightest chance of preventing Cnut from taking full control of England."

"And if the king gets wind of the plot, he'll strike," I said quietly. "They're afraid for their lives."

Winston nodded and added, "And not just *their* lives."

When I looked puzzled, he explained, "Whoever Osfrid met with is still alive. But only for as long as the meeting can be kept secret from Cnut."

Chapter 13

o the king is guilty after all?" I asked after draining my tankard.

"Perhaps, but probably not," Winston said, grinning at me. "And yet . . . kings can be hard to figure out. But upon closer reflection, I still don't think he did it. It's just not like him."

This surprised me. "Not like Cnut? Tell that to Tonild's father, and the ealdormen, and all the other thanes he's had assassinated."

Winston nodded. "Exactly. He had them mowed down. There are certain things a king has to do. But why did he do it? What was his goal?"

"God's grace?" I guessed. I didn't see what Winston was getting at.

"Priests talk a lot about that, yes," Winston said. "And I'm sure the good Wulfstan keeps Cnut's ears full of how he won the kingdom because he enjoys God's favor. So of course Cnut does everything he can to remain in the Lord's favor—just ask the monasteries and the Church. A few years ago, the monks at Ely Monastery were cursing Cnut as a battle-crazed Viking marauder. Now that he's been lavishing them with gifts, they're falling all over themselves with praise for him." Winston drank from his tankard. "But don't you find it odd, Halfdan, that God's favor never falls to kings *until* they've won, never before. Cnut received God's favor *by* winning. But *why* did he win, if God's favor didn't come until afterward?"

What a stupid question. "He was strongest," I said.

"He had the best soldiers, the best advisers, and the greatest yearning for power, yes," Winston said, rolling his now-empty tankard between his hands. "So, you see, it is *power* that makes him king. It's power he's after. That's what he cleaves to. And in the shadow of power is fear. Why do you think all these nobles are flocking into Oxford right now?"

"Well," I said, "the *Vikings* are coming for their promised share of the heregeld, which was why they fought, as well as the reason they chose to follow and then hail Cnut."

"But what about the Saxons, the Angles, the Jutes, and the nobles from the Welsh borderlands?" Winston asked. "What about the Danes who had kept their oaths to Ethelred and Edmund? All the peoples who have been conquered?" Winston paused. "*They* are coming out of fear of incurring the king's wrath, because they've seen what happens to people who oppose him. King Cnut does his killing in the open. He leaves no doubt that it is *his* avenging hand striking the blow. By wielding his power in such plain sight, he casts a formidable shadow of fear. The men upon whom that shadow falls scurry toward him, hoping that Cnut's power will not crush them the next time. That's why I believe the king when he says he's innocent in this case—because Osfrid was murdered *in secret*. But if we've guessed correctly, Osfrid did meet with someone working against the king."

Winston smiled wryly before continuing. "But does Cnut know that? Don't you think Tonild and Egbert are afraid Cnut will find that out? Isn't that why they're so reluctant to talk?"

Winston was making a good deal of sense.

"That all sounds well and good, but we have no proof."

"Oh, I wouldn't say that. And Cnut isn't entirely in the clear yet either," Winston said, as our waitress, Robin-No-Breast, stopped by the table.

"Yes?" Winston said to her.

"Are you two planning to have anything else to drink? If not, I have to ask you to leave to make room for other patrons," she said, her voice sounding lethargic from exhaustion.

People were standing all around us. The ale tent was evidently doing well these days.

"Bring us another two tankards," Winston said, squinting into the sun as he looked up at the wench before she scurried away for more ale.

"We'd better take stock of where we stand," Winston said, turning back to me. The girl returned and set the sloshing tankards on the table, grumpily taking the coin Winston handed her.

"Maybe Osfrid's brother did it," I suggested, wiping ale foam out of my beard.

"Maybe," Winston replied. "I'm sure many would find displeasure in being left out of their brother's will."

"Although in this case that doesn't really make sense," I said, scooting in closer to the table as an ale-swilling patron squeezed past behind me. "If Osfrid's brother had stood to inherit, then he might have had a reason. But Tonild is the heir."

"I suppose so," Winston said, nodding slowly. "But he may have had other reasons. We could look into what Osfrid and his brother each inherited from their father. Nothing fosters hatred between two siblings like the unfair distribution of an inheritance."

"What about Osfrid's brothers-in-law?" I suggested.

"The brothers of his first wife, who died so long ago? Hardly likely. Although we should probably find out whether Osfrid inherited anything from *her* and if he shared that inheritance with her brothers. If he did share, they would have no reason to go after him. If he didn't, well, that's another matter."

As I mulled this all over, I remembered what the king had said about the death of Osfrid's son Oslaf, who had been Cnut's hostage. "What about Thorkell?"

"Thorkell the Tall? The earl?" Winston looked at me, astonished.

"Well, he's taken out men before when they've opposed Cnut. And it was *his* stallion that killed the boy. Maybe Osfrid accused him as well as the king?"

"Hmm," Winston said, tugging on his nose. "Hmm. But he was in the Hall with the king when the murder took place."

"He's an earl! He has men for that kind of thing," I said, scoffing at Winston's gullibility.

"Good point," he conceded. "All right, then. If everyone else turns out to be a dud, we won't rule Thorkell out. Anyone else?"

I had another thought. "Perhaps Tonild herself?"

"The widow?" Winston asked, laughing almost contemptuously. "I just explained to her that her behavior toward Cnut had convinced me of her innocence."

"Which could have just been what it was *meant* to do," I said, raising my voice in my eagerness. Winston slowly lowered the palms of both hands to the table and leaned forward, signaling me to drop my voice to a whisper. I leaned forward as well. "How long were Osfrid and Tonild married?" I said. "Two, three years? And she was still barren. And Osfrid's other heirs are all dead. His eldest son died at a very young age, and the younger one died at birth. How old was Osfrid?"

Winston shrugged. "Well, you saw him—both quick and dead."

"How old are you?" I asked.

Winston's mouth slid open, taken aback. "A little over forty."

"Well, Osfrid looked to be a little older than you," I estimated. "Closer to fifty, I'd say. So he was running out of time to line up some heirs. What are a man's options if his wife is barren?"

Winston nodded in understanding. "Annul the marriage and disown the wife. Yes, you're right. If he had threatened to do that—or if Tonild was even simply afraid that he might—then that would be a very good motive."

"And a good reason not to tell us who Osfrid was meeting with yesterday," I added.

"If he was meeting with the murderer she had hired—yes, indeed," Winston said and then paused to sip his ale. His furrowed brow and pursed lips carved deep wrinkles into his face.

Finally he looked up. "All right. You go back to camp. Find out as much as you can about this Horik, if he even exists. But also find out what you can about Tonild and Osfrid and their life together."

"How am I supposed to do that?" I had trouble imagining Tonild's soldiers being especially forthcoming with me.

Winston's smile went beyond teasing as he replied, "Your eyes have scrutinized the chest of every single woman we've passed all day—not to mention ogling as far up their skirts as possible. If women are as fond of you as you are of them, I'm quite certain you'll be able to locate a scullery maid or a servant girl whom you can charm into gladly supplying you with all you could ever want—in terms of information, I mean."

I beamed at him and asked, "What are you going to do, then?"

"I'm going to run a couple of errands."

Fine, if he was going to be all secretive like that . . . Well, actually it didn't bother me at all. I stood up and handed my seat to a Viking who had been eyeing it for some time.

The hubbub in the camp had not died down while we'd been talking at the alehouse. Men were pushing and shoving and shouting at each other, and Cnut's housecarls were strolling all over the camp in small groups. The king clearly wanted to demonstrate that he had things firmly under control.

Instead of heading straight for Tonild's tent, I ducked left into the row of tents just before it. No one paid any attention to me. There were as many soldiers wandering around in worn clothes as there are rocks in a streambed, and I knew that as long as I didn't pick any fights, I would be left well enough alone.

I recalled yet another of Harding's lessons: To avoid confrontation, avoid making eye contact. That's how to move safely through a crowd of soldiers.

And it worked like a charm.

Tonild's tent came into view between the two tents to my right. Though the guards were still there, they were simply staring straight ahead, focusing on the area immediately surrounding the tent, and therefore took no notice of me.

The tent flap was closed. Tonild was presumably deep in prayer with her priest, and they'd probably remain there until her brother-in-law arrived.

I turned my back to her tent and headed toward the edge of the camp. The cooking bonfires were blazing out on the grassy meadow. Long worktables lined the cooking area, and lines of servant girls and boys were bent over them, hard at work. Some makeshift canvas awnings had been put up behind the worktables.

I wandered around, trying to eavesdrop. Eventually I thought I heard the name Osfrid, so I moved closer to the two servants, who were slowly turning a skewered sheep over the embers. When I asked whether they were Tonild's men, they looked at me, shrugged, and shook their heads.

Then it struck me that they might still think of themselves as Osfrid's men, but when I asked them if they served him, I got the same response. I realized that they'd probably just been discussing the murder, like so many others in Oxford that day.

A few minutes later, a leggy vixen came jogging across the grass. Luck was with me now. Her blonde hair billowed over her bare shoulders, her breasts jiggled gently against her linen top, and a pair of promising lips beckoned in her lovely face.

I hadn't forgotten that I had a job to do, but that was no reason to keep my eyes to myself. I stifled an exclamation of delight when she yelled to a little boy too tall for his shirt and dirty breeches that Lady Tonild wanted a flagon of wine right away.

The boy, who had been sitting aimlessly in the grass, instantly stood up and walked over to one of the awnings, where the vixen was waiting for him. They went inside together. The boy came back out with the requested flagon, and the vixen emerged a moment later holding a bronze cauldron in her hands. I guessed that the cauldron was full of sloshing water. And sure enough, she headed across the meadow toward the stream that ran along its edge.

To reach it she had to walk around a couple of tattered storage tents that stood about shoulder height. I hunched forward and ran to the right of one of them, hoping she would walk to the left of it. It worked. I straightened up and stepped in her way just as she rounded the corner. She crashed right into me.

Her cauldron smacked into my shin before jostling back into her and spilling dirty wash water all over her. She yelped in pain as the metal cauldron hit her ankle.

"What the . . . ?" I began, on my knees. "Are you all right?"

She looked at me in confusion. Tears were welling up in the corners of her eyes. "How, uh . . . oh, I'm so s—" she stammered.

"Sorry?" I said. "Don't worry about it. I mean, obviously you should have been looking where you were going, but I'm just fine." I moved on before she could realize that I too should have been looking where I was going.

"Here, let me help you," I said. I put my arm around her, just below her breasts, and carefully pulled her to her feet, picking up the cauldron with my other hand. With my arm still around her, I looked down at her wet clothes. "Were you on your way to the stream?"

She nodded and tried to free herself, but I didn't let go.

"Take it slow. Doesn't it still hurt?" I asked. She pulled free of me and took a step back.

"Ow!" she yelled, and I shot my arm out to keep her from falling.

"Yes, I'd say that definitely hurts. Is it your ankle?"

Another nod.

"Let me help you," I said again.

A handful of girls were standing by the stream, where I guessed the washing was done, so I gently steered her upstream toward a flowering hawthorn. My luck stayed with me: There was a pleasant, secluded little spot right between the tree trunk and the stream. I lowered her onto the sloping bank, knelt down, and took her warm foot in my hand.

"Is it bad?" I asked.

She nodded, but her eyes suggested that she was not in all that much pain.

I slid my hand up her calf, and although I encountered no objection, I stopped at her knee and gently ran two fingertips back down to her ankle. She shivered and gave me a quick smile.

I slid my hand up to her knee again, but this time I continued up to her soft thigh, paused, and then stroked her gently with the tips of my fingers all the way back down.

Her mouth opened halfway and leaned forward. "Stop," she whispered.

I flashed her a big smile, and then I leaned forward and pressed my lips to hers just long enough to feel her lips relax.

My hand came up to rest on her shoulder, and she bristled only slightly when I pulled her to me. Suddenly she stiffened. I realized she had bumped into the hilt of my sword, so I let go of her, undid my belt, laid it in the grass, and then turned back to her. She was watching me, an encouraging glint in her blue eyes.

I responded to her encouragement and pulled her to me once more, turning us so that she was lying in my lap with the stream behind her.

This time I let the kiss go on for a long time. She tasted good, fresh with a hint of bread, and her tongue was warm and playful as it moved to meet mine.

It was the sun and the shiny surface of the bit of stream flowing by the tree that saved us.

I'd kept my eyes open as we kissed and suddenly saw a sparkle in the water in front of me. I realized instinctively that it was the reflection from a shiny weapon, so I flung myself backward, clutching the girl to my chest as an ax sliced through the air above us. My back hit a man's leg, and I pushed the girl aside as I flung myself forward. I grabbed my sword by the hilt and leaped to my feet in an instant, tossing the sheath and belt aside as I did so.

The girl screamed, and the attacker cursed.

I recognized him when he pulled his ax back. It was the axman we had met in the hamlet a couple of days earlier, Toste he had said his name was. I met his next swing with my blade. I parried the ax handle down and to the side, feinted at his eyes, and slashed away at his legs. The blade reverberated in my hand as my sword struck his shinbone. As he screamed and teetered, I jammed the sword through his doublet into his chest. I twisted the blade and pulled it back out with all my might before he even hit the ground.

The girl was on her knees sobbing, her hands clutched to her mouth, but she was going to have to wait. I ran roaring up the slope, ducked under the hawthorn, and flung myself to the left, rolling over the ground. I was back up with my sword at the ready within two heartbeats.

There were no other enemies and no drawn weapons. Only two servant girls who stared at me wide eyed, each with a bundle of laundry resting on her hip.

I slid back down beneath the hawthorn to the girl and the Viking, who was shuddering, half his body engulfed in the stream. He'd lost his ax, his eyes were rolling back in their sockets, and he was hiccuping blood as his hands clutched his stomach, trying to stem the flow gushing from his stab wound.

"Who sent you?" I demanded, dropping to my knees beside him. His eyes narrowed.

"You . . . lied . . . to us!" he stammered while shuddering.

I nodded. Of course I had lied to him. It was true that I wasn't the lord of any estate, but I was certain that wasn't why he had just attacked us.

"Whom do you serve?" I demanded.

He stared at me in disdain. Blood foamed around his mouth.

"Where are your buddies?" I demanded.

His eyes mocked me as he wheezed, "I'll see you in Hel."

Ha. He didn't think that this counted as a heroic death in battle, and he therefore didn't believe he was about to enter Valhalla.

I shook him. "Who sent you?"

His eyes rolled up, unseeing, and his mouth twisted and opened, emitting a stream of blood. As he died, the sharp odor of shit hit my nostrils.

I swore.

The girl was still sobbing. I knelt down beside her, put my arm around her, and held her so close that her body stiffened. I stroked her hair back with one hand while caressing her cheek with the other. I whispered that everything was all right. She was safe.

Her body relaxed, and her forehead rested against my chin. As I raised her face toward mine, her eyes were welcoming, though still filled with tears.

"You're safe now," I told her.

She nodded. I gave her a quick kiss and then stood up. I glared angrily at the dead man, who stared up vacantly into the branches.

I heard footsteps in the meadow, followed by rough voices, ordering me to come out.

With my sword pointing down at the ground, I climbed up the slope from the stream and burst out from beneath the hawthorn. Four housecarls stood before me, their spears lowered. I gathered that the laundry girls now standing behind the housecarls had alerted them.

"My name is Halfdan. I am investigating the murder of Osfrid the Saxon on behalf of King Cnut. I was attacked and have killed my attacker."

The one on the far left barked that I should drop my sword.

"Hear me! I am in the service of the king," I stated.

"Now!" They came closer, the tips of their spears pointed at my chest.

I complied.

Then I spotted more housecarls running toward us. I sighed with relief when I recognized the one in front to be Godskalk. "There's a girl down there who requires protection," I told him.

I saw only two possibilities: That sack of shit Viking just happened to recognize me and wanted revenge because he had figured out I told him a lie. I rejected that possibility. If they knew I was lying, why wait to attack me? Why not pounce on me immediately and force me to fight? Regardless of how he had figured it out, he was clearly not the kind of person who hesitated to use his weapon. A man like that always thinks he's a better fighter than whoever he goes up against. A mistake that cost him his life.

The other possibility seemed more likely: He had been sent by someone who had seen me with the girl. Someone who wanted to stop her from saying anything to me.

I needed Winston to help me figure out what it was that she wasn't supposed to tell me.

Chapter 14

he girl was still sobbing, and didn't stop even after Godskalk had dispatched two mail-clad housecarls down to the bank to protect her. He hadn't asked any questions; he simply gave the order.

I wished I could go comfort her, but for the time being, she was going to have to manage on her own. Something had just occurred to me.

"Could you send a man up to that pointed tent up there?" I asked Godskalk.

He raised an eyebrow at me. Godskalk looked smart but not arrogant. He had a steadfast look in his eyes, his jaw was square, and his beard well trimmed. His chestnut-brown hair fell forward over his wide forehead under his helmet. Although he was draped in silver and gold, his sword's hilt was devoid of ornamentation—the weapon of a soldier.

"Tonild sent for a flagon of wine," I explained. I regretted not having realized the significance of this before. "Which must mean that her brother-in-law, whom she was expecting, has finally arrived. I think Winston wants to ask him a few questions, as well. I would really like the brother-in-law to remain in the tent until Winston has had a chance to speak with him. Ideally, I'd also like to avoid having him hear about what happened down here."

At a snap of Godskalk's fingers, three housecarls approached us. Godskalk gave them instructions to assume positions outside Tonild's tent and, in the name of the king, to ask anyone wishing to leave the tent to wait for us.

"But," he added for my benefit, "do not use force. Trying to forcibly restrain a Saxon nobleman could be the bump in the road that topples the king's cart."

I understood.

"Well, if he does leave the tent, perhaps someone could follow him," I said.

"You heard that?" Godskalk asked the housecarls, who nodded before rushing off to secure Tonild's tent. Godskalk then turned to me. "What about the girl?"

I thought quickly. "We'll have her stay down here by the stream for now."

It was surely best to keep the Viking's death under wraps for a while if we could. Unfortunately, I was forced to accept that our chances of doing so were as dead as herring in brine the moment I peered over Godskalk's shoulder and saw that the laundry girls who had raised the alarm were gone. I spotted them in the middle of an excited cluster of people in the camp. The gossip was too good for them to risk someone else being the first to share it.

I considered our options. The girl had been down by the stream the entire time, so it was unlikely that the laundry wenches had seen her. Maybe we could keep people from finding out she was still alive after all.

"Also," I said to Godskalk, "do you think you could send a man to fetch Winston the Illustrator?"

Godskalk nodded and dispatched yet another man.

I picked up my sword and meticulously rubbed it clean, first on some hawthorn leaves and then in the grass. Then I strode back over toward the stream bank and peered down at the girl, who had collapsed on the slope between two gruff-looking housecarls.

I skidded down, picked up my belt and put it on, and slid my sword down into its sheath. Then I let the housecarls know with a toss of my head that they could move along.

They sent a cascade of pebbles down the slope as they left, but they were soon out of sight. I could hear their voices, as well as Godskalk's, from the bank, so I felt safe from further attacks.

I lowered myself to the ground and put my arms around the girl. At first she tried to push me away, but then she went limp in my arms and rested her head against my shoulder. I turned us so that she faced away from Toste's dead body.

"My name is Halfdan and I'm on an assignment for the king. What's your name?"

"Fri . . . Fri . . . Frideswide," she said between sobs.

"You were named after Oxford's patron saint?" I asked her.

She nodded against my shoulder. "Yes," she said. "But every . . . everyone calls . . . calls . . . me Frida."

"And you're from Oxford?" I asked, sliding my hand around her shoulder and giving her a hug.

Another nod.

"So you haven't been working for Lady Tonild for very long?" My hand slid down her back and pulled her in closer.

She raised her tear-striped face from my shoulder, but gave no sign of wanting to pull away from my embrace. "For only two days," she replied.

Many noblemen had come without large retinues, choosing instead to hire servants upon arrival in Oxford.

"Is she a good mistress?" I asked Frida.

She shrugged. Servants were usually satisfied as long as they received a decent amount of food, earned more than a field hand's wage, and weren't beaten.

I suddenly discerned a new voice above us. Frida looked up in fear, but I pulled her to me, which she didn't resist. "That's just my partner—he's a friendly man, and he wants to talk to you. You can trust him."

Frida relaxed, and I felt her warm hand slip into mine.

A smile lurked on Winston's lips when he spotted us sitting so close.

"You really know how to follow an order, Halfdan," he teased.

I grinned at him.

"Winston, this is Frida. She works for Lady Tonild and was just attacked."

He looked at me with eyebrows raised. "*She* was just attacked?" he asked.

I didn't dare let go of her for fear she would turn around and burst back into tears at the sight of the Viking's bloody corpse. Instead I motioned for Winston to sit down.

With my mouth right up against his ear, I quietly explained why I thought Frida had been the target. When I finished, Winston nodded.

"Not bad thinking, Halfdan," he said and stood up. "Shall we go up to sit somewhere in the sun?"

I pulled Frida up, and keeping an arm around her waist, helped her up the slope. I pointed to a toppled alder tree a few feet away. Winston nodded and followed us. Once Frida was seated, I slid down next to her, rested my hand on hers, and explained that she should feel free to answer any question she was asked.

Frida, who was quite relaxed by now, made no move to pull her hand away from mine. She wiped her now dry tears away with her left hand, then looked at Winston with clear eyes.

"What are your duties, Frida?" Winston asked.

She shrugged. "Pretty much anything you can think of."

"You prepare food?"

She shook her head. "No, the cook the lord brought does that."

So Osfrid had wanted to make sure he would eat well.

"Do you wait on them?" Winston asked.

A nod.

"Do you scrub vegetables, clean fish and meat, scour and do dishes?" Winston asked.

Another nod.

A girl who did everything, in other words.

"Do you know any of the other staff?" Winston asked, sounding deliberately casual.

"A few. Most of them are also from here in Oxford," Frida said.

"Ah, I meant your lord's soldiers, actually," Winston said.

"Only the ones who grope me," she scoffed. Winston smiled at her.

"You don't like that?"

"Not if they smell and are all dirty," she said with a look of distaste.

"No," Winston said, now smiling at me. "I suppose not everyone has a nobleman's habits."

The girl didn't seem to understand what he was talking about.

"Is Horik one of the ones who touches you?" Winston asked.

"He's tried," she replied, holding her head high.

Winston and I exchanged looks. So he existed, this Horik.

"When did you last see him?" Winston asked.

Frida thought for a moment. "This morning, I think."

"I see." Winston closed his eyes halfway. "Could you be more precise?"

After a long silence, she nodded. "The lady had guests and sent for a flagon of wine. Shortly after that, the priest came out and spoke to Horik. They talked for a while, and then Horik left."

Winston's eyes met mine. So we were right. He had been sent away while we were in the tent.

"Just like that?" Winston said.

She stared at him blankly, not understanding.

"He just left?" Winston asked.

"Well, no. He went and got a knapsack first," Frida replied.

So he was long gone by now.

Winston asked a few more questions, in an effort to discover what Frida knew about the relationship between Osfrid and his wife, but she obviously knew nothing. He asked about guests they had hosted, but she couldn't tell us anything. He tried to wring more answers out of her—all for naught. As a scullery maid, she didn't even have access to the tent. She had to hand everything she fetched over to a steward, who then made sure that the lord or lady received it.

"This steward," Winston finally asked. "Is he from Oxford?"

Frida shook her head, explaining that Osfrid had brought his most important serving staff—cook, steward, and presumably his wife's lady-in-waiting—with him.

"What's this steward's name?" Winston asked.

"I don't know," she replied.

I eyed her skeptically. They had been working together for two days—not long, I realized, but surely long enough to learn each other's name. But Winston looked at me and shook his head.

"He's a household servant," Winston explained to me. "He wouldn't give a temporary scullery maid the time of day. How many domestic servants were you on a first-name basis with in your former life?"

I was going to snap back that I remembered quite a few of the servants' names, but the words froze in my mouth as I realized he was right.

"Frida, thank you very much for your help," Winston said as he stood up.

Godskalk and his housecarls were waiting for us, and we walked back across the meadow toward the camp together. When we reached the kitchen tents, Frida let go of my hand.

"Maybe we'll see each other again," I said, reaching out and giving her arm a squeeze.

"Maybe," she said, looking down demurely. "You know where to find me."

The three housecarls that Godskalk had sent up to Tonild's tent were standing at a suitable distance from the tent, putting up with silent glares from Tonild's own soldiers. As soon as Godskalk's team spotted us, one of them stepped forward and announced, "No one has left the tent."

"But do they know you're out here?" Winston asked. I had filled Winston in on my instructions to Godskalk's men on our way over here.

The housecarl nodded. "One of the lady's men passed a message inside. It was that one over there," he said, pointing out one of Tonild's guards, who looked back at us defiantly.

"We'll manage on our own from here," Winston said, smiling at Godskalk, who dismissed his housecarls with a hand gesture.

"And the girl?" Godskalk asked, before leaving to join the housecarls.

"She should be safe enough, I think," Winston said. "Presumably she's already told us whatever they wanted to stop her from telling us, or maybe she doesn't even know what she knows. In any case, whoever gave the order for the attack may already know that we've spoken with her—and if not, they'll know soon enough—so she should be out of danger now." Winston walked over to Tonild's tent flap but was stopped by the guard whom the housecarl had singled out.

"Would you kindly ask your lady to receive us?" Winston asked cordially.

We had to wait quite awhile.

When we were finally shown into the tent, Tonild did not get up out of her chair. Nor did the priest or the broad-shouldered nobleman who occupied the other chairs.

"I thought we were done," Tonild said flatly.

"I'm not here to see you, my lady," Winston said. Though he was standing stiffly, he sounded relaxed.

"You're not?" Tonild sounded surprised. "You do know that this is my tent, do you not?"

Winston and I had turned our eyes toward her guest. Filling the chair nicely, Osfrid's brother sat with his legs outstretched and appeared to be quite at ease. While his brother's hair had been only tinged with gray, Osmund's was wiry and steely gray all over. Though less fleshy, he had the same ruddy complexion as Osfrid.

"We're here regarding your brother-in-law," Winston said.

Osmund's eyes widened, but he didn't say anything.

"I'm sorry for your loss," Winston continued, still sounding cordial.

Osmund tipped his head slightly forward in response.

"You're intruding on our grief," Tonild said, scolding us more stridently than before.

"Only because it's necessary," Winston said. He hadn't taken his eyes off Osmund. "I'm looking for a soldier who works for you."

"I have a great many soldiers," Osmund said. He had a deep voice.

"This one is a Viking," Winston explained. "His clothes are worn and his doublet has seen better days."

Osmund shook his head. "I'm a Saxon. I have no use for lousy Vikings."

"An axman," Winston continued, undeterred.

"I don't know him," Osmund said.

"And dead," Winston finally said.

I trained my eyes on Osmund. Even given the dim light under the canvas of the tent, I would have been willing to swear his face did not twitch once during this exchange.

I shook my head at Winston, who sighed quietly.

"Well, surely not dead from disease," Osmund said. He was teasing us.

"Killed, in fact," Winston said.

"As Vikings are wont to be," Osmund said. His gaze moved over to me for the first time, coming to rest on my sword belt. "By you?"

I nodded.

"Well, then it's a good day for the Saxons," Osmund said. "Yesterday the Danes killed my brother; today an English sword has cut one of them down."

Clearly he knew nothing of my background.

"Well, it's not yet clear who murdered Osfrid," Winston said, looking around. Tonild, however, pretended not to understand what he was waiting for and continued to make us stand.

Osmund snorted in response, a snort that he only half stifled for politeness' sake. Then he said he was sure I had my reasons for killing a Viking in the middle of a town currently under tight lockdown by Cnut's housecarls.

I glanced at Winston, who nodded at Osmund. I noticed that Winston seemed to be keeping a close eye on Tonild.

"The Viking attacked a girl," I said, speaking aloud for the first time—in Saxon.

The nobleman's teeth flashed as he grinned. "Those Viking assholes have a habit of doing that. I suppose she was English?"

"Yes. It was the lady's girl," I said. Like Winston, my eyes were also focused on Tonild, who looked up in concern.

"My girl?" she asked.

I nodded.

"But . . ." the widow began, looking toward the back of the tent. A woman wearing homespun sat bent over her sewing on a daybed in the very back.

"A girl you hired here in Oxford," I explained. "Her name's Frida."

Tonild shook her head, drawing a blank. "Frida?"

Father Egbert leaned forward and said under his breath, "One of the temporary girls. She was hired to help out while we're here."

The widow seemed very confused. "And what . . . Why should I . . . I don't understand," she stammered.

Winston looked at me to signal that we were leaving and then bowed low before Tonild. "I apologize for having taken up your time, my lady," he said.

Once outside the tent, we exchanged looks.

"What now?" Winston asked, scratching his chin.

"We didn't get anything out of that," I said.

"Maybe not. And yet," Winston said, smiling to my surprise, "we learned that that priest fellow has an eye for the ladies and knows their names."

Chapter 15

inston glanced at me when he saw Godskalk waiting for us outside Tonild's tent. He was clearly wondering if I knew why he was there, which I didn't. Winston stopped and nodded politely to the housecarl.

"Do you have any news I can give the king?" Godskalk asked.

Winston shook his head. "No such luck. But we could use your help."

"Of course."

"A tall, redheaded warrior by the name of Horik has gone missing. Can your housecarls find him?" Winston asked.

"They can try," Godskalk replied.

I opened my mouth, then closed it again. I was going to remind Winston that Horik's hair was braided, but then braids can be undone.

Winston looked out at the throngs of people in the camp and turned to me.

"The man you killed by the stream, Toste, what about his companions from that night in the hamlet?" he asked.

"What about them?" I said.

"Would you recognize them?"

I thought about it. I hadn't paid much attention to that pack of masterless Viking dogs; they looked like any other highway robbers.

"If I were sitting across from them, maybe. Bedraggled ring mail, threadbare clothes, shabby sacks of dung."

"Just like scores of others," Winston said, smiling slightly. He turned back to Godskalk and continued, "In any case, we could also use your help with this matter. We encountered the man who was killed today once before, along with four others."

Godskalk nodded. "I heard you tell the king about them."

Had he been standing that close to us in the king's Hall? I remembered it differently—that he'd come rushing over to us only when Cnut yelled for him. But of course, the head of the king's housecarls was surely never out of the king's earshot unless he was under specific orders.

"Your housecarls are everywhere. Do you think they could they find these four men for us?"

Godskalk laughed. "Find four warriors who look like all the other warriors in this gathering of warriors from all corners of the realm? I doubt it."

"The man I killed had a Northumbrian accent," I said. The housecarl raised his eyebrows at me.

"Ah well, that certainly narrows it down," he said, rolling his eyes. "There are probably only a couple of earls, a handful of thanes, a hundred or so lesser noblemen, and who knows who else from Northumbria. And they've all brought retinues with them."

"Still," Winston said courteously. "Four masterless men—who are also broke—because otherwise they would hardly have tried to loot that hamlet."

"And that's what they were planning to do?" Godskalk said, suddenly keenly interested.

Winston and I looked at each other. Truth be told, I had intervened before the Vikings had a chance to make it clear whether they were planning to rob the farmers or pay them for a night's shelter. But I hesitated because I didn't want to put my head on the chopping block. Since I couldn't swear they were there to pillage the place, I made do by saying, "They lied."

"As men do," Godskalk said, bursting out laughing. "Did you expect them to tell the truth?"

"But they were without a master," Winston interrupted, "and judging from appearances, impoverished to boot. Could you at least ask the housecarls to keep their eyes open?"

Godskalk studied Winston for a long time and then nodded.

"Of course," he said. He began to turn away but then paused. "Oh, one other thing! The king has demanded that you pay him a visit at dusk."

"Thank you, we were already planning on it," Winston replied, bowing quickly.

After Godskalk had disappeared down the makeshift footpath, I looked at Winston, who looked back at me, puzzled.

"This Toste who I killed *wasn't* masterless, was he?" I asked.

Winston's eyes widened a little.

"Someone ordered him to kill Frida," I pointed out.

"Which means his buddies might be in the service of the same man."

"Toste *claimed* they served Thorkell the Tall."

"But he was lying?" Winston asked.

"I think so," I said with a shrug.

"Right. Let's keep that in mind," Winston said, looking toward the flap of Tonild's tent, which had just opened. "The easiest lie to crack is often the one right in front of you."

We turned our attention to the people coming out of the tent. Father Egbert emerged first, his hands folded around a cross, and was followed by Osmund's broad, sword-draped form, then six soldiers who were carrying the bier. Osfrid lay as we had last seen him, dressed magnificently with a sword between his folded hands. Tonild came out of the tent last and walked behind the body, her back straight and her eyes dry.

Winston and I were intrigued by her lack of tears. "Let's attend the burial," he said.

So, as the procession passed us, we joined it.

We had to stop at regular intervals on our way through the encampment, in part because the crowd was so thick, but also because many of the English wanted to pay their last respects to the dead by kneeling in silence before the bier for a few moments. Everyone seemed to know who it was—and was probably well aware of how he died.

Several Vikings paused briefly and nodded at the dead man, and a few even moved their hands over their chests in the sign of the cross. However, none of them knelt before the bier or raised their hands to make the pagan sign of the hammer.

Our procession moved just as slowly once we entered the town of Oxford itself. The narrow, twisting streets and lanes lined by wattle fences were filled with tradesmen; people pushing carts and handbarrows; women doing their shopping; craftsmen's apprentices and merchants' assistants;

and soldiers on their way to the taverns, either alone or in the company of girls, who were peddling their services on every corner. Housecarls were visible everywhere, stiffly keeping an eye on everyone.

Here in town as well, English and Danes alike paid their respects to the bier. I was most struck, however, by the fact that every housecarl straightened and bowed his head as the dead man passed by. Cnut clearly wanted everyone to see that he was sorry that this had happened.

As the procession crossed the square in front of the Hall on its way to the church, I noticed that the Hall's door remained closed. The king himself did not step out to pay homage to the dead.

We reached Saint Frideswide's and plunged into the cool darkness inside.

A small gathering was waiting. Everyone knelt as the bier came through. By the time Winston and I found a place to stand off to the right, my eyes had adjusted to the darkness, and I could make out all the faces.

There were quite a few women, as there always were at such events. I jabbed Winston in the side with my elbow.

"I think Osfrid might have had a way with the ladies," I whispered, discreetly pointing out the still-kneeling women.

"Nonsense," Winston replied, his voice even quieter than my whisper. "It's not unusual for devout, newly converted women to show their piety by attending *anything* that takes place in a church."

In addition to the women, I spotted half a dozen clergymen, each of whom had some role to play in the ceremony, judging by their behavior.

Two Saxon noblemen stood at the very front of the center aisle. After the soldiers had set the bier down before the alter, the two noblemen stepped forward and kneeled briefly before bowing in greeting to the widow and the brother of the deceased. They returned the greeting, though even in the dim light I detected irritation in Tonild's face.

Now Winston was the one jabbing me in the side.

"Those are the brothers-in-law—the brothers of Osfrid's first wife, Everild," he said. Now I knew what Winston had been up to while I'd been with Frida.

Before I could respond, my attention was diverted by a commotion by the front door. A man entered and I reflexively grabbed for my sword before

I remembered that all our swords were lined up neatly against the wall of the church outside. My initial thought was that a heathen Viking warrior had been ordered to slay the several temporarily unarmed Saxons in the church. But I was mistaken.

I recognized the heavy head and stooped silhouette almost before I noticed the wool collar. Archbishop Wulfstan himself had come to do Osfrid the honor of performing the service.

At first I assumed that Cnut must have sent his archbishop as a sign of his solicitude, but the way Father Egbert, then Tonild, and finally Osmund greeted him made me realize my mistake; it's quite natural for an English clergyman to want to bury an English nobleman.

A good deal of mumbling and singing ensued, followed by a few swings of the censer, and some sprinkling of holy water before we eventually left the church, with the dead man in the lead.

Winston and I hung back, in our unobtrusive position. Amid the flock of pious dry-eyed women, I was startled to see one with tears streaming down her cheeks.

I was about to point her out to Winston, but saw that he had already noticed her, too. A short while later, as we stood graveside in the grass-covered cemetery, we didn't take our eyes off her. After Wulfstan had said his final words and sent the dead man to Paradise, purified by intercession and holy water, she stayed on her knees slightly longer than the rest of the group.

I turned to Winston, but he was watching Tonild, who was walking dispassionately away from the grave. She shot the weeping woman an icy look and then left the cemetery.

We didn't speak until we were back in front of the church.

"Was that woman going to be Osfrid's third wife?" I asked as I put my sword belt back on.

Winston bit his lip thoughtfully. "Maybe."

"What did you find out about the brothers-in-law?" I asked, thinking he would be impressed that I had guessed what he had been up to.

"Not enough, but I'm not done yet," Winston said. Suddenly he turned serious. "Follow her and find out if our guess is correct."

"What are you going to do?"

"You didn't notice, but Osfrid's former brothers-in-law didn't leave with Tonild and Osmund. I'm thinking the brothers-in-law are probably on their way to some tavern. Since I'm thirsty anyway, I figure a seat at their table might tell me what I want to know."

I was thirsty, too. But the prospect of comforting a grieving young woman was more appealing than even the fullest tankard of ale, so I nodded to Winston and set off. I found the woman walking slowly down one of the narrow lanes.

Chapter 16

 had the impression she was fairly young when I saw her in the cemetery, but now that I was following her from behind, I could tell that she was older than I'd first thought, despite her bouncy gait and swaying hips. She walked with purpose and dignity, elegantly maneuvering around all the piles of manure and various other obstacles, finally stopping where an alley intersected with the narrow street we were on.

In three long strides, I caught up to her and could see her face. She had a broad forehead, gray eyes, a slightly plump nose, and a heavy chin. Though the hair that peeked out from beneath her head linen was dark and full, fine wrinkles around her eyes and the corners of her mouth revealed her age.

Over thirty, in my opinion.

Seemingly lost in her own thoughts, she didn't notice me looking at her. After carefully checking that no one was coming down the alley from either side, she continued straight on the narrow street.

I fell back a few steps and followed her without difficulty. Now I focused on her clothes. Her head covering, I noticed, was covered with fine embroidery. I noted the high quality of the weaving in her cape and the weight of the cloth in her dress. In her blue dress, red cape and pale leather shoes, she looked, all in all, like the sort of upper-class woman who would appeal to a man like Osfrid—but her age? I rejected the idea that she was meant to replace Tonild in Osfrid's bed.

The woman's gait slowed. Then she stopped altogether and looked around. She began walking again, and turned right abruptly onto a wider street, which, much to my surprise, led us back toward the square between the church and the Hall. Had she noticed me? Did she now want to return to a more crowded area?

No, that wasn't it. She continued across the square, where a group of noblemen were lined up in front of the Hall, which was now being guarded by quite a few more housecarls than before. Cnut apparently wanted to address the witan in private, and he was not going to make it easy for any English enemies to attack.

Once across the square, the woman stopped and carefully studied the buildings on either side of the street, then nodded to herself, and walked on at a steady pace.

I suddenly understood: She was not familiar with Oxford, had taken the wrong road, realized this, and found her way back to the church to start again from a familiar location.

Sure enough, she was once again walking with purpose, looking neither left nor right.

Her grief at Osfrid's burial had appeared genuine. If she hadn't been bidding farewell to a lover who had promised her a golden future as a nobleman's wife, then what had caused her tears?

When the woman stopped in front of a post-and-plank house guarded by heavily armed men, I had my explanation: Her future was indeed dead, but not because she had been promised gold and green woodlands as Osfrid's future bride. She had to have been his mistress—perhaps of many years— and she had just buried the only financial security she had ever had in the world.

If that was the case, she had less reason than anyone to want Osfrid dead and buried. However, she might know something that would help Winston's and my investigation.

Men often speak more freely with the women they choose as mistresses than with the ones who share their tables and beds before God and the world, because a wife is not chosen for love. Spouses' hands are tied at the altar to advance a family's interests and its hunger for land. A mistress, by contrast, is usually a woman the man truly loves but whom the family refuses to acknowledge with a bridal crown.

Isn't that precisely what people suspected of King Cnut? Rumor had it that he actually loved his first wife, Ælfgifu, and that he had only married Emma for her connections to her brother and her strong Saxon affiliations.

The same rumor held that he only found his way into Emma's bed to produce an heir—but that he made his way into Ælfgifu's bed any way he could.

And now here I was, following a woman who has been forced to accept a life in the shadows as a nobleman's secret lover. Osfrid had evidently not been the man Cnut was, brazen enough to be openly married to two women.

As the woman walked up to the door of the sturdy building, two guards snapped to attention and opened it for her. Once she had entered and the door closed behind her, I casually walked up to it.

Neither of the guards made any move to open it for me.

Their eyes were cold, their faces expressionless.

"What do you want?" one of them asked dismissively.

"It's important that I speak with the lady who just went inside." I intentionally relaxed my lips so that my Saxon sounded more southern, more like the guard's dialect.

"Oh, it is, is it?" the guard retorted.

Neither guard showed any sign of movement.

"So, if you would either let me in or let her know," I urged.

"The lady, you said. Don't you know her name?" the guard asked.

"Unfortunately not. But perhaps you could enlighten me?" I smiled politely.

They exchanged sarcastic smiles.

"Get lost," he said.

I was going to have to get serious.

"My name is Halfdan, and I am acting on behalf of King Cnut," I announced.

The guard on the left, who still hadn't uttered a word, spat on the ground. The spokesman curled his lips in a mocking smile and said, "Free Saxons live here. Cnut can order Danes around, but he has no authority over Saxons."

I considered my options. I had no chance on my own. And I knew that Cnut's housecarls wouldn't forcibly enter a home that was openly hostile to the king's authority. Cnut was striving to create harmony throughout his kingdom; his soldiers forcing their way into a Saxon home definitely would not help.

So I shrugged and strolled away, trying to appear as nonchalant as possible.

As soon as I'd rounded the nearest corner, I stopped, waited a bit, and then slipped back onto the street, making my way to a stone archway across the street from the house. From here, I could keep an eye on the building without being seen.

It seemed that the guards at the door hadn't noticed me, as neither one made any move to come over and shoo me away. Instead, like their colleagues posted at the corners of the building, they behaved like proper soldiers, not given to slacking off or chitchatting with each other. They remained vigilant, their hands hovering just above their sword hilts.

I kept well in the shadow of the archway, smiling amiably at anyone walking by who stopped to look at me in an effort to give the impression that I was entitled to be there.

The sun drifted steadily across the sky, and the door across the street remained shut. I'd begun yawning from boredom when I spotted a nobleman walking up the street accompanied by four guards.

He stopped outside the post-and-plank house and looked around, which enabled me to see his face before he walked up to the door. The guards opened it promptly without asking him a single question.

I was wide awake now and remained so until Osmund stepped back out onto the street.

I was torn. Should I follow Osmund and ask him to explain what he was doing in the house where his dead brother's mistress was staying, or should I stay here and hope for an opportunity to speak with her?

I chose the latter. We already more or less knew what Osmund was up to, and, since noblemen are not in the habit of discussing their relatives' personal business with strangers, he would probably refuse to answer any questions about the woman anyway.

Then a thought struck me. Osmund and Tonild must have expected the mistress to have enough class to stay away from Osfrid's funeral. The cold look she had gotten from Tonild made that very clear. And yet Osmund showed up here now. Why? I saw two possibilities: Either he wanted to scare Osfrid's mistress away, or he wanted to pay her off so that she would leave.

I had no doubt the woman was quite alone in the world. Though she obviously had enough money and connections to secure accommodations in a nobleman's house like the post-and-plank building across the street from me—a building whose owner I hadn't yet identified—she was nonetheless lowly enough to walk through Oxford without so much as a boy to attend to her.

The door across the street opened again, and a young, nobly dressed man stepped out. He nodded to the guards and disappeared down the street.

After that, nothing happened for quite a while, and I started thinking about going in search of Winston to give him my report. However, I thought that Osmund's visit might prompt the woman to come out again before nightfall, so I stayed put.

My patience paid off.

When the woman finally stepped out, I was surprised to see that she wasn't dressed for travel. She was wearing the same outfit as before, and wasn't carrying a duffel bag or even a knapsack. She nodded to the guard, and I suddenly realized I might have a problem. If she headed down the street to my right, I was going to have to walk past the guards to follow her, and I doubted they would let me do so without intervening.

I held my breath and cursed under my breath when she headed right. I looked around, and my eyes fell on a wide-bladed grain shovel hanging in the archway. I grabbed it and held the blade up in front of my face, then twisted my sword belt to move my weapon around to my right side. I hunched forward slightly, and walked slowly past the guards, who watched indifferently as I passed.

Once I was a fair way down the street, I tossed the shovel aside, moved my sword back into place on my left hip, and surveyed the street ahead of me. Luck was with me. I spotted the woman and began to follow her.

Something caught my eye over the twig fence to my left. It was the nobly dressed young man who had left the house before the woman. He appeared to be bickering with a couple of Vikings in the yard. I didn't have time to stop and help some nobleman's brat, and since four broad-chested house-carls had just turned onto the street, I decided to leave it to them to protect the boy from getting the beating he seemed to be itching for. I hurried on after my prey.

When she stopped in front of a merchant's stall under a wide canvas aw-ning and started examining the wares for sale, I approached her.

"My lady," I said, "you don't know me, but it's important that I speak to you."

She turned around, confused, and furrowed her brow when she saw my unfamiliar face.

I gave her my best smile. "I'm sorry for your grief, my lady, but perhaps I can help to assuage it. My name is Halfdan, and King Cnut has asked me and my companion to investigate the murder of your beloved."

Her gray eyes widened, until they were absolutely round. "My beloved?"

I nodded. "Lord Osfrid, the Saxon."

I saw fear, despair, and—to my surprise—amusement flit across her eyes.

"Osfrid, my beloved?" she repeated.

I gave her another nod and an encouraging smile.

"You seem to be mistaken," she said, her mouth twitching and her lips narrowing. "I'm Estrid, Osfrid's sister."

Chapter 17

he last time I had felt so dumb was many years before, when my father—with barely concealed glee—dismissed a farm girl's claim that I was supposedly the father of the baby she was expecting.

After grilling me thoroughly, he laughed the girl out the door, telling her that it wasn't going to be *that* easy to get her hands on a nobleman's silver. Then he chewed me out in front of Harding and several of his pals for not knowing that cuddling with a girl is not enough to get her pregnant.

"Open your eyes, boy!" my father said condescendingly. "You've seen bulls and stallions and boars and dogs. You ought to know that unless the cock really plunges in properly, there's not going to be a calf, foal, pig, or puppy."

I was only sixteen winters old, with nothing more than peach fuzz on my face, when my father and brother had mocked me for not knowing how a man lies with a woman. I had just been thoroughly trounced once again, standing before this Saxon lady, and my ears were every bit as red now as they had been then.

"My . . . my lady . . ." I stammered. "Forgive my blunder."

Her gray eyes shone, not from tears, as I had feared at first, but evidently from amusement. Her bosom rose and fell the way it would in someone doing everything they could to keep themselves from laughing.

"Maybe things would have turned out better if I *had* been his mistress," she said, reaching up and wiping her eyes with a pale hand.

"My lady?" I asked, trying with all my might to recover from my own foolishness.

She didn't respond. Instead, she stared attentively at me and then asked, "The king asked you to investigate my brother's murder?"

"Yes, yes, I know," I sighed. "You and your family are convinced that Cnut ordered Osfrid's death."

"I don't really care what my family thinks," she said, her voice suddenly surprisingly steely. "As far as I'm concerned, my brother is dead and that's the end of it."

It occurred to me that a conversation with Osfrid's sister might be just as helpful as one with his mistress, so I looked around for somewhere we could talk. The stall before us appeared to be much better stocked than Alfred's—obviously not all merchants were being charged the large share of the heregeld that Alfred was. Behind the stall, I spotted three tables with benches.

"Let me buy you a drink to make up for putting my foot in my mouth," I offered.

Estrid eyed me, her amusement only barely concealed. "Or in exchange for information."

"My lady," I said, holding out my hand to her. "I would gladly buy you a tankard for both of those reasons."

She raised her own soft hand, gave mine a squeeze, and then—to my astonishment—led the way and sat down at an empty table. A stooped carpenter, his apron strewn with wood shavings, was seated at one of the other two tables with a young man who I guessed was probably his son or apprentice, because his clothes were also covered with sawdust. At the third table, three housecarls each clutched his tankard in silence.

I asked Estrid what she would like to drink, and she replied that a cup of mead would do her good. I walked over to the counter, a sturdy oaken plank resting on three sawhorses. Behind it stood a colorfully dressed bristle-haired man, whose belt held a knife with a nicely carved bone handle next to a heavy leather purse.

When he opened his mouth, I understood why his stall was so richly stocked compared to Alfred's. He spoke Danish, not English, and judging from his accent, he was a relatively new arrival from the old homeland east of the sea, not a third-generation Dane from the Danelaw, in northern and eastern England.

The mead he served was a golden-honey color and smelled sweet and strong. The enticing scent of malt wafted up from my ale. Both drinks were poured almost to overflowing.

"My lady!" I said, raising my tankard to her. "Would you allow me to start from the beginning?"

She looked downright jovial now. "By all means, Halfdan Who-Serves-the-King."

I briefly explained how Winston and I had been in Cnut's Hall when Tonild burst in with the news of her husband's death, how Winston had made some observations at the scene where the body was found, and how the king had put us on the case.

Estrid listened in silence, with one hand under her heavy chin and her eyes attentively on my face. When I'd finished, she sipped her mead and asked how she could help. I answered that I was glad she was *willing* to help.

"Halfdan!" she said, sounding vaguely weary, as though she had been trying to convince me of something for a long time. "My brother is dead. Do you somehow think I want him to lie unavenged in his grave?"

"Well, good," I said, leaning forward as though speaking in confidence. "Why did you say it would have been better if you *had* been his mistress?"

Her mouth hardened, then she replied, "A man makes sure that his mistress is provided for after his death."

I stared at her. What had Winston said earlier? That Tonild wouldn't care if Osfrid had a mistress as long as the mistress didn't inherit anything. Estrid obviously thought more highly of noblemen. On the other hand, Tonild had claimed that she was Osfrid's sole heir, after the monastery got its share.

"My lady," I said. I hadn't taken my eyes off her. "English law does not allow a daughter—let alone a sister—to be left without some accommodation. And English law does still apply, does it not?"

There was no trace of jollity in her eyes now. "For the time being. But that only holds true if the daughter and sister are full-blooded."

"Oh," I said, already suspecting what I was about to hear. "Please do tell."

It was an oft-told tale of a nobleman who "forgot" to make provisions for his mistress's children, and then the legitimate children refuse to recognize the rights of the natural-born children.

"And your mother? I mean, you just said—" I began.

"I know what I said." Estrid's eyes filled with tears. "My mother was named as an heir, but she died before my father. When he died, my half brothers refused to recognize that I had any claim. I wasn't even mentioned."

Something didn't add up.

"So, am I to understand that Osfrid trampled on your rights and refused to recognize your claim to any inheritance from your father, but you still want to avenge his death?"

Estrid's eyes welled up again as she explained, "After our father died, Osmund convinced Osfrid to ignore my inheritance rights. But Osfrid was an upstanding man, and he nonetheless took it upon himself to provide for me."

"So Osfrid was supporting you," I said, taking a drink. The ale was strong and I decided not to overdo it. I could quench my thirst later with the usual brew.

Estrid nodded. "It was thanks to Osfrid's first wife—Oslaf's mother. She was a God-fearing woman and she convinced her husband to do right both by me and by the Lord."

I remembered the look Tonild had given Estrid by the grave. "And Osfrid's *second* wife?"

A flicker of hatred gleamed in Estrid's eyes, so fleeting that I almost missed it. "Tonild doesn't want Osfrid to have a past—no first wife, no son, and no sister."

"So Tonild convinced Osfrid to stop supporting you?"

"You didn't know him," Estrid said, shaking her head reproachfully. "Osfrid kept his word. Though Tonild didn't like it, he made sure that I received a sum of money each year."

I scooted in to let the exiting carpenter and his young assistant past. The young man was supporting the older one, who wasn't going to last long if he habitually drank so much in the middle of the day that he needed help walking, I thought. No one wants to pay for crooked carpentry.

"So Tonild is both a gold digger and jealous of her husband's past?" I asked.

Estrid laughed, a frank laugh that made the housecarls turn around in surprise.

"Tonild's father was one of the wealthiest of the Saxon nobles. He refused to pledge his fealty to Cnut, a stance for which he paid with his life."

Tonild had already told Winston and me that. But then I realized what Estrid was saying.

"You mean the king seized his land and property?" I asked. Estrid nodded.

"When Osfrid married Tonild," she said, "he was marrying into an expected fortune. Tonild was Wighelm's only child, you see, and she used to really lord her wealth over Osfrid. She was an extremely wealthy young woman when she entered into the marriage. But less than two years later— after her father refused to follow Cnut and was killed and the land and properties had been seized—she was far less eager to discuss who had brought the most into the marriage."

We were interrupted by a polite voice saying, "Excuse me." I looked up and saw that it was the nobly dressed young man from earlier. It seemed that he had escaped his dispute with the Vikings unscathed, presumably with the help of those housecarls. As I scooted my bench in again so that he could get by, Estrid greeted him with a tasteful nod.

"You know each other?" I asked her.

She shook her head. "We're just staying in the same lodging house."

"So you no longer have any financial support?" I asked.

"Basically," Estrid said with a tired smile. "I had anticipated this might happen when Osfrid died, so I have set aside a little nest egg. Perhaps enough to convince an abbey to let me serve as a lay sister."

I could hear in her voice and see in her face that this wasn't the future she'd hoped for, and wondered whether her tears at the funeral were the result of grief for her dead brother or the fact that her income source had just dried up.

"And Osmund?" I asked.

Her eyes hardened. "My surviving brother just paid me a visit to inform me that he did not intend to continue what he called 'Osfrid's foolish flood of silver.'"

I raised my eyebrows.

"Yes," she smiled wanly. "That's what he called the few pennies Osfrid had allowed me to accrue."

"The few pennies? How much are we talking about?" It was a brazen question and one that I didn't think she would answer.

I could tell that she didn't think she would either, and yet she shrugged and said, "A pound of silver a year."

Which was no small sum. Not by a long shot. I could live well, albeit not quite like a nobleman, on a pound of silver. A farmer could support a family on that. It was hardly surprising that she had been able to set some money aside.

But I knew from experience that a pound of silver was also a lot to have to give up. While I had still lived safely at home, I had paid no attention to money or wealth. But in the years since, I had learned what it meant to live without.

Then something occurred to me. "Do you have your own estate?"

"No," she said, playing with her mead cup. "My mother left me a house with a kitchen garden, a poultry run, and the right to keep geese and ducks in the meadow down below." The look in her eyes seemed to say: *You see? I'm not hiding anything.*

She was quite well-off by any measure. Not rich, but by no means poor. I remembered her soft, pale hands. She obviously did not look after the poultry or other household work herself. She must have had at least one servant girl at home, wherever that might be.

And that "little nest egg" probably wasn't insignificant, either. I had a hunch that she shared her sister-in-law Tonild's fixation with money. And yet, she had been walking around Oxford unescorted.

That confused me until I realized that she didn't want to advertise her wealth. Both Osmund and Tonild were meant to think that she was living hand to mouth. I was meant to think so, too—and maybe even take pity on her. Her comment about becoming a lay sister at an abbey had to be a ruse, as well.

She was a woman who knew how to play the hand she was dealt. But that still didn't make her a suspect. It would be quite a stretch to think that she was behind her brother's death, given that he had been the only secure source of income she had.

"So," I said, returning to my conversation with Estrid, "Osfrid must have been disappointed when Cnut's housecarls seized his father-in-law Wighelm's properties, thereby eliminating any chance of his receiving a large inheritance from him." I figured I might as well find out what I could.

"Osfrid?" Estrid said, shaking her head haughtily. "No, he wasn't like that. He didn't marry Tonild for her money."

I cocked my head, curious.

"Heirs are the greatest riches a nobleman can have," Estrid explained.

"Precisely the kind of riches Osfrid was not blessed with," I said. A smile that could be characterized as a tad malicious slid over her lips.

"Tonild is barren," she said.

I took advantage of her hatred for her sister-in-law and asked, "Was it very important to Osfrid to have an heir?"

Estrid snorted condescendingly. "Didn't I just say heirs are the greatest riches a nobleman can have?"

"So he might have considered acquiring heirs some other way?" I pried.

Yet another snort, but this time seemingly at her dead brother's expense.

"Osfrid was too straitlaced for that. Faithful as a turtledove. As far as I know, he didn't even *look* at other women during either of his marriages."

"But would he have considered an annulment or a divorce?" I asked.

Estrid shook her head, then her eyes widened. My question had evidently made her realize something.

"If he'd thought about that and then shared that possibility with Tonild," she said, leaning forward and giving me a wink, "I'm sure Tonild would have had something to say about it."

She gave me a withering look, but I stared at her blankly, wondering what she meant.

"You really don't know what I'm saying?" she asked, now teasing me. But she continued with her vitriol before I had a chance to respond.

"Maybe what you found in the merchant's shed *was* her response," she said.

Chapter 18

he afternoon was more than half over, and my stomach was growling, reminding me that aside from the ale I had drunk with Winston I hadn't had anything since breakfast.

My curiosity about what Alfilda would soon be setting on the table lured me back to the tavern. Our hostess was being assisted by a full-bosomed girl, whose charms were unfortunately marred by a toothless smile, which she nevertheless let me bask in as I squeezed my way over to a table between a foul-smelling monk and a scrawny, fidgety tanner who smelled no more inviting than the friar. Most of the customers only had drinks in front of them—ale or mead, or wine from the looks of their cups—but when I requested food, Toothless nodded and brought me a nice, thick slab of bread covered with ham and grilled onions along with a tankard of malted ale.

The tavern was doing brisk business and the room echoed with all the languages and dialects spoken throughout Cnut's vast North Sea Empire, his Viking realms to the east and north and across the great sea west of Ireland. Squeezed in among the Oxford craftsmen and merchants were countless noblemen's hired soldiers—who preferred the inns in town, where they could escape their masters' keen eyes more easily than they could at the ale stands in the camp.

It wasn't every day that a powerful king visited Oxford, and in addition to the presence of all of the most prominent noblemen in the kingdom were those who simply saw potential for personal advancement by appearing wherever the king was. The Oxonians appeared to be enjoying all the excitement in their midst and had set their regular work aside to rub elbows with the warriors and noble troublemakers, some of whom had helped burn the town to the ground not so long ago.

Standing in her apron among the cooking kettles and ale kegs, Alfilda seemed to be in her element. Her eyes kept scanning the men and tables. A nod from Alfilda would dispatch Toothless to clear those of customers who had just emptied their tankards and were just sitting around people watching.

The bread was pleasantly sour, the onions sweet, the ham succulent, and the ale so satisfying that I would have liked to stay for another. But my eagerness to find Winston and hear his report on Osfrid's former brothers-in-law won out over my thirst. I reluctantly got up and walked over to the hostess, who had just straightened her back and wiped the sweat off her brow with the back of her hand.

"Good day to be running a tavern," I said as she smiled at me in recognition.

Her auburn hair danced over her shoulders as she confided in me that she had had more customers that day than she normally did in a week. "And," she continued, "you and your companion are lucky I'm a woman of my word. I was offered four times as much as what you're paying for your room."

I didn't bother mentioning that our being on a special assignment for the king might have played a part in her willingness to stick to her agreement. Instead I made do with asking if she'd seen Winston.

"Your charming companion?" she asked with a wink. She lost me there for a second, as it almost seemed as though she were interested in Winston. Unsettled, I nodded. She replied with a shake of her head.

"Not since the two of you left together," Alfilda said. Then her eyes widened and she smoothed her apron before giving me a playful shove and walking back into the crowd in the tavern.

I turned around and recognized Godskalk, who nodded subtly at the hostess before turning to me.

"Where is your partner?" he asked.

I smiled obligingly at the housecarl. "I wish I knew," I said. "I'm looking for him myself."

Godskalk rubbed his square jaw. "You asked me to keep an eye out for a red-haired warrior."

I nodded, curious to hear what he'd say next.

"Come with me," he said, spinning on his heel and heading straight out the door. I gave Alfilda an apologetic look as I followed him. From the look on her face, I could tell that she knew he was Cnut's housecarl and thane, and she must have felt slighted when the powerful warrior left without enjoying so much as a sip of ale. If word got out that Godskalk drank at her tavern, she would attract other customers—because everyone knows that men like to rub elbows with the powerful whenever they can.

We had hardly made it out the door when we practically crashed into Winston, who ignored the housecarl, and looked straight at me. "There you are, Halfdan! Good, let's get caught up."

He was puzzled when I shook my head. When I had explained, he turned to Godskalk. "You found this Horik guy?"

His response was more of a grunt: "You tell me."

I'd had to sidle and push my way through the throng in the streets before, but following Godskalk was more like trailing in the wake of a dragon ship. The sea of humanity simply parted before his broad silhouette. It wasn't that he seemed menacing—or even particularly fierce, really—but even those who didn't recognize the captain of the king's housecarls moved out of the way of such a clearly powerful warrior.

I could tell from Winston's furrowed brow that he had come to the same conclusion I had, namely that whatever condition this Horik turned out to be in, he would probably not be up to helping us with our investigation. And no doubt Winston shared my anxiety that, even though we were finally going to lay eyes on this man, it would probably be some time before he would be able to answer our questions.

When we reached the square in front of the Hall, Godskalk did not turn toward the king's residence, but instead cut diagonally across it, and then ducked between the freshly tarred wall of a house and a half-destroyed fence. He continued up the narrow lane that ran along the pitch-scented houses and stopped at another fence, behind which stood two housecarls in peaceful conversation. Godskalk bent to pass through the opening in the woven twigs.

The soldiers stiffened at the sight of their thane, greeted Winston and me with brief nods, and then stepped aside so that we had an unobstructed view of a manure pile swarming with flies.

"Is this your man?" Godskalk asked.

Our eyes followed where he was pointing. A soldier in Saxon garb lay sprawled on his back over the dunghill, his vacant eyes staring up at the sky, not noticing the swallows flying above. His sword belt was taut, the hilt deep in the sheath, and his tunic was covered with sweat stains. His breeches were tucked into his low leather boots, and the hair that protruded from beneath a well-maintained helmet was plaited into two thick, red braids.

Winston looked from the dead man's slit throat over to me and then back at Godskalk. "It's hard to know. We've never met him."

Godskalk narrowed his eyes. "He's Saxon, a soldier, and a redhead," he pointed out.

Winston nodded.

"But we're going to have to—" Winston began, but then he turned to me and asked, "Did that priest Egbert do this?"

"Maybe," I said. "Should I . . . ?"

Winston nodded, but as I turned to leave he stopped me. "Wait! Maybe it's best if we don't let them know we found him . . . in case it *is* him," he added. Then his eyes returned to Godskalk's uncomprehending face.

"We need someone to tell us if this is Horik," Winston explained. "But the person or people responsible for killing him wanted to keep us from talking to him. I think it might be a good idea to leave them in the dark about whether Horik has been found."

Godskalk shook his head skeptically. "Why?"

Until that moment, Winston had looked very serious, but now a smile played across his lips.

"It's just a thought," Winston said.

Godskalk stood completely still. He looked at the body, glanced up the passageway and back at the dead man, then surveyed the little courtyard we were standing in.

"I think you're wrong," he said.

"Really?" Winston's eyebrows shot up, intrigued.

"Osfrid's body, you'll remember, was hidden away in a shed," Godskalk said.

Winston and I both nodded and then looked at each other. Winston was the first one to figure out what Godskalk was getting at.

"But this man has been left right out in the open," Winston said.

Godskalk nodded. "No attempt was made to hide this man's body. On the contrary, he was dumped in an open courtyard behind a fence that isn't tall enough to keep anyone with business in the passageway from seeing him."

I cleared my throat. "It seems you are unaware that Osfrid's body was moved from the location where the actual murder took place?" I asked.

"No," Godskalk said, shaking his head. "I assumed he was killed right there in the shed."

"Which makes sense," Winston said quickly, fingering his beard. "Who found this man?"

"The woman in the house here," Godskalk said. "You see that window?"

The window was right over the dunghill.

"Whoever dumped the body here knew that it would only take a glance out that window for him to be noticed."

There was no longer anything subtle about the way Winston was scratching his beard. "This man wasn't killed here?" Winston asked.

"How should I know?" Godskalk said with a shrug. "That's the kind of thing *you're* supposed to figure out."

"All right," Winston said. "But I'd still like us to keep quiet about this for now." He turned to me and grinned. "Do you think Frida is up to looking at one more dead body?" he asked.

Now it was my turn to shrug.

"Well, fetch her," Winston said. "Meanwhile, I'm going to take a look around."

It was far more cumbersome to make my way through the crowd now that I no longer had Godskalk to clear the way for me. I was motivated, however, since I was heading in search of an attractive servant girl, and it didn't take me long to reach the outskirts of the camp where I had first seen her.

Luck was on my side. Frida was bent over a cooking fire, keeping an eye on that same brass cauldron, whose contents gave off a promising scent. When I placed a hand on her shapely buttock, she straightened up with a jump, and slapped my arm with the ladle she'd been using to stir the cauldron.

"Leave me alo—Oh, it's you," she said.

"Didn't I tell you we might meet again?" I said. When I moved to kiss her, she made up for slapping me by opening her lips to mine. The kiss was as frisky as before.

"Are you free to get away for a few minutes?" I asked. "I could use your help with something."

She gave me a disappointed look. "*That's* why you're here," she said with a pout.

I shook my head. "That's why I'm here *now*."

"So you say." She still sounded disappointed.

"I mean it. Are you free to leave?" I asked, winding an arm around her shoulder and giving it a squeeze.

"Here," she said, handing me the ladle and walking over to a nearby lean-to. As she disappeared inside, I peered into the cauldron, stuck the ladle in, and gave it a tentative stir.

Fortunately, she returned quickly. "You've obviously never stirred a stew," she teased.

She was right about that.

A moment later, a filthy wench with mud-splattered legs came over to us and silently took the ladle from me. As she petulantly began stirring the stew, Frida led me away toward town.

When we reached the passageway, I stopped. I had deliberately not mentioned the nature of the help I needed, and had changed the topic every time Frida asked on our way there.

Now I put my arm around her. "You saw a dead man earlier," I said gently.

Her eyes widened.

"Was that your first?"

She shook her head. Then in a subdued voice she added, "He was the first person I ever saw be killed."

"But you've seen dead men before?"

"One, who'd fallen off his horse," she said. "Why?"

I told her that I needed her to look at a dead man now and tell me whether she recognized him.

"Recognize? Is it someone I know?" She shuddered in my embrace.

"I don't know," I said, putting my finger to her lips. "I'm not going to tell you who it is. Will you do it? For me?"

She nodded, and I gave her a quick kiss.

Winston was leaning against the wall of the house, and Godskalk was standing next to him. The guards were gone.

The sun had sunk behind the buildings, and the flies had disappeared with it. Frida's face froze when she became aware of the dead body in the yard.

With my arm still around her shoulder, I led her over to it. "Do you know him?"

She gasped. "It's him! Horik, the one you were asking me about."

I heard both Godskalk and Winston inhale.

"Thank you, my girl," Winston said, placing a hand on her shoulder. "Halfdan will walk you back. But would you do me a favor?"

She nodded.

"Would you keep this a secret for the time being?"

Once she had promised to do so, Winston looked at me. "Hurry back now," he said in a teasing tone. Unfortunately, I knew he really meant it.

I took my leave of Frida by her cooking fire once the filthy wench had sulkily handed the ladle back to her. But before I left, I promised to come back and see her again as soon as I could. A promise I planned to keep, given the farewell kiss we shared.

Chapter 19

found Winston bent over the dunghill. Godskalk was leaning against the wall of the building, watching him, and the two housecarls I'd seen earlier were waiting in the narrow lane as three other housecarls carried a borrowed door into the fenced area. Winston looked up as I approached him.

"He was killed here," Winston said. "See?"

He poked around in the dung with his foot, and I saw the bloodstain under the straw and shit.

"Then the killer covered up the blood?" I asked.

Winston nodded and looked at me, even though it didn't make any sense.

"If you're right," I began, "and the killer wanted the body to be noticed, then why cover up the blood?"

Godskalk cleared his throat. "It's easier to explain why you have manure on your shoes than blood," he suggested.

That thane had a head on his shoulders. I quietly kicked myself for not having thought of that myself. Since the killer had maneuvered the body onto the dunghill, there was no way he could have avoided stepping in dung. But, before doing so, he had covered the blood with straw to make it safe to step there.

Winston nodded at the housecarls. "You can take him away."

They loaded Horik's body onto the door and were about to leave when Winston stopped them with an upheld hand.

"Wait a moment," he said, looking around. Godskalk and I watched incredulously as he walked over to a pile of trash in the corner of the yard and started rooting around in it. Eventually he held up a tattered horse blanket. "Cover him with this. It would be best if we could keep this to ourselves for a while."

"Where are they taking him?" I asked

"To the church," Winston said, stepping over to the fence to speak to the waiting housecarls. "If anyone asks, he died of sickness," Winston instructed. We watched as they carried the dead man away.

"Why do you want to keep it secret?" I asked.

He gave a small shrug. "It may not be important, but I want to see how Tonild reacts when I tell her about the murder, and I want to make sure she doesn't hear the news through the rumor mill first."

"But what about the woman who found him?" I said. "Surely she's already shared the biggest event of the day with her neighbors and friends."

"No, Godskalk made sure of that," Winston said.

"The woman's husband is a housecarl," Godskalk explained when I looked at him. "He knows how to keep his mouth shut, if I ask him to."

That explained why the murderer's plan for everyone to find out about the dead man in the yard hadn't worked. The wife of a housecarl would obviously notify her husband before running all over town spreading gossip.

"Speaking of asking," Winston said, placing a hand on Godskalk's arm, "Would you mind having your last two housecarls here question the people living along this lane? I'd like to know if anyone saw anything—though I doubt they did." Winston could tell from my face that I didn't understand the reason for his doubt, so he added: "We haven't seen even a single curious onlooker this entire time."

Godskalk had already nodded to his men, who turned on their heels and headed off down the passage. Then he reminded us, "And perhaps you two will remember that the king would like to see you."

Winston nodded. "I haven't forgotten. But let us pay Tonild a visit first."

"So someone is killing men and leaving them out in plain sight," I summarized for Winston, speaking softly so that I wouldn't be overheard as we pushed our way through the crowds.

Winston gave me a look. "That's not how I'd put it."

"No?" I said, stopping in surprise.

"No," he said, grasping my arm and pulling me along. "Someone is killing *Saxons* and leaving them out in plain sight."

Osfrid and Horik. And Frida, too, if I hadn't been there to prevent it.

Well what did that mean? Was Cnut behind it after all? Had a Dane seen this as his chance to kill off some English enemies?

Or could it simply be a coincidence?

It didn't sound like Winston thought that was the case.

When we reached Tonild's tent, I was struck by another possibility: It could also be an Englishman killing off defectors.

Tonild's guard wouldn't let us in.

"Lady Tonild is in mourning for her husband and would like to be left alone," he said, his face as stiff as a woodcarving. The guards behind him didn't so much as twitch.

"And yet I must insist," Winston said, his voice quiet, but firm.

Laughter, shouts, girls squealing, hoof beats, and whinnying could be heard all around us. Though the camp hadn't grown much in size since that morning, everyone had obviously decided to enjoy themselves as they waited for the king to open the joint session of the Witenagemot and the Thing.

A variety of cooking scents mingled, and smoke from the countless cooking fires danced in the breeze between the tents, swirling like elvish maids. A chaotic jumble of servants, farmhands, and clergymen's housekeepers were carrying casks, jugs, bowls, barrels, cans, crocks, and pots to and fro, while soldiers, noblemen, ladies, lads, and well-guarded maidens sat in the grass or traveled between tents to visit one another. Only the Saxon widow's tent sat silent and closed amid the frenzy.

The guard did not respond. Winston bit his lip.

"I'm here on official business for King Cnut," he said.

The guard emitted a scarcely audible snort.

"Would you like me to send for the housecarls?" Winston asked.

The soldier shrugged. "Be my guest. If you think they would dare barge into the tent of a grieving English widow, that is."

He had a point. I could tell that Winston realized that as well. There was no way Danish royal housecarls were going to force their way into Tonild's Saxon tent. Cnut's express desire to create peace between his peoples precluded such an action.

Winston tried again. "If you could just let Lady Tonild know that I would like to see her, then she can make up her own mind."

The guard was unwavering. "I don't need to let her know. The lady does not wish to be disturbed. At all."

I spotted a familiar face over the guard's shoulder. Winston was so preoccupied with trying to figure out how to get past this guard and his many well-armed colleagues that he didn't notice as I walked off.

Frida lit up when she saw me, but then the gleam in her eyes faded. "I don't have time," she apologized.

A platter she was holding confirmed that. It was heaped with thick slices of roast beef. A manservant stood behind her holding another, equally heavily laden platter. Judging from the smell, I guessed that his was full of lamb.

"Lady Tonild certainly has a healthy appetite," I joked, smiling at Frida.

Frida opened her mouth, but an elbow from the lamb man shut her up.

"The lady's affairs are not the concern of strange soldiers," the manservant said, giving Frida another push.

I followed them with my eyes as they made their way to the front of the tent, where a guard flung the flap open for them. I waited for them to come back out, but when they did the manservant had a firm grip on Frida's arm and forced her past me. There had already been one attempt on her life that day, and I didn't dare push my luck. I had to hope the bastard simply thought I was a girl-crazed soldier looking for a beddable wench.

Winston hadn't gotten any closer to the tent door when I returned. The guard appeared bored, but no less vigilant.

"Let's go," I said.

Winston turned to me in surprise. "Absolutely not. I need to speak with Tonild."

"Which we're obviously not going to get to do. Let's go," I repeated.

Winston's eyes widened when I winked at him. I gave the guard a snide look and walked off. Winston followed.

"What are you winking about?" he whispered as soon as we were out of earshot.

"She has guests," I informed him.

"Guests?" he asked, bewildered.

I told him about the heaping platters of meat. "Which is funny," I added, "because I've heard grief makes you *lose* your appetite."

Winston rubbed his chin. "We have to find a spot from which we can keep an eye on the tent."

I'd already figured that much out.

"Is your wench of the day nearby?" Winston asked.

"We have to steer clear of her," I said somberly. After an insult like that, he didn't deserve any further explanation. I looked around. "There!"

A narrow opening between the backs of two tents facing away from Tonild's, it was the perfect spot. We could sit between them, hidden from sight, with an unobstructed view of Tonild's tent. We could use the time to fill each other in on what we'd each learned that day.

Chapter 20

e were well hidden between the tents. Someone passing by would only see us if he looked right between them, and even then the shadows would likely keep him from noticing us. The tents' heavy wool cloth muffled sound so we could speak relatively freely as long as we didn't raise our voices. The din of the camp had died down now that most of its inhabitants had filled their bellies and switched to ale, mead, and wine. Winston sat up very straight and kept his eyes on Tonild's tent.

"You talk, I'll keep watch," he said.

He listened silently as I described my meeting with Estrid, my mistaken assumption about her relationship to Osfrid—which brought a faint smile to his lips—and my subsequent conversation with her.

"So she is actually Osfrid and Osmund's half sister, and she *confirmed* that Osfrid might have been planning to take a new wife?" he asked.

I shook my head, but then I realized his eyes were still trained on Tonild's tent.

"No," I said aloud. "I planted that idea in her head, and she elaborated on it. There's little love lost between her and Tonild. In fact, she took great delight in hinting that Tonild might be behind the murder."

"But you don't think Tonild did it?" Winston asked.

"How would I know?" I scoffed. "I'm just saying that Estrid would like to think it was Tonild."

"Well, do you think Estrid did it?" he asked.

I knew he was going to ask me that. "Hardly," I said. "Why cut off the hand that feeds you?"

"Good point," Winston said, rising up into a crouch as Tonild's tent flap was flung aside, but it was only another servant, who hurried across the grass in long strides.

"And Osfrid fed her well, you say?" Winston asked.

"A pound of silver a year," I told him. "I know a good many people who would kill for a sum that great."

"Hmm," Winston said, his eyes leaving the tent for a moment to give me a teasing look. "Yes, I'm sure you probably do."

"There is something I've been wondering about, though," I hastened to add, ignoring his remark. "Why is Estrid intentionally making herself appear poorer than she is? I mean: a pound of silver a year, a house with a kitchen garden, and a poultry farm. She's not poor."

Winston chuckled to himself. "She told you the answer to that one, herself. She knows that Osfrid's death means her source of funding has just dried up, and now she's turning to the only option she has left: the abbey. All the abbeys I'm familiar with value silver every bit as much as those of us who live out here in the lay world. If the good Estrid lets word get out that she is a wealthy woman, any prioress or abbess will charge her accordingly."

We sat in silence for a while. I was just about to ask Winston to tell me what he'd gleaned from the brothers of Osfrid's first wife when he continued, "And there was one question you *didn't* ask that Estrid answered all the same."

Winston's eyes were twinkling in the twilight, but, infuriatingly, I couldn't figure out what he was referring to.

"The question of why Estrid, an illegitimate daughter of a nobleman, wasn't married off to advance the family's interests."

That thought hadn't even occurred to me. I chewed my lower lip in frustration and waited a moment before opening my mouth.

"Let me keep watch now while you fill me in," I said.

Osfrid's first wife, Everild, had two brothers: Ulfrid and Torold. Their father, Beorthold, had been an ealdorman under King Ethelred in the shires of East Anglia. For various reasons, Ethelred had had this Beorthold assassinated by none other than Eadric the Grasper. Ethelred and Eadric had used compurgators to swear they were innocent of the killing, and were acquitted. Ethelred and Eadric recognized Ulfrid and Torold's claims as Beorthold's heirs, but, enraged by the murder of their father, the brothers had switched their allegiance the moment they came into their inheritance. They sold off their property in East Anglia, forswore their allegiance to Ethelred, and pledged fealty to Morcar, a thane in Northumbria, which was not a fief of Ethelred's.

Later, after Eadric had murdered Morcar as well, King Ethelred sent a message to Ulfrid and Torold in which he told them that they had been sufficiently penalized and that he would accept them back into the fold. But now, furious not only about the murder of their father but also that of their patron Morcar, Ulfrid and Torold swore they would never serve Ethelred again. They stayed on their lands in the Danelaw to the north, and their loyal warriors repulsed attacks from the south more than once.

When Ethelred the Unready died, his son Edmund Ironside sent a message to the brothers that, as far as he was concerned, all that business was history and water under the bridge and so on and so forth. Ulfrid and Torold realized there might be some benefit to being King Edmund's men, rather than continuing to live as Englishmen without a patron in the Danelaw, so they sold off their lands and property and returned to Wessex, where King Edmund treated them honorably.

In serving Edmund, however, the brothers refused one thing: they would never associate or join ranks with the "bloody ealdorman Eadric," who had their father's and Morcar's blood on his hands. At the Battle of Assandun, Ulfrid and Torold fought loyally on foot in the ranks of King Edmund. Ulfrid later admitted his deep regret that he had refused to serve with the traitor Eadric—because if he had, Ulfrid could have axed him from behind when Eadric turned his back on his countrymen and joined Cnut.

After Edmund Ironside's defeat at Assandun, Ulfrid and Torold continued to serve Edmund loyally to the bitter end. Their reputation of integrity was so great that Cnut recognized their claims and rights in Wessex without hesitation, which is why no one grumbled when Ulfrid and Torold assumed their rightful seats in the Witenagemot.

"And what about their sister, Everild?" I blurted out.

"It is just as Tonild said. Everild married Osfrid and bore him a son. She then died in childbirth with her second child."

The tent door opened again, but it was only one more servant coming out.

"And did Osfrid leave Ulfrid and Torold anything?" I asked.

"He did," Winston replied. "Whether they think they got their fair share is another matter. But yes, he left them something."

"Hmm," I said, staring at the tent and its stonelike guards. "So Osfrid had a good relationship with his brothers-in-law?"

"It seems so. And yet . . . Ulfrid said . . ." Winston hesitated, until I gave him a look to continue. "When the conversation turned to Everild's death, Ulfrid spat on the ground and said it was lucky for Osfrid that Everild had died giving birth to a son."

"What did he mean by that?" I asked.

"That a nobleman can't have enough sons," Winston said, suddenly leaning forward. "Hey, something's happening over there."

The guard by the tent flap was scanning the area.

"So what would have happened if Osfrid had let their sister die giving birth to a daughter?" I asked.

"I'm sure you can guess," Winston said, standing up.

The guard had flung the tent flap aside, but the expected stream of noblemen did not emerge—rather, one lone man stood in the opening, waiting for the guard to gesture for the man to proceed.

I strained my eyes. I'd seen him before, but it took me a moment to place him. "I know him."

"Who is he?" Winston asked, not taking his eyes off the tent's entrance.

"He's staying in the same lodging house as Estrid," I explained.

"Is that all?"

"He also came in and had a drink at the market stall where Estrid and I were drinking," I added.

"And what was he doing in Tonild's tent?" Winston asked.

Winston's guess was as good as mine, so I didn't bother answering.

"Follow him," Winston said. "I'll wait here and see if anyone else comes out."

But as I stepped out into the path between the rows of tents, I suddenly found myself face-to-face with five housecarls who did not look as though they planned to step aside. Their leader, a bald, one-eyed man, flashed me a hostile smile.

"You're the guy who's with that Saxon painter, right?" the one-eyed Danish warrior asked me.

There was obviously no point in denying it, so I nodded.

"Where is he?" the warrior asked.

Before I had a chance to think, my eyes flitted to the space between the tents.

Winston stepped out and asked, "Are you looking for me?"

"For both of you. The king requests your company," the housecarl stated.

"Please tell King Cnut we'll be right there, we just have to . . ." Winston began.

"Now!"

I did mention there were five of them, didn't I?

The king was seated at a table in the middle of the Hall with three other men.

Archbishop Wulfstan's stooped silhouette leaned over the table to Cnut's right, his hand resting on a sheet of vellum in front of him. A richly dressed Saxon nobleman with curly hair and broad cheekbones stood to Wulfstan's right, leaning forward on the back of a chair. I couldn't help but notice that he wore a very attractive sword.

Thorkell the Tall was seated to the king's left, leaning back in his chair.

The king looked up when we entered, but the guard who had escorted us into the room put his hand on Winston's arm to indicate that we should wait.

Wulfstan was speaking urgently to the king, who sat with both hands squarely on the table before him, listening attentively. Thorkell's posture—

reclining in his seat with his ass scooted out to the edge of his chair—suggested that he wasn't interested in what the clergyman was saying, but I noticed the tension in his eyes and understood that his relaxed stance was all for show.

The Saxon nobleman beside Wulfstan had his elbows on the chair back and his cheek propped in his hand, so I had difficulty discerning the expression on his face. Still, I got the impression that he was following the conversation attentively.

Wulfstan's creaking voice was low, so only a few scattered words reached my ears. Words like *law, all men, God-given,* and *righteous.*

Finally he stopped talking.

The king sat in silence for a while, his hands resting on the table, then he looked at us.

"My learned archbishop is very preoccupied with the law. As am I. I would like to achieve the best possible conditions for unifying the assembled witan and noblemen of the realm. Can you bring these conditions about for me?"

Though the king's eyes were directed at me as well as Winston, I did not speak. Winston, however, stepped forward and responded: "You gave us three days, my lord, and we have used only the first of them."

"So your answer is no?" Cnut asked.

Winston nodded.

"Out with it," the king instructed.

"My lord?" Winston seemed startled.

"What have you found out so far?" the king asked.

Winston's eyes scanned the Hall, which was filled with housecarls, women, servants, noblemen, soldiers, Saxons, Danes, and Vikings. Everyone was silent, their eyes trained on us. They all knew what was at stake.

"Nothing worth reporting, my lord," Winston said.

"Nothing?" The king stood up and slammed his fist against the table. "*Nothing?* In a whole day you have learned nothing? Is that why you hesitated to come despite my summons? Because you've been loafing around instead of doing the job I asked you to do?"

Then he clapped his hands together with a resounding smack. "Is that how it's going to be in this country? People simply disregard what the king asks for?"

The Saxon nobleman next to Wulfstan removed his hand from his cheek, and I saw a smile flicker across his lips.

"My lord," the nobleman said.

The king turned to him with a jerk. "Ealdorman Godwin."

So, this was the famous Godwin Wulfnothson, the most powerful ealdorman in England since Eadric died.

"I am certain no one is disregarding your orders," ealdorman Godwin said. "Surely there's a reason for these men's reticence."

Cnut's gaze returned to us and was almost palpable on my skin. "Well, is there? A reason, I mean?"

Winston hesitated, then took another step forward. "My lord, Oxford is full of men who are waiting for you to convene the Witenagemot and the Thing. In the meantime, they pass their days doing what has always been the preferred occupation of the idle: gossiping. If I mention our suspicions to you here tonight"—at this, Winston paused to look around the Hall—"by tomorrow morning everyone in town and beyond will have heard the rumor that I already have my eye on the murderer. My suggestion is that you let us carry out our assignment discreetly. In return, you have my word that as soon as I know anything for certain, I will come to you immediately."

The king shook his head, unconvinced. "Am I not the king? Am I not within my rights to demand your compliance? Are you not expecting silver in return for obeying me?"

"Yes, my lord. And if you command me to share with you what my companion and I have discovered today, I will do so. But I would ask that you let us work in secrecy for now."

The king scanned the Hall and found what he was looking for. I hadn't noticed Godskalk before, but he had evidently been there the whole time. "You said you found another man dead," Cnut said to Godskalk.

"Yes." Maybe Godskalk knew more about kings than Winston—and that a brief answer was best.

"A Saxon," Godskalk added.

"A Saxon soldier. Yes," acknowledged Winston.

"Who served Osfrid?" Cnut asked.

"Yes," Winston replied.

"And you," Cnut said, his eyes falling on me now. "You killed a Dane today."

"A Dane who was trying to murder a young girl, my lord." I forced myself to remain calm as my eyes met Cnut's.

"A Saxon wench?" the king asked.

I nodded.

"Three people murdered, and one who only barely escaped death. And you still don't think you owe me a report?" the king continued.

"That's not true, my lord. We do owe you a report, just not yet," Winston said, appearing utterly calm, which was clearly provoking the king.

But before the king had a chance to boil over, Wulfstan placed a hand on his arm and pulled the king toward him. Wulfstan whispered into Cnut's ear, and after a while the king pulled his arm free and straightened back up.

"All right. Have it your way," Cnut announced.

Winston bowed slightly, and I followed suit.

"But find the murderer or you will lose my favor," Cnut said, his voice like a stone sliding across fresh ice.

Once we were back outside, I began to open my mouth but was silenced by a shake of Winston's head. He held his breath until we reached the middle of the square. Once he felt that we were sufficiently far from anyone who might overhear us, he exhaled loudly, whistling like wind racing through a knothole. Then he turned to me and said, "Yes?"

"You play high stakes," I said.

"Yes, and we both stand to lose," Winston replied. When I raised my eyebrows at him, he explained: "If we don't have our hands on the murderer by the day after tomorrow, we're going to need a faster mount than Atheling to escape the king's rage."

Chapter 21

didn't like it. And the more I thought about it, the less I liked it: We had made an enemy of the king. Cnut's words echoed in my head: *or you will lose my favor.*

When a powerful man warns that you'll be losing his favor, it's already half lost. From now on every word we said would be scrutinized, and even if we did manage to find the murderer, no one would ever forget that a lowly painter and an equally lowly and landless nobleman's brat had stood in the king's way, refusing to bend to his will.

People would remember the murdered noblemen, but for every thane or ealdorman killed, dozens of commoners would pay the ultimate price as well.

King Cnut understood the power of fear. To preclude further treachery, Cnut had had Eadric the Grasper assassinated the year before, and this had been highly effective, "encouraging" dozens of noblemen to swear fealty to Cnut. A wide swath of battle-dead soldiers, sword-slain farmers, sliced-up Saxons, and mutilated Jutes had all driven the noblemen's subjects to fall into line, as they'd seen that the king was willing to clear not only the trees but also the brush from his path. Countless Saxons and Danes had ended up blowing into the king's fold as a result.

The bodies of an insubordinate illuminator and his insignificant assistant would demonstrate what befell those who opposed the king.

I said nothing.

Winston demanded that we stop by the stable so he could make sure his bastard of a mule was doing all right. I followed him in silence.

Atheling didn't even look up when Winston patted his brisket; he simply continued munching the sheaf of oats that I was sure he had stolen from his pitiable, bullied neighbor. When Winston moved out of the way after petting his beast, Atheling glared at me with his yellow eyes. I spit at the mule and followed Winston out. Evidently reassured that Atheling was fine, Winston pushed his way through the narrow, crowded streets.

Alfilda greeted us as though we were old friends. She assured us that our room was still waiting for us and that no one else had occupied it, but felt compelled to remind us that she could have made a good shilling by letting us share our bed with two other people.

The tavern was packed even though it was late. Everywhere I looked, soldiers, merchants, and craftsmen were reaching for plates and bowls and taking long quaffs from full tankards of ale, while noblemen were tucking into slices of roast beef and legs of lamb. Though most of them preferred wine, which they poured from leather flagons, a small number sat with mead cups in their hands.

Our hostess led us to a small table at the very back of the room, then returned with a dish of meat, some bread, and two tankards of her malted ale.

Though I had eaten that afternoon, I was ravenous and dug in silently. Winston shared my hunger, for he too devoured his meat and bread, washing it down with big gulps of ale. He was evidently unconcerned by my silence. Instead of talking, he looked curiously around the tavern, sizing up everyone in the room.

Finally we both pushed ourselves back from the table, inhaled deeply, leaned back, and stretched out our legs.

Winston gave me an indecipherable look and said, "Well, out with it."

"Out with what?" I asked, muffling a burp behind my hand.

"With whatever's bothering you. You look like a cloud that can't shoot off its lightning. Is it that wench?"

I scoffed. As though worrying about a wench could weigh me down.

Winston leaned across the table. "Something is definitely bothering you."

"Did you really need to turn the king against us and make him our enemy?" I blurted out before considering my words.

"Oh, I see," Winston said, leaning back and giving me a half-annoyed, half-satisfied look. "So that's what you think I did?"

"A person who refuses to obey the king is not a friend of the king," I griped, flinging my hands up in irritation.

"But not necessarily his enemy," Winston said calmly.

"We're losing his good graces," I exclaimed.

"If we don't come up with the murderer—then, yes, that will indeed be true. But does that come as a surprise to you? Did you not already realize that?" Winston asked.

Now I was offended. "Well, yeah," I said. "But there was no reason to flaunt it in his face like that."

Winston didn't respond. He sat watching me for a long time, as though contemplating whether it would be worth his time to explain.

Finally he scooted closer to the table again, leaned toward me, and said, "Actually, *yes*. I do believe there was every reason to provoke the king. Have you given any thought to why he asked us to investigate this murder?"

"Because you demonstrated that you could think when they found Osfrid's body," I said. Winston himself had heard the king say that. "And because you're a Saxon and I'm a Dane, as the king pointed out," I said.

Winston shot me an arrogant look. "You need to learn that the high and mighty in this world rarely mean what they say. True, you do not have the same experience I do. I've worked for archbishops, priors, and abbots. Many, if not all, of them are noble-born, like yourself—not that your lineage seems to be doing you much good these days."

He ignored the look I gave him. Did I deserve to be mocked just because the nobler aspects of my bloodline had been buried along with my father and brother?

"And, you see, churchmen like that, " he continued, unmoved, "often say one thing and mean something else altogether. 'Of course you can paint it any way you want it,' they'll say. 'Certainly we'll pay your expenses, Winston,' they'll say. 'We'll pay what we think it's worth,' they'll say. But such statements are rarely reliable. It's the same thing when the king says he wants the murderer found—he may actually prefer that the murder never be solved. I mean, so what if a Dane killed a Saxon? Angles and Saxons have been killing Danes and Vikings and vice versa for as long as anyone can remember. What's one more death here or there?"

"But the king wants reconciliation," I protested. There, I *had* been paying attention.

Winston shook his head. "Cnut wants unity. He wants everyone to agree that he's the king. He wants the various parties to agree how the country should be governed. Cnut is being honest when he says he wants law and order to prevail. But he wants it to be *his* law and *his* order. Cnut is happy enough to let Wulfstan say whatever he needs to say about traditional Saxon law and the like, and Cnut is happy enough to let the Witenagemot and Thing adopt Wulfstan's recommendations. But he'll only let them do that because once the law is adopted, the king is the one who will uphold it."

I didn't understand. "But what does any of that have to do with Osfrid's murder?" I asked. "If we solve the murder, that can only help Cnut push through whatever he wants adopted, right?"

"Maybe. Depending on whom we identify for the crime," Winston said eagerly, but quietly. "Let's suppose we find out there was a feud between two Saxon noblemen. That would suit the king just fine. Or, maybe we find out it was a Dane exacting a thoroughly justified revenge. The king could live with that, as well, because in both cases it's just a murder like so many others, and the noblemen won't make a fuss about it.

"But, Halfdan," he continued. "Suppose we find out that the whole thing is more complicated. What if the English are still hoping Cnut will come up a few votes short out in the meadow in a few days? Or maybe there are Danes who would rather that Cnut be a weak king than a strong one? Thorkell the Tall has said very little in our presence, for instance. Don't forget that he opposed the king until not long ago, fighting for his own power."

"I wonder if Cnut hasn't thought that Thorkell is just biding his time?" I asked. "What if his loyalty to Cnut is just an act?"

"So you see, my young Danish friend: If we were to reveal something like that, evil itself would be loosed into our midst. That *would* create obstacles to unity and agreement, and the gathering of noblemen might turn into a witch's cauldron of discord, accusations, and open fighting."

"But . . ." I began.

Winston gave me a look of encouragement.

"Well, but then why ask anyone to solve the murder in the first place?" I asked, still mystified.

"Because it demonstrates Cnut's good will," Winston said, a strained smile on his face. "Because then he can tell the noblemen, 'I asked a couple of clever men to investigate the murder, but unfortunately they haven't been able to get to the bottom of it.' And everyone will say what a shame that is, but no one will be able to claim the king didn't do his best. And then, we're just two unknowns, so the king can snap his fingers and be done with us if we fail. If he'd asked any of his own loyal men to look into the matter, their failure would reflect poorly on him."

Winston was starting to make sense. "So you really think the king doesn't want us to succeed?"

Winston shook his head. "No. What I'm saying is that it's one possibility that we have to consider."

"But why . . ." I said, still trying to understand, "why provoke Cnut by standing up to him like you did?"

He gave me another aggravatingly overbearing smile. "Because I'm *actually* planning on finding the killer," he said.

My face must have betrayed my incomprehension, because he continued, "If the king wants to find out what we've learned, that *might* be because he's honestly interested in finding out, but it *might* also be because he wants to know how much freedom he can give us to investigate.

"If we tell him there may be a plot against him," he said, "he will be forced to act. And whether he must strike deeply into the English ranks or slash his sword among his own Danish noblemen, any retaliation against a plot from either party will ultimately sabotage Cnut's chances of creating unity.

"So our only real choice is to keep everything we learn to ourselves and not open our mouths until we're sure about our facts," Winston said. "We *had* to stand up to him so that he doesn't compel us to disclose anything, thereby showing we're not afraid—but we also had to stand up for our right to perform the job *he* asked us to do, which we *shall* do."

"But we don't care if he succeeds in convincing his council of noblemen," I said, starting to think I might be the tiniest bit afraid, but I didn't see any need to mention that to Winston.

"We don't?" Winston asked, somberly shaking his head. "We don't care if our fellow countrymen are thrown to the wolves again? If Cnut fails, all hell will break loose in this country *yet again*. This land has been ravaged by war for as long as I can remember. Right now, right here, *this* is the first real peace I've experienced. Cnut may not be the *best* candidate to be crowned king of all the peoples in this land, but he is the *only* candidate. So I'm hoping that we find a murderer the noblemen won't really care about."

"And what if we find out there *is* some kind of plot?" I asked.

Winston sighed. "Then we'll need to decide whether we're going to share that information with the king."

"In other words, peace is more important than law and order?" I asked.

Winston didn't respond right away. After a long silence, he nodded and said, "Yes, I do believe it is. But of course we'll make that decision together, if it should come to that." He sighed again. "And, fortunately, there is one small sign that Cnut might honestly want us to solve the murder." He looked into my puzzled eyes. "If the king had really wanted to pump us for information—to prevent us from solving the murder, if that suited his purposes—he would have been wise to meet us in private so that only he could hear what we had learned. But he questioned us in the Hall surrounded by his retinue, his earls, his soldiers, the servants, and anyone else who happened to be around. That suggests that he's being honest."

Now it was my turn to sigh. "Let's hope so. I really don't want to lose his good graces, as he threatened."

"Me neither," Winston said, a cunning smile playing across his lips. "So I guess there's only one thing to do."

"What?"

"Solve the murder."

Chapter 22

he crowd in the tavern had thinned out while Winston and I were talking. Only a few people were left, slurping up the last of their stew and bread. At a long table in the middle of the room sat six strapping, battle-seasoned soldiers. Though they had healthy appetites, I noticed they hadn't drunk more than a single tankard apiece since Winston and I had sat down.

Suddenly four more soldiers walked in the door, all with the same fearless demeanor, cocky, reckless manner, and sturdy swords hanging at their hips as the first six. The first group got up and left the tavern and the four that had just arrived took their places. Alfilda brought them bowls of the hearty stew right away. Toothless had scarcely set their tankards down in front of them when another three men walked in. Two of them were also soldiers, but the third immediately stood out to me because of his peculiar appearance.

Though not ostentatiously dressed, he was obviously wealthy. He didn't wear a sword or ax, but rather, had a short dagger tucked into a silver-inlaid leather belt around his narrow waist. When he pulled off his blue cap, he revealed a few scant curls stuck to the top of his head. I couldn't help but notice that he kept his thick wool doublet on despite the fact that it was quite warm inside.

But it wasn't his clothes that caught my attention: It was his body that was so striking. It looked as though it was made up of two halves that didn't go together.

From the waist down, he was slim, if not emaciated. In his red leggings, his legs looked no thicker than willow twigs, giving the impression he was staggering around on chicken legs, and his waist was so narrow that I would swear I could have reached my hands around him and touched my fingertips to each other.

His torso, however, was barrel shaped. His potbelly hung out under his doublet and shirt, his chest was broader than I could reach around with my arms, and his face was fleshy, puffy, and red. His eyes—blinking between the fatty folds of his lids—were black and keen, and his mouth was wide and round, with thick lips under a massive Roman nose.

Winston was sitting with his back to the door, but my wide eyes made him turn around.

"There's a man you won't forget," he mumbled. "I passed him this afternoon."

I watched as the man sat down at the end of the soldiers' table and noticed the deferential looks they gave him.

"Who is he?" I asked Winston.

"The devil if I know," Winston replied, shrugging slightly. "He was standing in the doorway of an imposing-looking house on the square in front of the king's Hall. He was surrounded by soldiers, and the door to the house was well guarded."

So he was a nobleman who had reason to be protected by guards and who, judging from the spread on their table, evidently treated them quite well.

I turned my attention back to our conversation. "Have we actually gotten any closer to solving this murder, then?"

Winston inhaled deeply. He held his breath for a bit and then snorted, making a sound that reminded me of the one otters make before they emerge from the water, exposing themselves to the hunter they know is waiting on the bank. "We need to talk to that young lout who's lodging in the same house as Estrid—that lout who paid Tonild a visit," he said, standing up to go, but he stopped when he saw my upheld hand. "What?" he asked.

"It's nighttime," I said. "They're not going to let us in." I ignored Winston's nod. "The men guarding that lodging house don't give a rat's ass about King Cnut's orders."

"Hmm," Winston said, sitting back down. "A shame you didn't find out any more about him from Estrid."

I felt a surge of rage. "Yes, what a shame that I didn't ask her to tell me about every single man we ran into. How was I supposed to know that that guy was going to go visit Tonild? At the time he was just like any other dumb guy who just happened to greet her."

"Didn't she mention that they were staying in the same lodging house?" Winston asked.

I gave a tired sigh. "Well, yes. But how many people are staying there? It's some kind of Saxon hostel."

Something tingled in the back of my mind, a memory, something I had noticed but not thought important at the time. I remembered Estrid had only said that they were staying in the same lodging house. Did that matter?

Winston eyed me with curiosity, but I held up my hand to keep him quiet. That young man had come out of Estrid's place, walked past the guards unhindered, and even nodded to them, the way a man does when he has nothing to hide.

I had seen him once again later on while I was following Estrid. He had been bickering with some Vikings, but I had left it up to the house-carls who were on their way up the street to save him from a thorough drubbing.

I held my breath. That was it! Had I interpreted what I'd seen correctly? Was he just a young Saxon noble who had stepped on the toes of a few Vikings and then refused to apologize? Or . . . ?

I looked across the table at Winston, who was wondering with a raised eyebrow what I was thinking about.

"That lout was scolding two Vikings in the lane," I finally said.

"Vikings?" Winston furrowed his brow and leaned back. "Do tell."

Winston listened with his eyes closed as I recounted what I'd seen. When I was done, he kept his eyes closed, and looked as though he were asleep. Only his breathing told me he was awake.

Finally he opened his eyes. "We'll speak to him first thing in the morning."

"Well, I don't see why it's *that* important," I said.

"You don't?" Winston asked, a haughty look twinkling once again in his eye. "Well, you may be right. But still, this is the first time we've seen a Saxon interacting with Vikings. Or vice versa. So far we've observed only deep divides between the Saxons on the one hand and the Danes and Vikings on the other. It may not be significant. But you were puzzled by it yourself when you recalled it just now," he said, then paused. "Besides, what else do we have to go on?"

I thought about it. "There is one thing," I said hesitantly, unsure how my thought fit into the big picture, but Winston gave me an encouraging look. As I started to explain myself, the idea gradually became clearer in my mind. "Well, first we had Osfrid, then Frida, then Horik. So . . . a thane was murdered . . . Then someone tried to kill a young wench, presumably to shut her up . . . And then a Saxon soldier who had been accompanying the thane was murdered."

Winston's mouth gaped as he struggled to understand what I was getting at. "And?"

"Well, that's it," I said, growing more confident. "If Osfrid was murdered because—and what do I know?—of jealousy, general malice, ill will, or maybe even by a robber who was just after his money . . . well, then it should have just ended there, right?"

Winston realized his mouth was open and closed it with a snap. He stared at me, tugging on his nose. Finally, I detected nascent comprehension in his eyes. "But it *didn't* just end there, did it?" he said. "Someone is killing *witnesses*. It is someone so powerful that he has shamelessly killed not one person, but three! Well, killed two and almost killed another—thanks to you, Halfdan. There has been a trail of dead bodies through the middle of Oxford when not only the king himself is in residence but dozens of housecarls are patrolling the city, which means this cannot be the work of just one person. Yes, yes. I think you're right. This is not about jealousy, hatred, or revenge. This is a plot to overthrow the king."

I nodded, pleased at having worked it out correctly.

"Yes," Winston said again. "Now we just need to figure out whether the plot is Saxon or Danish or—who knows—maybe Viking. And what you observed has just made that a little harder for us to do."

I looked at him blankly, but then I saw what he meant: We now had an unexpected and enigmatic connection between a *Saxon* and some *Vikings*.

The tavern had quieted down. Aside from the soldiers and that strange no-bleman who was with them, there was only one other man left, a clearly inebriated Viking. With a great deal of effort, Alfilda managed to get him onto his feet and guide him toward the door. He became agitated and tried to yank his arm back. I stood up, but Alfilda didn't need any help. She got him under control with a solid punch to the kidney, and escorted him out the door while he was still moaning. She came back in and flashed me a smile that meant, *I'm woman enough to run my own tavern, thanks.*

The soldiers stood up now, bid their nobleman a quiet farewell, and headed for the door, which flung back open just as they reached it. The drunk Viking staggered forwards, screwing up his eyes to try to spot an evidently blurry Alfilda from across the room, but the first soldier stopped him and, following a nod from the hostess, dragged the bastard back out again.

The Viking grumbled loudly outside until we heard a smack, and then peace once again settled over the inn and its narrow street. The funny-shaped nobleman stood up. He nodded aloofly to us, headed for the rear door that led to the hallway, and disappeared, leaving us with only the di-minishing sound of his footsteps.

Alfilda put the buxom Toothless to work cleaning up then grabbed an empty tankard and a pitcher of ale and brought them to our table. She sat down, poured a round, and raised her tankard to us. "Closing time."

We raised our tankards back to her.

"Who's your other guest?" Winston asked, wiping the foam from his lips.

"Oh him," Alfilda smiled roguishly. "He's a man it might pay off to se-duce—if he were for sale, I mean. Which I happen to know he isn't. He's King Cnut's most trusted man in Oxford these days."

Winston and I exchanged glances.

"But who is he?" I asked, now wiping the foam from my own mouth.

"His name's Baldwin, and he's the king's master of accounts," Alfilda said.

That didn't help me at all, and I said as much, but Winston just nodded to himself.

"That well-guarded house across from the king's Hall?" Winston asked.

"It houses the heregeld, or what's come in of it so far," Alfilda said. "There are still two days until the deadline."

That explained the brutish and incorruptible-looking guards.

"So the king is collecting the heregeld here?" I asked, fishing a fly out of my ale.

"The king is sticking to his agreement," Alfilda said. "Seventy-two thousand pounds of silver, plus an extra ten and half thousand pounds specifically from London, need to be in that building by nightfall the day after tomorrow."

Winston smiled wryly. "We're a rich people in a rich country."

"Add the thousands of pounds we've bled out in recent years, and this is what I own now," Alfilda said, showing us the empty palms of her hands.

"And Baldwin is responsible for all the silver?" I asked, setting the fly on the table and crushing it with my thumbnail.

"Baldwin does all the computations and counting. The Witenagemot and the Thing won't meet until he's satisfied," Alfilda explained, shoulders drooping. I could tell she was tired. And yet she didn't miss a thing going on around her. She turned to Toothless, who had just run a rag over the last table. "That's great, Emma. You can go to bed."

The serving girl with the same name as the queen didn't have to be told twice.

When the door had shut behind her, Alfilda continued, "But the king *is* a man of his word. You have to give him that."

Winston and I both cocked our heads, wondering what she meant.

"There was news today. Haven't you heard?" she continued. We shook our heads.

"Cnut sent his fleet home, just like he'd said he would."

"Home? To Denmark?" I asked. That didn't seem plausible.

But yes, Alfilda assured me it was. After Cnut had repelled an attack by an unaffiliated fleet of Viking pirates, just a month ago, the Witenagemot had stated unanimously that the Saxons would not negotiate with Cnut if his entire fleet were just sitting there threatening to start harrying England again. Cnut had promised to order a good portion of his fleet home as a sign of good faith, and there had just been an announcement that Cnut had actually done so.

"So Cnut is leaving the country defenseless?" I asked. That was just as hard for me to grasp. If he wanted to be England's king, he had to be able to defend the country's coasts.

"He's keeping forty longboats here, but that's all," Alfilda said, rubbing her neck.

That was probably enough. Under the command of Thorkell or the king himself, that many longboats would be a devastatingly effective fleet—if the enemy consisted merely of a few Viking warlords out plundering, that is. But if the Vikings decided to launch a full-scale attack, forty ships would be nothing.

But where would such an attack come from, anyway? Cnut was the most powerful Viking king in all the Nordic lands. His enemies had either been defeated or spread to the four winds, and he had won over the only force he needed to fear—the Duke of Normandy—through marriage.

The English would now realize that the king planned to live up to his word. *See?* was his message, *I don't need a fleet to subdue England. The country is mine, and I will govern it with the consent and support of Saxons, Angles, and Danes alike. You can see that I keep my word. Now you keep yours. Send me the heregeld, and meet me in the meadow outside Oxford so that we can decide together how to govern the country.*

Winston's eyes met mine and he nodded.

"Yes," Winston said, "it seems that the king is a man of his word."

Chapter 23

don't know long I'd been asleep when Winston's thunderous snoring woke me up. He had told me to just give him a shove. I sighed. It was pitch black, and even straining my eyes, I couldn't make out the window in the wall.

I rolled over.

The penetrating rumble rattled the blankets; I rubbed my ears.

I jabbed him in the side with my elbow.

"Huh, what?" he grunted.

"You're snoring," I told him.

The bed boards creaked as he rolled over.

I drifted off to sleep again and then woke with a start.

I did my elbow trick again.

I didn't know how much time had passed, but I was becoming increasingly tense and irritated. Every time I jabbed him, Winston abruptly sat halfway up in bed, sounding chipper and well rested. A pale outline of the window started to take shape in the wall as the spring morning dawned.

I got out of bed, cursing. I wrapped myself in the blanket and walked out into the hallway, but my companion's codfish-out-of-water gasps could be heard even from there. I wondered if anyone in the whole building could possibly be sleeping.

I bit my lip. I was tempted for a moment to open the nearest door and crawl into bed with whoever happened to be in there, but instead I headed toward the tavern door.

Alfilda woke me. Our hostess was already fully dressed, while Emma, mid-yawn, stared sleep-drunk at me in the doorway behind her.

"Are you afraid of an attack?" Alfilda asked me.

I sat up. My back ached, and my body felt heavy from lack of sleep. Though I'd wrapped the blanket tightly around me, it hadn't made the hard, oaken table any softer to lie on.

"Attack?" I yawned.

"Weren't you lying here in the tavern keeping guard?" Alfilda asked, blowing some life into the coals on the baking stones.

After shaking my head to wake myself up, I explained why I was lying on her table.

She laughed as she laid some kindling over the coals. "I know how that goes. My blessed husband snored until the house shook."

"What did you do about it?" I asked, now on my feet.

She poured some ale into a cauldron. "There are lots of other rooms here. He found his way into one of them every time."

I excused myself and headed to the well. After drinking a dipperful of water, I washed myself, snorting from the cold. It was a bright, crisp morning, and the swallows were chattering between the thatched roofs.

Winston was sitting at the table when I returned, looking shamelessly well rested.

"So you abandoned me?" he asked, warm ale dribbling from the corner of his mouth.

"Well, I hope *you* slept well," I said, sitting down heavily.

He drizzled golden, slow-flowing honey over his slice of bread. "The blanket was nowhere to be found, but once I put on my doublet and warmed up again, I slept marvelously."

We spent the rest of the meal in silence.

The tavern began to fill up with other guests. Baldwin the Master of Accounts was the first to arrive. After giving us a brief, reserved bow, he sat down at a table by himself, and began to bite off carefully measured mouthfuls of bread. He chewed them rapidly and methodically, like a squirrel, rinsed them down with ale, and had finished eating in the time it took me to cover a single slice of bread with honey.

As he left, likely on his way to accept more heregeld deliveries, several other customers walked in. A monk who had achieved a certain high rank within his monastery—judging by the silver cross on his chest—was accompanied by a novice with a little peach fuzz on his chin. The older friar talked steadily, but the novice didn't open his mouth except to take bites of his bread.

A gray-haired man, who comported himself with a certain dignity and greeted neither us nor the monastic duo, studied the slices of bread in front of him for a long time before cautiously biting into one of them. Then he started to eat with the expression of a man who'd just been served a bucketful of ants. He was on his second slice when a flabby woman who hadn't yet put on her head linen joined him. She, too, had gray hair, but with a black stripe that ran from the top of her head to just behind her right ear. They ate in silence, hardly glancing at each other, completely indifferent to everything and everyone around them.

Winston finished his tankard and looked fondly at Alfilda, who had taken a seat next to him to chat between her duties. Winston said it was time to start the day.

The day was warming up nicely, and people were already out and about as we stepped into the street. We strolled at a leisurely pace over to the square. The king himself was standing outside in front of the Hall, surrounded by housecarls and a small flock of men who looked like craftsmen and merchants. Winston took one look at them and declared that they must be locals who were either trying to curry favor with the king or who had been summoned to pay some additional share of the heregeld. We watched as Cnut slammed his fist into the open palm of his other hand, hurling angry words at the man in front of him. Then he began to walk up the road that led north, the whole group following behind him like a flush of ducks.

We were about to turn west into the lane that led to Estrid's lodging house when a cart came rumbling out of the lane toward us. Judging from both the deep wheel tracks it was carving into the dirt and the heavy breathing of the oxen beneath their yokes, the cart was carrying a heavy load. We stopped to wait for it to pass. When it groaned to a stop in front of the house where Baldwin the Master of Accounts was waiting out front with his armed guards, we realized that the cart must be delivering some of Cnut's eagerly awaited heregeld.

Winston and I continued on down the lane toward Estrid's lodging house, where we were stopped by the guards at the door. I couldn't tell you if they were the same guards from the day before. I hadn't studied them all that closely, and none of them seemed to recognize me now—but that's how it is with guards.

"Could you please inform Lady Estrid that Winston the Illuminator, the companion of Halfdan, with whom she spoke yesterday, would like to speak with her?" Winston asked them politely.

One of the guards promptly turned on his heel and went inside to deliver Winston's message. Why were they so quick to do Winston's bidding when they hadn't given me the time of day yesterday? It could have been because Winston looked less menacing than I did—he wasn't carrying a sword, after all. But I suspected the real reason was that Winston actually knew the name of the lady, which I had not known the day before. It seemed to do the trick, as it only took a few seconds for the guard to return and wave us in.

The interior of the house was every bit as spacious as it appeared from outside. Though it was not as grand as the royal Hall Cnut was staying in on the square, it was by no means the smallest hall I had ever been in. A fire was burning in the hearth in the middle of the room. Bunk beds lined the wall, beside which were bundles of clothing marking where the visiting nobles were sleeping. Men were sitting on the beds and on the benches lining a long table that occupied the middle of the room on the far side of the fire from us.

Although a few women sat at the table with the men, most of the women in the room were servants walking purposefully back and forth. Estrid stood up from the table and came toward us with an ingratiating smile. Over her shoulder, I spotted the young man we had come to speak with.

"So you have more to discuss with me?" Estrid said.

As Winston bowed briefly, I wondered how he was going to get us out of this pinch.

"Just one simple question, my lady," Winston said, in his customary polite tone. "And I would ask you to forgive that it may be a bit lewd."

Her eyes widened.

"But," Winston continued, undeterred, "I don't have time to couch my words more delicately since—as you know—the king has charged me with solving your brother's murder."

Estrid stood silently, making no effort to find a place where we could sit down.

"I'll just ask you straight out then," Winston said, lowering his voice. "Why haven't you, a nobleman's daughter, ever been married?"

Her head, which she had bashfully lowered, jerked up. The rage in her eyes was almost palpable.

"I warned you it would be a frank question," Winston said, his voice soothing and gentle.

"A question that has nothing to do with my brother's murder!" she said shrilly.

"All the same, in my experience it's impossible to know what details will end up being important in a case like this," Winston said.

I glanced over at the young man we had come to talk to and thought he might be looking at me.

Estrid's heavy chin quivered; then, in a steady voice, she said, "Even natural-born daughters need a dowry. None of my brothers ever felt the need to provide me with one."

"Thank you for your candor," Winston said, bowing gracefully and looking at me.

"My lady," I said. The look she gave me was hardly friendly, but I continued anyway. "The young man who greeted you when we were having our drink yesterday—who is he?"

I didn't think she was going to answer me. It seemed that she was debating whether to do so or not, as she studied me silently for a moment. Perhaps she hoped that divulging that information would shut us up.

"Ranulf," she said, and turned on her heel and walked away.

I raised my eyebrows and looked at Winston, who was rubbing his chin. No one seemed to find it odd that we were still standing there, even though the person we had come to speak with had left us. I saw Ranulf stand, rest his hand momentarily on his neighbor's shoulder, and make a remark that made the other person laugh.

He then crossed the floor, not toward us but in the direction of the door. I nodded at Winston to indicate that we should follow him and we set off.

Once we were safely back out in the lane, we looked right and then left. Ranulf was walking purposefully up the narrow street, and we followed suit.

Before reaching the open square, he turned right into another narrow lane, apparently unaware that we were on his tail. He stopped to wait for a drove of pigs being herded down the lane, then continued on and turned into a side street. He appeared to be headed toward a little church about a hundred paces from the corner.

"That isn't Saint Frideswide's Church," I said.

"No, it's Saint Ebbe's."

Young Ranulf crossed the cemetery and disappeared inside. Winston nudged me with his elbow, so I took off my sword, passed it to him, and followed the lad in.

It was dark inside the little church, which was illuminated only by a single window in each of the side walls and the back wall and the two lit candles on the altar.

The room was empty apart from me and Ranulf, who was kneeling before the altar.

I exited quietly and found Winston, who was sitting on the wall that surrounded the cemetery. I retrieved my sword, and reported, "He's praying."

A contemplative look came over Winston's face. "Like someone praying for forgiveness for committing the sin of murder?" he asked.

I shrugged my shoulders. I'd wondered the same thing myself. There was only one place a murderer could go to find salvation for his deed.

"Well," Winston said, sliding off the stone wall and then leaning against it, "there's only one way out of the church. We'll let him finish praying before we question him."

Chapter 24

he street outside the church cemetery was buzzing with activity. Oxford was inundated with people scurrying in all directions. Surely they all had some destination in mind, but from my perspective—leaning back, trying to appear relaxed, watching them hurry by—they seemed as aimless as rats.

Trying to appear relaxed. I couldn't take my eyes off the church door for more than a second at a time because the crowd was so thick that someone who knew he was being watched could easily slip away, hidden in the swarming mass of humanity.

Winston sat in silence. He had plucked a straw blade, which he was sucking on with his eyes half shut, but when I looked over at him, I could tell that he was just as intently focused on the church door as I was.

Even so, we almost missed Ranulf's exit. A heavily laden cart came to a halt in front of us. Its driver started whipping his two broad-necked oxen, screaming for them to move along, which didn't do the least bit of good.

As I stood up to peer over the cart, three horsemen rode past on the other side of it. Enormous and armed, they were no doubt housecarls out on the king's business. Regardless, my greatest concern was that they were completely blocking my view.

As the rump of the last horse finally moved out of my line of sight, I saw the church door swinging back into place in its frame. Had someone just gone in? Or out? My eyes darted up and down the street, and there—about a dozen paces down from the church—I spotted young Ranulf's back. I brought Winston to his feet with a curse and broke into a run to catch up with our quarry.

Winston panted behind me as I caught up to the lad, fell into step with him, and waited for Winston to catch up to us.

Ranulf glanced at me, but showed no sign of recognition. He continued along at the same pace until we reached the square in the center of town. The Hall sat silent, but guarded. Activity was lively, however, in front of Baldwin's treasury. A line of heavy-looking, ox-drawn carts snaked out from it, each of them surrounded by tough-looking housecarls. An even more intimidating-looking group of guards stood at the door, their hands never far from the hilts of their powerful swords.

Ranulf crossed the square to an alehouse, where he took a seat beneath the awning. He was served a tankard, and then simply sat there in silence.

I looked at Winston, who shook his head, indicating that we should hold off on approaching him. "Let's see if anyone comes up to him," he said.

But it seemed that Ranulf had just been thirsty, because quite some time passed and no one met up with him. When it looked as though he was almost done with his drink, Winston nodded and we stepped under the canvas awning.

Ranulf looked up as our shadows fell over him and then scooted over to make room for me next to him. Winston took a seat across from him. Recognizing me from the street, he narrowed his eyes at me.

"Are you following me?" he asked.

Before I could respond, Winston leaned across the table. His voice was quiet, but earnest: "Did you receive the absolution you were seeking?"

Ranulf's eyes widened and he stared at Winston agape.

I hadn't really paid that much attention to Ranulf before, having guessed that he was no more than twenty. But now that I was so close to him, I realized he was a fair bit older than I'd first thought. The wrinkles at the corners of his mouth indicated a man beyond his youth, and the steady look in his eyes indicated a man not easily bested.

He was dressed as a nobleman, with his breeches tucked into short boots. His shirt was made of fine wool, as was his sleeveless coat, which hid an elaborately worked sword hilt. He wore his brown hair in a helmet cut, and his powerful hands matched the rippling muscles that were just visible beneath his shirtsleeves.

"What in the world are you talking about?" Ranulf asked in a steady voice.

"In the church earlier, when you were praying," Winston said, still quietly.

"So you *are* following me," Ranulf said and started to stand up, but the hand I put on his shoulder stopped him. I never found out whether he was strong enough to shake my hand off because he immediately sat back down. "I'm Ranulf. Who are you?"

Winston nodded to himself. "That's a reasonable question. I'm Winston, and this is my partner, Halfdan. At the king's behest, we're investigating the murder of a man named Osfrid, whom you knew."

"And what does that have to do with me?" Ranulf asked.

So he didn't deny knowing the dead man.

"Probably nothing," Winston said, nodding to a lanky man with an oversized leather apron tied around his belly who appeared tableside. "Three ales, please," Winston said and turned back to Ranulf. "But we'd really like you to answer a couple of questions all the same."

Ranulf raised his eyebrows. "Ah, so that's what you want. How long have you been following me?"

"Since you left the lodging house." Winston had obviously decided that honesty couldn't hurt.

"Did you follow me into the church?" Ranulf said, not protesting when the servant replaced his empty tankard with a full one.

"Yes and no. Halfdan followed you in, but then came right back out so as not to disturb your prayers."

Ranulf exposed his teeth in a sarcastic smile. "So you think your tactfulness entitles you to ask questions."

Winston responded simply by shrugging.

"Wait a minute," Ranulf said, his facing suddenly lighting up with understanding. "Absolution? Are you implying that I killed Osfrid and was praying for forgiveness?"

"That is a possibility," Winston said.

Ranulf shook his head haughtily. "Not for me, it's not. I don't slink around killing men in secret."

"But you do go visit their widows," Winston said pointedly.

"Yes," Ranulf said, looking from me to Winston, with a puzzled look on his face. "Of course."

"Of course?"

Ranulf leaned back and studied us, as though he were contemplating whether he could be bothered to take the trouble to explain. He took his time, drank, wiped his mouth, drank again, wiped again, and then looked straight at Winston, who was waiting calmly for an answer.

"Tonild is my sister," he said.

Winston's eyes met mine. There seemed to be no end of relatives popping up in this case.

Something wasn't right. I tried to put my finger on a foggy recollection, but it slipped away from me, and I sat back with a vague sense that it had been important.

"Your sister?" Winston said with a nod. "Yes, then I understand."

"Thank you. Now, perhaps you will excuse me?" Ranulf said. He finished his ale and stood up.

"If you wouldn't mind holding on for one moment," I said, trying to put my finger on the thought that had escaped me. I stood up and pointed to the bench.

But it was not to be. Ranulf turned his back on me without uttering a word and was already three paces away when my vague recollection finally crystallized. I walked up behind him, put my hand on his arm, and said, "Yet you didn't attend your brother-in-law's funeral." He looked annoyed.

"That's my own concern," he said.

"And ours," I said. Winston had jumped to his feet and run around the bench as quickly as a cat to welcome us back to the bench.

"Would you please sit back down as Halfdan asked? Otherwise we will have to summon their help," Winston said, pointing to four housecarls who happened to be walking past.

Ranulf eyed Winston for a long time before sitting back down on the bench without a word.

It had been a falling-out over land. The story Ranulf reluctantly told us has been told before and will be told again. A nobleman's wealth is land. Land is what he covets most, and his enemies are often the result of disputes over land.

When Cnut had ordered Ranulf's father assassinated, Ranulf decided, like so many other Saxon noblemen, to throw his lot in with Cnut, and swore allegiance to him.

Cnut accepted Ranulf's oath, returned a portion of his father's seized property, and hinted that the rest could be won back through loyal service and fulfillment of his oath. But Cnut did not return the family's ancestral home, an estate in Kent that had been in the family for three hundred years, ever since King Eadbert had bestowed it upon their ancestor, Ranulf the Elder, and it had passed to the eldest son in each subsequent generation since that time.

"What happened to the estate?" Winston asked.

I was fairly certain I knew the answer already but let Ranulf confirm that Cnut gave the estate to Tonild. Thus she brought her family's ancestral home with her into her marriage with Osfrid. Predictably, this infuriated Ranulf, who felt it should rightly have been his. First he tried negotiating to get it back, but he eventually resorted to begging.

"What about Osfrid?" I asked.

"Osfrid just laughed at me and promised that he and Tonild would name their first son Ranulf," he said, practically spitting out the words.

Osfrid could not have insulted or dishonored Ranulf more if he'd tried. Not only did Osfrid hold the family's ancestral home, he was now threatening to take the name Ranulf and pass it down on the female side—this despite the fact that Ranulf was walking around, alive and well and presumably fully capable of producing an heir, who should have been entitled not only to the name Ranulf, but also to the family estate.

Though Osfrid was his brother-in-law, Ranulf swore he would never see him again. Ranulf's oath had cost him dearly: Tonild, his sister, was welcome to visit him, but Ranulf never again set foot in the same building as Osfrid.

"And *did* Tonild visit you?" Winston asked. Ranulf explained that Osfrid had forbidden her to do so and that their visit the night before had been the first time that he and Tonild had seen each other since the falling-out.

I wanted to ask if he had appealed his case to Cnut directly, but I bit my tongue—it obviously more than suited the king's purposes to sow strife between two Saxon noblemen.

"So you weren't praying for Osfrid in Saint Ebbe's?" Winston asked.

Ranulf was quiet for a moment and then sighed deeply.

"My wife died three weeks ago," he said. "My prayers were for her and the child who killed her."

Winston's voice was kind: "A son?"

Ranulf nodded.

We sat in silence for a long while, until Winston said, "I understand that this is difficult for you, but I'm wondering if you wouldn't mind answering just a couple more questions."

Ranulf flung up his hands, indicating that he didn't really care one way or the other.

"There are a lot of people staying in that lodging house with you," Winston said. "Who owns it?" Winston asked.

Ranulf looked up in surprise and explained that it was owned by a thane by the name of Edmund of Wessex. This Edmund didn't live in the house, himself. He was too old and infirm to come to Oxford, but obviously not too old to care about money, since he let anyone stay there who wanted to. As long as they were Saxon.

"And Estrid is staying there as well?" Winston asked.

"Estrid?" Ranulf gave him a blank look.

"The woman I was sharing a drink with yesterday behind that market stall. You said hello to her," I explained.

"Oh," he said. He didn't seem especially interested.

"She's Osfrid's sister," I informed him.

He shrugged faintly. "I don't know anything about her aside from the fact that she's staying in the same lodging house."

"And Ulfrid and Torold?" Winston asked, looking down at the dirt, as though the question weren't important.

Ranulf raised his eyebrows, wondering who they were.

"The brothers of Osfrid's first wife," I explained.

"I don't know them," Ranulf said. "But yes—I guess there are two men by those names staying in the house, as well."

I could tell from Winston's eyes that he did not believe Ranulf any more than I did.

If there's someone who believes for even an instant that a nobleman—be he Saxon, Angle, Jute, or Dane—would not have a firm handle on who his relatives' relatives are, then I've got a mule to sell him. The ties that bind relatives together, no matter how weak, are what determine inheritances, and no nobleman can help but be aware of even the smallest twig on the thinnest branch of his family tree.

But to my surprise, Winston did not press the issue. "Thank you for your help," was all he said.

Ranulf stood and bade us a polite farewell.

Winston waited until he was out of earshot and then asked me, "What was it that Estrid said yesterday when you asked if she knew our friend Ranulf?"

"That they were just staying in the same lodging house," I said.

"That's right," Winston said, nodding to himself. "Perhaps they're both telling the truth . . . but I wonder whether it's more than a mere coincidence."

"That they're telling the truth?" I asked, confused.

Winston shook his head vigorously. "That four people who all have reason to want Osfrid dead are staying in the same lodging house."

I didn't respond because something else occurred to me.

"I'm surprised that you didn't ask Ranulf about the squabble I noticed him having with those Vikings yesterday," I said.

"Yes," Winston replied casually. "There's a time and a place for everything."

Chapter 25

e left the alehouse and roamed around for a while. Winston hadn't opened his mouth since his remark about there being a time and place for everything, and I just followed him as he wandered around, seemingly quite aimlessly.

We plodded down first one narrow lane, then another, turning more or less randomly into other lanes. We stopped and stared at a strumpet quarreling with a customer who thought he had not received enough for what he'd paid. We browsed the wares of a couple of market stalls, whose proprietors glanced fleetingly at us and then ignored us, since it was evidently obvious that we didn't intend to buy anything.

I looked over at Winston several times, but he never looked back; he just kept strolling along with me at his heels.

The sun was approaching its midday zenith, and my stomach started rumbling, reminding me that the tankard of ale I had emptied during our chat with Ranulf had not been enough to satisfy me.

When we returned to the square, I stared hungrily at the stall where we had had our ale, but Winston didn't seem afflicted by the same need for sustenance, wet or dry. Suddenly he stopped in the middle of the crowd and drew something in the dust with his foot. Then he sighed, and continued on toward the Hall.

I was speculating whether he was planning to pay the king a visit, but just as we reached the Hall, he turned and followed the length of the building toward the entrance to another narrow street that was blocked off.

The barrier consisted of half a dozen housecarls, who were clearing a path for the king himself, who had just emerged from the narrow street onto the square. He was followed by the same assortment of citizens we'd seen him with earlier, deep in conversation with a mason in a leather apron who was listening attentively to the king's words with his head cocked. The men around them were either speaking softly among themselves or leaning in closer in an attempt to eavesdrop on the mason and the king.

The king turned around in front of the door to the Hall, which brought the whole procession to a standstill, and held his hand out to the mason. "So then, Ralf, and the rest of you—we are in agreement."

They nodded eagerly. The mason quickly surveyed the rest of the group, then cleared his throat and responded in a deep voice, "We will build a rampart crowned by a palisade. My lord will pay for the materials. We will provide the labor."

Cnut nodded. "The people of Oxford will sleep more soundly. To the south you are already protected by the river. To the north there will be this fortification. And," he continued, raising his voice, "we shall take on this work and other work like it to benefit all the peoples of this land." His words were clearly meant for everyone present. "Together we will make this country strong, and we will start by strengthening this town so that it may withstand its enemies."

Cnut paused and bowed his head slightly, acknowledging the shouts of praise being lobbed at him. When he turned around to enter the hall, his eyes fell on us. "Time and tide wait for no man," he told us.

I glanced over at Winston, who bowed quickly.

Neither of us opened our mouths, I because I had no idea what to say and Winston for his own reasons—or maybe he had come up just as short as I had.

After the king had disappeared into the Hall, the men in our midst, who had evidently just completed a walking tour of the new town fortifications, all started talking at once. From what I could tell, they were all praising him. Not a single one among them was complaining about being asked to do loads of work for free to secure Oxford against the same kind of attack that Cnut and his father had launched against this town nine years earlier. An attack that had left the town in ruins.

Cnut had taken the first step toward achieving unity between the Saxons and the Danes when the Witenagemot and the Thing met the day after next. Although Oxford's residents would not be participating, they would be present, and a rumor would race through the crowds—soon reaching the ears of the nobility—that the conqueror king was using his silver to fortify his kingdom for the good of *all* its inhabitants. Anyone who thought they might get clever and point out that Cnut had just collected that silver *from them* would be wise to remain silent.

Winston suddenly turned to me and said, "It's no use."

I stared at him. "Huh?"

"They're lying. Every last one of the people we've talked to," Winston railed.

That did seem entirely likely.

"Do they think we're so stupid we can't tell?" Winston asked, his lower jaw jutting out menacingly. "All these noblemen with their half sisters, brothers-in-law, and dead spouses. Murdered fathers and stillborn sons. Well, they can all just revel in their own shit."

And to my great surprise, Winston turned on his heel and made a beeline across the square. I followed him, waiting for him to say more, but he remained silent. He simply stormed through the narrow lanes until I eventually realized he was headed back to Alfilda's tavern.

"Hey, that's a great idea," I said.

He scowled at me.

"That way we can get something to eat," I clarified.

"Harumph," he muttered, spitting on the ground.

Wasn't he planning on getting something to eat?

The look he gave me now was just as ominous. "They can all just revel in shit, I said."

"Uh, you mean the *king*?" I asked hesitantly, nervously casting a quick glance around.

"Cnut and all the Saxons and all the Danes. Not to mention all the Viking pirates, kings, ealdormen, earls, noblemen, and widows." He'd reached the tavern door. He turned and all but shouted, "Get out of here!"

"But . . ." I stammered.

"You heard me. Get!" He slammed the door shut, just missing my nose.

My chest tightened in indignation. I kicked the door open, causing everyone inside to look up, and caught up to him in two steps. My strong grip on his shoulder forced him to turn around. "A day and a half!" I began, on the verge of losing my temper. "We only have a day and a half left and you're . . . you're wasting . . ."

I felt him go limp in my grasp. He made no move to physically resist me. Suddenly he didn't seem angry anymore. He just looked at me calmly and said, "Let go."

I let go.

"Thank you," he said.

"Maybe now we can talk?" My anger was making me sound kind of choked-up.

He waved me off, turned his back on me, and headed into the tavern. The whole place had gone quiet during our tense little exchange, but the patrons all suddenly started chatting again. I glared at Winston's back, cursed loudly, flung the door back open, and left.

Outside I kicked a rock across the street. To hell with him!

I noticed an overturned handbarrow across the street. I leaned it against the wall of the building, sat down on it, and forced my breathing to return to normal. I was not going to let myself attract the king's rage because of some lousy illuminator's whims.

Once my breathing had calmed, I started thinking. Although Winston was more gifted in this arena than I was, I wasn't entirely inept.

What had Winston said after Ranulf left us? That's right! Could it be a coincidence that four people, each of whom had reason to want Osfrid dead, were all staying in the same lodging house? And then I thought what a coincidence it was that they were all Saxons. And what had Winston meant when he said there was a time and place for everything? And shouldn't we go find out what Ranulf's disagreement with the Vikings was about?

Suddenly my thoughts turned to Frida. I could picture the curves beneath her dress, and imagine her fresh breath on my neck. Should I?

I stood, my mind made up. But when I reached the square, I didn't turn down the lane toward the tent camp. Even I had the sense to realize that bedding a wench in the middle of the afternoon when I was supposed to be hard at work solving a murder would probably incur the king's wrath.

Chapter 26

he heat of indignation was still surging within me as I strode down the lane, seething at that louse of an illuminator, who didn't seem to give a damn about pissing off the *king*.

Well, if Winston was just planning on farting his time away in taverns, then apparently it was going to be up to me to get to the bottom of things. And I was convinced there was only one place to start—back at that Saxon lodging house.

I slowed down as I approached, forcibly containing my rage. Still working to cool down my rapid breathing, I stopped a couple buildings away from the lodging house. Then I walked in calm, steady strides toward the door, and faced the icy stares of the guards.

"I have some business with Lady Estrid," I announced, utilizing Winston's trick from earlier that day of mentioning her by name. "My name is Halfdan."

One of the guards, broad-nosed and one-eared, considered me in silence. His companion turned his sizeable back to me and disappeared inside.

I didn't have to wait long.

"Lady Estrid wishes to have nothing to do with you," he announced.

I bit my lip, but retreated when they crossed their spears in front of the door. I walked on up the lane, out of their sight, and then stopped. After a while I strolled back nonchalantly and found the archway I'd stood in during my stakeout the day before.

As far as I could see, there were two possible reasons for Estrid's refusal to see me. One—she was simply tired of our coming and going; two—she had something to hide.

There was a lot of traffic in the lane, which made it easy for me to stay hidden but also frequently blocked my view of the lodging house. At one point I pulled a little farther back into the safety of a shadow in the archway, and noticed a stone mounting block someone had stowed to help a person mount a horse. I stepped up onto it.

Not only was I better hidden but I now had a better view over the heads of all the foot traffic in the lane. However, it was difficult to balance on my perch, and it wasn't long before the muscles in my legs started protesting. So I had to climb down at regular intervals to avoid leg cramps.

I don't know how much time passed—only that I'd been on and off the stone several times—when I was finally rewarded for my efforts. Though several people had exited and entered the lodging house door, I hadn't recognized any of them until two noblemen stepped out side by side. It was Ulfrid and Torold, the brothers of Osfrid's first wife.

They strode purposefully down the lane, looking neither to the side nor behind them. I had no trouble following them through the crowded streets, and the crowds made it easy for me to blend in should one of them look back.

I had plenty of time to wonder where we were going. The two brothers repeatedly gave way to carts, shoppers, drunken men, whores, horsemen, and housecarls in groups of various sizes. They weren't headed in the direction of the tent city, which had been my first guess, nor were they headed toward the king's Hall—which didn't surprise me—and it seemed that neither of them was hungry or thirsty, because my hope that they would turn into a tavern or an ale tent went unfulfilled.

I could smell the mud of the Thames and recognized the street leading down to the ford. It occurred to me with a prickle of anxiety that the men might be leaving town, but then I realized that if that were the case, they wouldn't be on foot. Sure enough, they didn't cross the ford but walked right past it into a narrow passageway that was so dark it hid them from my sun-blinded eyes. I cursed, thinking I'd lost them.

An empty lot—where I assumed that someone hadn't been able to afford to rebuild whatever had been there before Cnut and his father torched the town some years back—created a sunny patch in the passageway, and I easily made out the two tall silhouettes of my quarry once they got that far. I sped up a little to make sure that I didn't lose them again when they reentered the passageway's shadows beyond the sunny spot. But then they suddenly turned around and looked behind them.

Fortunately I happened to be at a spot where two buildings abutted each other. One was set back a little from the other, and without thinking, I flung myself into the shadow created by it, waited a dozen heartbeats, and then stuck my head out again.

They were gone.

I cursed. Then I realized they must have entered one of the buildings, because I could see that there were no empty lots or cross streets where I had last seen them standing. I walked slowly forward.

The buildings down here by the river, far from the center of town, were run-down and rickety, and none of them was more than a single story high. Judging from the small number of people in the narrow passageway, I guessed that these buildings were mostly warehouses and the like. I was just beginning to wonder what the two brothers could be doing in this neighborhood when I heard voices behind the wattle-and-daub walls of a building that was more run-down than most.

I pressed my ear to the wall. The men I heard inside did not seem to be standing immediately on the other side of the wall, but I nevertheless made out three distinct voices. Two Saxon voices, which I guessed and hoped were those of my two noblemen, and a deep, almost rumbling Danish voice that was doing most of the talking—in a tone that suggested extreme dissatisfaction.

Though I had no trouble understanding the languages, it was impossible for me to hear exactly what they were talking about. I could only make out a few words here and there.

". . . that was stupid . . ." one of the Saxon voices said.

". . . murdering a girl could . . ." also said by a Saxon.

". . . didn't . . . understand . . . orders . . ." said in Danish.

". . . the king . . ." said in Danish.

". . . Witenagemot has to . . ." said in Saxon.

Then it happened. I didn't see him, didn't hear him, didn't sense him. He appeared so suddenly that he could have fallen from the sky. I don't know why Vikings make mistakes—I just rejoice when they allow me to save my own life.

The day before by the stream, it had been the reflection of the ax in the water that had saved me. Today it was the sound of a sword being drawn from its sheath. If he had had the good sense to pull his sword out in advance, before he was on me, I would have died without ever knowing what hit me.

As it was, the quiet whistle of the blade made me jump to the side, drop to the ground, and roll. When I saw the sword glint above me, I kicked both my feet straight up, and cursed loudly as my toe struck his arm. I rolled away from my assailant's hissed curses and got to my knees. I drew my sword as I leapt to my feet.

The Viking swung his sword in a huge arc. I escaped the blade by flinging myself backward, striking my shoulder on the wall behind me as I did so. I lunged and jabbed my sword in under his outstretched arm into his stomach. I felt the resistance as my blade made contact, and then drew the edge of it across his soft abdomen, hearing his cry of pain and then the alarm being sounded behind me as the men emerged from the building.

Ulfrid and Torold glared at me in shock. The Dane they had been talking to cursed and yelled for them to get out of there. Then he howled at my attacker to finish me off before running down the passageway himself, followed closely by the two Saxon brothers.

The Viking roared—from pain or rage, I didn't know or care—and started hacking at me with such strong, rapid blows that he drove me backward up the passageway. He swore nonstop, feinting at my face and sneering scornfully as I feinted at him. When I pulled my sword up, he brought his own down onto it, knocking my sword out of my hand and me to the ground.

And then he made his second mistake.

I had instantly realized he was a better swordsman than I was. As I lay there in the dusty passageway, still reeling from the blow that had knocked my sword out of my grasp and into the dirt, tears of rage formed in my eyes at the knowledge that he needed only one more strike to finish me off. I was lying on my back, trapped against a wall, and I shouldn't have had the slightest chance of escaping his sword.

But then he took a step back to taunt me before killing me.

"You Danish scum!" he swore at me in Danish. "Not so cocky now, are you?"

And it was then that I recognized him. He was one of the four Vikings who had let me scare them into submission in that hamlet where Winston and I had spent the night on our way to Oxford. Stupid-shit Viking, scared by a fake Danish nobleman. I cursed the fact that I was to die at his hand.

"You killed my friend. Now it is your turn to die," he taunted me, striding forward and raising his sword.

I saw a glint of sunlight reflect off the blade, tensed my abdominal muscles against the blow that was coming, and closed my eyes. Then I kicked as hard as I could, straight up into his crotch.

The pain forced the air right out of him—and he emitted a whistling sound like that of a pig bladder deflating after children blow it up and then poke a hole in it.

When I opened my eyes, I saw his eyes rolling upward as he doubled over in pain. He twisted his knee out a little, in an attempt to maintain his balance despite the searing pain in his balls. I kicked him a second time and watched as he staggered away from me. I leapt up, grabbed my sword, and brought it down at his neck.

Just as the sword bit into him, someone knocked me down and a rough voice ordered me in Danish to release my sword—something I had no intention of doing. Damned if I was going to kill one stinking Viking just to let his buddy do me in.

"Lie still," another voice ordered, also in Danish. Then a very strong arm forced the wrist of my sword arm up and twisted it so that I screamed in pain and released my weapon. I was pulled up onto my feet and looked first at the dying man, blood spurting from the gash in his neck, then at the five housecarls who surrounded me.

I realized there was only one thing to do if I wanted to avoid either being killed on the spot or left to rot in a dark, filthy jail. I looked into the eye of the one I decided was their leader and said, "I am Halfdan. Take me to the king."

Chapter 27

he housecarls treated me roughly, but not brutally. Their leader had had them disarm me but did not insist that they tie my hands behind my back. As we walked up the lane, no one laid a hand on me or tried to force me along, probably due to the fact that I was walking along between them quite voluntarily.

The housecarl who took custody of me didn't say a word. He didn't acknowledge my requests, but simply signaled his men and me with a toss of his head to keep moving. After leading us through countless narrow passageways, lanes, and streets to the square, he did not head toward the Hall as I'd expected him to, but instead turned in behind it. He stopped at a building that I guessed was the housecarls' quarters, judging from the large number of behemoth soldiers sitting, standing, and lying in the grass in front of it.

I took a couple of quick steps, caught up to him, and grabbed his arm. I repeated my demand to be taken to the king. He walked away without a word—much too easily for my sense of self-respect—and barked at two housecarls standing outside a massive door. He stepped aside as the door opened and someone shoved me in from behind.

When I turned around to protest, I found myself staring at the door, which had already been shut behind me. I was immersed in darkness, with the only faint light coming through the slits in the shutters covering a window. The room was very small. When I stretched my arms out and turned, I could touch all four walls. There was no chair, not so much as a footstool, and there was certainly no bed.

I thought about yelling to the housecarls outside, putting up a stink about who I was, and demanding again to be taken to the king, but I realized I would be wasting my breath. The housecarl who had brought me in knew who I was, he'd heard me demand to see the king, and he'd simply chosen not to care.

I sat down on the dirt floor, leaned back against the rough-hewn wall boards, and began mulling over the fact that another of those Vikings I had recently sent packing from that Saxon hamlet had shown up out of the blue with his weapon raised, very obviously trying to kill me.

And here we'd been thinking it was significant that everyone we'd met during our investigation was Saxon. I very calmly rejected that theory: Clearly there were at least a couple of Vikings involved.

I mulled over what I had heard through the wall before I was attacked: Osfrid's brothers-in-law meeting with a Dane. I assumed that the Viking who attacked me was a guard, and when he saw me eavesdropping on his employer, he was ready to murder me on the spot. The question was whether he wanted to kill me because I was eavesdropping or because he wanted revenge. After all, I had killed his buddy after making a fool of him and his pals by lying to them.

I convinced myself it was the former. He attacked so quickly, there was no way he had a chance to recognize me first. It was just such a coincidence that his colleague had tried to do the same thing the day before.

I thought back to the snippets of the men's conversation that I'd been able to hear from outside.

They'd been talking about something that was "stupid"; they mentioned that "murdering a girl could" something; and they had said something about not understanding orders.

Could the order have been that *I* was supposed to be murdered?

I was the one who had assumed the Viking was trying to kill Frida. Why had I assumed such a thing? I thought back to the seconds after I killed the axman. I had dismissed the possibility that he had randomly recognized me and decided to exact revenge, because I had thought that a man like him would simply have drawn his weapon the instant he remembered me and not stalked me down to a secluded spot on the riverbank. That's why I had assumed he was targeting Frida.

But now things looked different.

I had told Cnut the day before that I had killed a man who was trying to kill a young girl. So I was the one who had started that rumor. Based on what I had overheard, even the people who were trying to kill me had believed it. That would explain what the Dane meant by "not understand the order."

I suddenly realized that Winston had been right in refusing to tell Cnut what we had learned. Winston had said, "If I mention a suspicion tonight, tomorrow the rumor will be all over the place." Boy, had he been right about that. Yesterday I had said aloud something that turned out to be wrong, and now even the people issuing my attackers their orders believed what I had said to be the truth.

Who had heard me say that yesterday? The king. Jarl Thorkell. Ealdorman Godwin. And the archbishop. As well as everyone else who had been close enough to hear us in the Hall.

But not everyone in the Hall had reason to want me dead.

Only the person who was afraid of what I knew wanted that.

I stood up, suddenly struck by a thought. I pounded on the door and yelled that someone should send a messenger to Winston at Alfilda's inn.

Whatever I knew, Winston knew it too.

When they finally opened the door of my cell, a pale yellow moon was drifting across the sky, and I was hungry in a way I hadn't been since I had started working for Winston. Godskalk was standing in the doorway.

"At last!" I said, stepping toward him, hunger screaming in my belly. "Does anyone know where Winston is?"

No response. The housecarl turned on his heel and led me around the Hall to the front door, where the guards admitted us. I noted that no other housecarls followed us.

Winston was waiting in the Hall. I have no idea who told Winston where I was, but I had to admit I was very relieved to see him. He was standing calmly before the king's chair, looking relaxed with his hands behind his back and his head cocked, and watched me as I walked across the room. I stopped beside him and found it difficult to keep the resentment out of my voice.

"I had to kill another man. What have you been up to?"

"Painting," he replied.

I opened my mouth to give him a piece of my mind, but stopped when the king cleared his throat loudly. Cnut was sitting in his chair. Wulfstan was at his side, as usual. Godwin sat behind him to the right, Thorkell to the left. King, Church, Saxon, Viking.

"Have you decided to make a habit of killing Danes in my town?" Cnut asked me, his eyes fuming with anger.

"Only when they're trying to kill me," I replied. I hesitated slightly and then decided that I might as well cast the stone. A dog that's been hit just might bark. "It is not my fault that my cowardly attackers are lesser warriors than myself."

The king appeared disinterested. The archbishop shook his head sadly. The smile that any Saxon would allow himself at the death of a Viking played over Godwin's lips. Jarl Thorkell yawned.

"Please continue," Cnut said, his tone more of a command than an invitation. I looked at Winston, who indicated that there was no longer any need to hold back what we knew so far. So I briefly recounted how I had followed the two Saxon brothers, how they had met with a Dane, how I had been attacked, and what came after that.

Cnut listened in silence. By the time I had finished, Cnut did not look any less angry.

"So you followed those two because you believe they're guilty of Osfrid's murder?" Cnut asked.

I snuck a glance at Winston, but he remained perfectly still.

"I followed them because I had to do *something*," I said.

The king scoffed. "So it was simply a coincidence that you happened to follow them?"

"Actually, yes," I said. I decided I didn't care what Winston thought. "My partner, Master Illuminator here, had returned to the tavern, and I needed to do *something*."

"And I'm supposed to believe that?" The king's face showed that he did not.

"That is the actual, plain truth," I said with a shrug.

Cnut turned his attention to Winston.

"You went back to the tavern? So you haven't been working on the assignment I gave you," Cnut said accusingly.

"Yes I have," Winston replied with a quick smile. He ignored my look of astonishment. Hadn't he just said he'd been painting?

"And are we any closer to an answer?" Cnut asked, not taking his eyes off Winston.

"Possibly," Winston replied. "As it so happens, I believe that I will be able to see the truth soon."

I surveyed the ealdormen and the earls again. None of them so much as twitched. And yet Winston had just turned himself into an even more obvious murder target than me.

The king looked back at me.

"So you are not claiming that these two brothers . . . Ulfrid and . . . and Torold . . . are *not* murderers?"

"I am claiming that I don't know whether they are or not," I said, quickly adding, "Just as I don't know whether other people are. Or are not."

"Hmm," Cnut said, squeezing the armrests of his chair. "And this Dane you mentioned?"

I had spent a good portion of my time in lockup thinking about him. I had gotten only a quick glance at him before he disappeared down the passageway, but he hadn't looked familiar. Aristocratically dressed, of course, in his early thirties, possibly a little taller than me, light brown hair.

I shook my head. "I hadn't seen him before."

"But you would recognize him?" the king asked, persistent.

I thought about it. "Maybe."

"Maybe?" Cnut's hand was shaking. From anger?

"My lord," I said, trying not to sound too impudent. "I was fighting for my life. To be perfectly honest, I was more concerned with my attacker's sword than trying to remember people's faces."

He gave me a stern look. Behind the king I saw Thorkell smile. Maybe since he was a hardened warrior himself, he thought the king should have anticipated my response. After all, it wasn't as though Cnut hadn't experienced his share of battle. A warrior knows that a man whose attention wanders while he's fighting for his life dies.

"And the dead man?" the king asked.

I looked at Winston, who very subtly shook his head. Had he really just shaken his head? I stared, dumbfounded, but sure enough, it was followed by a faint nod. I swallowed my surprise and looked around at the others— who were all watching me, curious to hear my answer. No one seemed to have noticed Winston's nod. So I took a deep breath, exhaled, and lied.

"I didn't know him either, my lord."

I hoped Winston knew what he was doing. We made eye contact briefly and his lips curled into a smile. I was just trying to interpret that smile when the king spoke, his words ominous.

"You have one day left, Winston the Saxon. One day."

Godskalk handed me my sword as we left the Hall.

Chapter 28

 was struggling with hunger, surprise, and curiosity, but before I managed to put words to any of it, Winston had already gotten several paces ahead of me, and I had to jog to catch up to him.

"Do you want to . . ." I began to ask.

He eyed me critically and said, simply, "No."

I stopped short. Winston rushed off ahead of me, never even turning his head to see if I was coming. When he disappeared around the corner, I realized there was only one thing for me to do. My anger growing steadily, I followed him.

Alfilda's tavern was quiet when I stepped in the door. The only people there were a couple of drunk Vikings, who were just settling their tab with the lovely-chested Emma, and Baldwin, Cnut's master of accounts. Baldwin nodded briefly to me, yawned noisily, and stood up just as Emma bolted the door after the Vikings. Uttering a quiet "good night," Baldwin exited through the back door that led to the guest rooms. Winston and I were the only guests left in the tavern.

Winston sat down at the table farthest from the front door. There were already two tankards on the table, and when I sat down opposite him, Alfilda appeared with a steaming bowl, which she placed in front of me.

"I'm betting they didn't feed you," she said.

I gave her a look of gratitude, then dug into the stew, which was full of meat and flavored with onions. A wonderful rye bread that was perfect for soaking up the sauce accompanied it.

I ate for a long time. Before I had joined Winston's service there had been days when I curbed my hunger by filling my stomach with creek water, which would tide me over for a short time before the hunger started tearing at my gut. Winston and I had been eating so well I was out of practice at feeling hungry.

I finally pushed the empty bowl away, downed the last slab of bread, and burped into the back of my hand, then sent a benevolent look across the table to our hostess. As my stomach filled, my anger abated.

Alfilda, who had apparently sent the serving wench to bed, took my empty bowl, set it clattering into a basin full of water, and then returned to take our empty tankards.

She brought them back filled with fresh ale and sat down quite matter-of-factly next to Winston, who was rolling his tankard in his palms fast enough to slosh the ale. Then he pushed his tankard aside and looked at me for the first time.

"So. We were wrong," he said.

At least he acknowledged the "we" part of it. I nodded. But why was he suddenly willing to talk about it now and not earlier?

"There were people around before," he said, sensing my question. He seemed amused that I'd been annoyed. "In the future we will speak to each other only when we're sure no one can hear us."

I noted that his rule didn't seem to apply to Alfilda.

Winston took a drink and continued. "The situation is not as simple as it appeared. Is this a plot involving both Saxons and Danes?"

As though I could answer that! Besides, I had my own questions. I looked at Alfilda, who was leaning against Winston so that they were sitting shoulder to shoulder.

"You've been painting?" I asked him.

I noted a faint ripple at the corners of his mouth.

"In the past I've found I think best when I'm painting. So, yes, I've been painting."

He reached awkwardly behind him to a shelf, pulled a scroll off it, and passed it to me. I untied the ribbon and watched the parchment unfurl. It was a painting of the king, as he lives and breathes. I felt uneasy. It was unnatural to be able to remake a human being as a small likeness like this. I almost expected this miniscule Cnut to start talking or walking across the paper. I handed the scroll back to Winston.

"And would you say that was the case today?" I asked.

He seemed puzzled.

"That you were able to do some good thinking while painting today?" I explained.

"Oh—uh, yes. Well, plus I had help."

Now it was my turn to look puzzled. Winston turned and looked at Alfilda.

"You weren't here, but our hostess was happy to listen to me. And she helped me," he said.

Who was it who had slammed the tavern door in my face? And who had told me to leave? And now he was scolding me for not having been here? I opened my mouth to give him a piece of my mind but was stopped by his upheld hand.

"Don't scold me about that which you don't understand," Winston warned.

"What the hell do you mean by that?" I said, anger sizzling in my ears.

He sighed, but it was obvious I felt I deserved an explanation.

"You saw the king's picture," Winston said. "Whose responsibility is it?"

What on earth was this man talking about?

"What 'responsibility'?" I asked, wide-eyed with confusion.

"When the plough boys plough a planting furrow crooked, the plough driver can scold them. When there's a defect in the hull of a clinker-built ship, the master builder can blame the carpenter. When the wall of a building collapses, the master can admonish the journeyman. When the shield wall yields, the thane can fault the soldiers," Winston explained. "But if a drawing doesn't turn out the way it should, the painter has only himself to blame. So every picture I paint is a test of my own strength.

"And I live as I paint," he said, pausing. "You think I sent you away because I wanted you gone."

"Which is a reasonable assumption," I interrupted grumpily.

"That's where you're wrong. I sent you away so that I could be by myself. So that I could look at the case as though it were a painting I was about to create. And while I painted, I looked at the case anew."

He wasn't making any sense. Had he not just said that Alfilda helped him?

"Yes," Winston said, seeming to know what I was thinking. "Although I paint alone, I realized that I cannot do everything alone. When it comes to this investigation, for instance, you and I need each other."

"Well, you could have come and found me, couldn't you?" I pointed out. I couldn't interpret the look he gave me.

"I could have, but Alfilda was here. I didn't know where you were."

"I was locked up in a cell," I fumed.

A nod.

"I came to get you out as soon as I heard," he said.

"Well, you certainly took your time," I said, glaring at him, irritated. He flashed me a fleeting smile.

"The king made me wait. He was busy with 'more important things,'" Winston said, winking at me. "But I made good use of the time I spent waiting."

I wavered between a persistent rage at his conceited implication that there was something I didn't understand and curiosity about what he'd been up to. Eventually I nodded.

"Well, out with it," I said.

"Godskalk summoned me and told me that you had been taken into custody, and why. I demanded to speak to you, which I was not permitted to do. Then I demanded to be taken to the king but was told that Cnut would see me as soon as he was done with whatever he was doing. And when Baldwin entered the Hall, I found out what that was. I decided to put my time to good use, so I ignored Godskalk—who at first tried to keep me in the Hall—and demanded that he have me taken to the body of the man you killed. I was rather surprised to discover that I recognized him."

I shivered in my chair.

"You hadn't guessed it was another one of those Viking bastards from that hamlet?" I asked.

"How could I have?" Winston said, looking disgruntled.

"No, maybe not. But then you recognized him, as I did. So what I don't understand . . ." I went silent, thinking what to say next, but I still couldn't see an explanation for why Winston had wanted me to lie about that. "Why didn't you want me to tell the king that I recognized him?"

"Ah," Winston said, leaning back. Now he looked quite pleased with himself. "Have you ever considered the possibility that when these Viking scoundrels attacked, not only once but twice, *you* might have been their intended target?"

"Well, yeah . . ." I told him my new theory that the first Viking's ax hadn't been meant for Frida but for me.

"I had exactly the same thought when I was standing there looking at that body today," Winston said.

"I actually demanded that they send word to you," I continued. "Because if I'm in danger, so are you."

"Which is why you should be quiet," Winston said with a nod.

I raised my eyebrows.

"Do you remember what they said when you asked those bastards back at the hamlet who their master was?" he asked.

As if I would forget something like that. "Jarl Thorkell," I said.

"And who was sitting in the Hall?" Winston pointed out.

"But when the Vikings said they were Thorkell's men, we didn't believe them. Well, I didn't anyway. They were just throwing the earl's name around to get me to shut up," I said.

"Mmm," Winston said, chuckling. "I noticed you didn't keep your promise that you would mention them to Thorkell." Suddenly he grew serious. "But what if they were telling the truth? Maybe they *do* serve Thorkell. Not as loyal warriors—they were too shabby for that—but maybe he contracts his dirty work out to them. The jarl must have plenty of foul deeds he requires assistance with, so maybe they are willing collaborators he uses for jobs like that."

"If that's true, then Thorkell is mixed up in this whole thing," I said.

Winston nodded. "In which case it would be phenomenally stupid of us to let him know that we recognize his henchmen."

One of the things I had been thinking in the cell was that Winston and I had been mistaken to assume that this was a purely Saxon matter, and I said as much.

"I had the same thought while I was painting," Winston said, looking at me approvingly. "I did say that to you earlier, didn't I? That we were wrong."

"But you really think that Thorkell, the king's most loyal earl, is involved?" I asked. It didn't seem likely to me.

"Loyal?" Winston shrugged skeptically. "His most powerful earl, no doubt about that. But Cnut would be wise not to put too much faith in Thorkell. It wasn't all that many years ago that Thorkell was the most formidable Viking in England. I'm sure he still remembers. And he's never made any attempt to hide his willingness to serve whoever benefits him most. Thorkell was loyal to Ethelred, for instance, but only until he thought Cnut would make a better master—or one who could bring him riches and power."

Winston's words made sense. Like many other warlords, Thorkell simply changed sides whenever it suited his purposes.

"So he's involved?" I asked.

"We would be wise not to overlook that possibility, in any case," Winston said.

"On the other hand," I said, "if Thorkell decided that his future is with Cnut, then the ax-wielder and his pals must have been lying."

"In which case there would actually be no harm in letting on that we recognized them," Winston said.

I looked at Alfilda, who was sitting next to Winston in silence. Silent, but alert, that was obvious.

"Our hostess helped you, you said?" I asked.

Winston placed his hand over Alfilda's.

"Alfilda listened to me for a long time as I ran through everything that's happened since we had our first audience with the king. I wanted to see everything in context, so did some thinking aloud while I painted."

"So she listened to you. I understand that," I said. But I obviously hadn't made myself clear. What I wanted to know was *how* she had helped. "But you said she 'assisted you'?"

He smiled at me.

"Alfilda pointed out that only one of the killings is important."

"Osfrid's, of course," I said.

Another tolerant smile, which annoyed me until I realized that he was tolerating his own shortcomings—and not only mine.

"No," Winston said. "The *reason* Osfrid had to be killed is what's important. Once we know that, we'll know who the murderer is."

Well, if Osfrid's death wasn't the important one, which one was? It couldn't be the ax-wielder from the day before or his buddy earlier today. Which left only one possibility.

"Horik?" I asked.

"Yes, Horik, who was with his master, Osfrid, the day he was murdered. So why was Horik killed?"

"Because he saw the murderer?" I asked, biting my lip.

"That is safe to assume," Winston said and then suddenly yawned. "But as Alfilda pointed out to me earlier, there is something even more important than Horik's death."

Winston paused and gave me a look of encouragement, waiting for me say what that something was. I shrugged in annoyance. Then it suddenly hit me, and I realized what Alfilda was on to.

"Who knew we were looking for Horik?" I blurted out.

"Exactly!" Winston said, looking at me triumphantly. "Fool that I am, I didn't see that detail hidden in the bigger picture. Tonild and Father Egbert were the only ones who knew we were interested in Horik."

"So did Frida," I was forced to point out.

"A mere servant girl," Winston scoffed. "She had no idea why we were even asking about Horik. Could she have ordered to have him killed?"

"We asked Godskalk to keep an eye out for Horik," I pointed out.

"So are you suggesting the king's housecarl killed him?" Winston said, sounding almost amused.

"Godskalk had his housecarls asking around for Horik. I don't think we mentioned that they shouldn't let on that you and I were the ones who wanted to talk to him," I said.

"You're right," Winston said, biting his lip, "but I still think that Alfilda is looking at this the right way." Winston looked at her warmly. "Housecarls know how to ask after a man without revealing too much. Tomorrow we'll look for the footsteps that must lead from Tonild's tent to the pile of manure where Horik's body was found."

He stood up, yawned, and said, "I'm going to take a piss."

I was tired, too. But there was one thing that still needed to be said.

"Those two Vikings had more pals," I reminded Winston.

"Yes, and presumably they'll want to kill us, too, if they get orders to do so," he said, turning around in the doorway. "We won't leave each other's side tomorrow, and you will make sure your sword is at the ready."

Chapter 29

hat night I slept like a rock. Winston was still outside when I crawled into bed, and I was so exhausted that I didn't hear him come in—or any of his confounded snoring. I woke up alone in bed, wrapped snugly in the blanket, but I found him at our regular table in the tavern, where he greeted me looking as chipper as I felt.

Alfilda and Emma were busy distributing bowls of porridge and steaming tankards to customers, and I was soon scarfing down a bowl of porridge mixed with chunks of bacon. I washed it down with honey-sweetened ale so hot that it burned all the way to my stomach.

Winston had apparently finished eating a good deal earlier. There was no bowl in front of him, and his mug was more than half empty. While I ate, he sat comfortably on the bench, leaning back against the wall, relaxing and scanning the room. His whistling was irritating me, but I held my tongue to avoid starting this important day off on the wrong foot.

I licked my horn spoon clean and dropped it into the clay bowl with a dull clatter. Then I pushed aside my mug and sat up straight.

"So, are we off to see our favorite Saxon widow?"

Winston took his eyes off Alfilda, who had just placed a bowl in front of the master of the accounts.

"That's where the trail begins," he said.

"This is our last day," I said, thinking it best to remind him in case he was considering whiling the day away painting.

"Then we'd better get busy," he replied.

As we stepped out into the street, I instinctively dropped my hand to the hilt of my sword and pulled the weapon out slightly. It moved easily in its sheath, just as Winston had suggested it should.

The tent camp was oddly quiet. It wasn't that the trampled pedestrian streets through the grassy meadow were any less crowded or that there were fewer people in the stalls or fewer guards in front of the noblemen's tents, but unlike the day before, there were no new processions of noblemen arriving with their retinues, no shouting from men as they erected tents and fenced in horse pens. Everyone who was entitled to attend the joint meeting of the Witenagemot and the Thing had arrived, and all were waiting for the next day to dawn.

We found the tent but were stopped by a guard as soon as we stepped inside the rope railing that had been set up to delineate the public areas of the camp from Tonild's temporary residence.

"I have business with Tonild, the widow of Osfrid," Winston said, looking quite relaxed. I held my right hand across my abdomen so that it wasn't far from my sword.

"My lady does not wish to speak to you," the guard said in a thick accent I had trouble placing and squinting at me.

Winston straightened up so that his head was even with my shoulder. His blue eyes were resolute and his voice firm.

"What Lady Tonild wishes does not matter. Tell her that I will force my way in if she does not allow me to enter."

The guard's eyes swiveled over to me. He opened his mouth in a cocky grin and tilted his head toward the door of the tent ever so slightly.

"You're going to force your way in there?" he asked, incredulous.

Winston waited until four of the guard's colleagues had stepped over to back him up.

"You may need a few more men to resist a dozen housecarls," Winston said.

"You are a Saxon," Lord Squinty Eyes said, furrowing his brow. "You have no influence over housecarls." His voice took on more strength as he spoke, as though he were convincing himself of his own words.

"I'm here on behalf of the king," Winston said without raising his voice. "Take your lady my message, or prepare to encounter the king's housecarls, as well as his rage."

The guard decided to comply. After ordering his colleagues to keep an eye on us, Lord Squinty Eyes disappeared through the tent flap. We waited for a while. The four guards stood silent as a wall between us and the tent, their faces immobile. Winston stared down at the turf while I surveyed the surrounding area. I didn't see what I was looking for.

At long last the tent flap was flung aside and the guard emerged. He waved us closer. Just as we stepped up to the opening, the priest came out and started to walk away after nodding curtly in our direction.

"I would prefer that you stay, Father Egbert," Winston said, stopping at the entrance.

"Unfortunately I can't," Father Egbert replied, although nothing in his face suggested that he actually found it unfortunate.

"Halfdan!" Winston cried.

"My companion expressed a request. Now I'm giving an order," I said, placing my hand on the priest's arm.

Lord Squinty Eyes took a step forward but stopped as I stated firmly, "I, too, am acting on behalf of the king."

The priest tried to twist his arm free but relented when I tightened my grip on it. I trained my eyes on the guard, who eventually gave a resigned shrug and stepped aside. Father Egbert went limp in my grasp when he realized no one was going to fight for him, and he allowed me to lead him back into the tent.

Tonild was waiting for us, seated on a chair in the middle of the tent where Osfrid's bier had stood two evenings earlier. She was alone apart from a girl sitting in the shadows by the wall of the tent, a "girl" who, much to my disappointment, had dark hair and was older than Winston.

Tonild's eyes widened a bit when she realized the priest was with us, but she didn't say anything. Her eyes followed us aloofly as we strode toward her across the carpet of grass. She didn't open her mouth until we had both greeted her with polite bows.

"You're imposing on me, Winston," Tonild said, a tad acrimoniously.

"*Imposing* is a big word to use regarding a person who is here on behalf of the king," Winston said, his voice gentle. They looked each other in the eye for a moment. Tonild broke the eye contact first.

"Are you aiming to be seated at the Witenagemot, my lady?" Winston asked, his voice still mild.

"The Witenagemot?" Tonild asked, clearly confused. "Since when have women held seats at the Witenagemot?"

"And yet you're still in Oxford," Winston noted, eyebrows raised. Arrogance blazed in her eyes.

"My husband was murdered! Did you think I would leave before learning the name of his killer?"

"Well, would you like to know his identity?" Winston asked.

Tonild started to stand up. Her mouth hung open. Her eyes expressed a hint of uncertainty.

"Would I like to? Of course I would like to know who killed him."

Winston looked from her to the priest and asked, "Why?"

Tonild was the very picture of confused befuddlement.

"Why? *Why* do I want to know who killed my husband? Are you mad?"

"Why? Do you want revenge? Wergeld? Or merely to know the truth?" Winston asked, continuing to speak calmly.

"I . . . I . . . The truth, of course."

"So that is more important to you than the wergeld?" Winston asked.

I was trying to figure out where Winston was going with these questions. Did all this talk bring us any closer to explaining what had happened to Horik?

"It . . . It . . ." Tonild sat back down and exhaled slowly. "Of course I want the truth. My husband was a good and powerful man, and he should not lie unavenged in his grave. The truth will bring us to his murderer. Once we know who that is, we will know if he can pay the wergeld or if my family will be forced to seek revenge in some other way."

"Your family, yes," Winston said, his eyes narrowing. "Your brother, Ranulf, whom Osfrid denied the right to the family's traditional land. A man who hasn't seen you—in how many years? Who didn't seek you out until after your husband's death? Do you mean to say that Ranulf will be the one exacting revenge? Or do you have other relations?"

Tonild's eyes were sorrowful, and showed no trace of arrogance.

"No," she admitted.

"Your brother Ranulf," Winston continued, "is someone who had good reason to want Osfrid dead."

"Ranulf would never kill someone in secret," Tonild said in disgust, standing to lend more weight to her protest.

"No," Winston exhaled. "Not many would. And yet someone did."

"Not my brother," Tonild said, sitting back down heavily.

"You say you want to know the truth," Winston said. "And yet you refuse to meet with me, one of the men tasked with finding out who did it."

Winston tugged on his nose, but Tonild said nothing as her eyes darted from Winston to me. I realized with some surprise that what I had interpreted as arrogance was, rather, fear. And I understood the reason for her fear even before Winston continued.

"Because you're afraid that Ranulf *is* the murderer," Winston said gently, which may have explained why Tonild's eyes suddenly filled with tears. "You fear the truth, Lady Tonild. You're afraid to face it head-on." Winston continued speaking as though to a child. "But no doubt Father Egbert will agree with me that the truth—however terrible it might turn out to be—is the only thing that can set you free."

Winston paused and gave me a look that essentially meant, *Keep quiet, Halfdan.*

For a while, the only thing we could hear in the silence that settled over us was our breathing. Then a soft sobbing interrupted it. Father Egbert took a step toward his lady, but was stopped by Winston's outstretched arm. We stood in silence, waiting for the sobbing to subside.

"You see, my lady," Winston said firmly now, but slowly, "the truth might have cause to upset you if your fear turns out to be justified. But if you never learn the truth, the doubt will be more unbearable. If I can show you that your husband's murderer is someone other than your brother, you will be able to breathe more easily. If I do find that it was your brother, you will live in a seemingly unendurable hell—for a time. But if you never learn the truth, you will have to live with the uncertainty for the rest of your life, wondering, *Did my brother kill my husband?* So, worst-case scenario, what I am offering you is profound, but finite, despair instead of a lifetime of hell."

Silence descended over the group once again. Though I saw the priest's lips moving, he remained silent. Winston's eyes were attentively focused on Tonild, whose hands covered her eyes.

Finally the nobleman's widow straightened up, dried her eyes with the back of her hands, and looked Winston straight in the eye.

"And you can give me the truth?" she asked.

"I can find it out at least, if you are willing to help me," he said, tugging on his nose again.

Tonild looked at Father Egbert, who had not uttered a word up to this point, and then returned her gaze to Winston.

"And you expect me to believe someone like you, who is being paid by the king?" she asked skeptically.

"You have no choice but to believe me, because I am your only chance to learn the truth," Winston said firmly and loudly.

Tonild looked over at me, and I tried to look back at her boldly, like a man who was a part of that only chance.

"Fine," she said. "What do you want to know?"

Chapter 30

irst I'd like to know why your husband and your brother had a falling out," Winston asked.

We were seated at a table at the very back of the tent. A runner had been sent to fetch ale for us and a flagon of wine for Tonild, who sat dry-eyed at the end of the table, the very picture of a gracious hostess.

I'd had a little fun, too. Frida had been promoted and had started waiting tables for Tonild the day before. She obviously had no idea who her lady's guests were, and since I was sitting with my face hidden in the shadows, she assumed I was just another unknown nobleman as she poured my ale. When I pinched her shapely buttocks, she blurted out an involuntary squeal, which resulted in an angry look from Tonild. When I followed the pinch by gently caressing her delightful rump, she stepped quickly away from me, but she stopped when she recognized my voice.

"You could at least say hello to the man who saved your life, Frida," I teased.

Her eyes looked angry, but she was smiling and blew me a kiss just as the tent flap fell shut behind her.

"My brother thinks Osfrid cheated to get his hands on the land and the estate that has been the seat of our family for as long as anyone can remember," Tonild said, taking a small sip of wine and then setting down her goblet, which was inlaid with red and green stones.

I looked at Winston and could tell that he too had noted her word choice.

"And you *don't* think so?" Winston asked, pushing his mug aside.

"Cheated? No," Tonild said with a sigh. "The king gave it to Osfrid before Ranulf pledged his allegiance to Cnut. Actually, Cnut gave it to us on our wedding day, in my honor as well as Osfrid's."

I remembered that Osfrid and Tonild had gotten married the same day that Edmund and Cnut had made their big pact.

"Which I suppose Ranulf understood?" Winston asked.

Tonild shook her head, at which point Winston nodded.

"My brother has been luckier than most. When our father was killed, he realized, like so many other noblemen's sons who suddenly found themselves fatherless that year, that there was only one way out. He hurried to the king, swore his allegiance to him, and in return received a portion of the lands and estates our father had owned, as well as the promise of more if he served the king faithfully. Cnut had already demonstrated his iron fist and Ranulf understood the king's message. Cnut has a very effective way of tying young, Saxon noblemen to himself—through expensive gifts."

I nodded at her approvingly. She was right, after all. She took another sip and then continued.

"Ranulf is brave, loyal, and ambitious, and Cnut has deeded him more land since then for his loyalty. But Ranulf is also proud and views the fact that the family's costliest and oldest property is not his as a defeat. So he got it into his head that Osfrid had improperly come to own what should rightfully have been his, and there were bitter words between them."

"Yeah, like when Osfrid offered to name his firstborn son with you Ranulf. Ouch!" I said.

Winston gave me a look, but I didn't care. A Saxon painter may not be able to appreciate what an insult that would be, but as an aristocrat by birth, I could feel in my bones how I would have reacted to such an affront.

"Gossip!" Tonild gasped, opening her eyes wide.

"Not according to your brother," I said.

"My brother hears what he wants to hear. I was there the last time he and Osfrid spoke to each other. Ranulf pointed out that the estate had always been owned by someone named Ranulf, but he ultimately accepted that Osfrid had more of a claim to it since it had been given to him by the king. Then Osfrid conceded that he might not have any children before he died, given his age. He concluded by saying that if that were the case, the estate would fall to me and I would be free to give it to my brother."

Winston and I looked at each other in surprise.

"Do you mean to say that your brother is claiming the *opposite* of what was actually said?" Winston asked.

Tonild nodded.

"My brother's eyes, ears, and heart are sealed with pitch on this matter. He sees, hears, and feels only what he wants," she said.

Winston and I exchanged looks again, and I could tell that he was thinking the same thing I was: *Didn't she just give her own brother a motive to kill Osfrid?* Perhaps.

"But Ranulf didn't kill him!" Tonild added, her voice impassioned.

Winston and I looked at her.

"He didn't?" I discerned a skeptical undertone in Winston's voice.

"No," Tonild said, shaking her head. "Ranulf is everything I've said, but he's also honest. The very idea of deceitfully murdering even an enemy is alien to him."

"I will do what I can, my lady, to prove that you are correct," Winston said.

Which, if you had asked me, was a somewhat hasty promise.

I looked from Winston, who sat lost in his own thoughts, to the priest, who hadn't spoken since we'd entered the tent, to Tonild, who was sitting, proud and silent, with shiny, but dry eyes.

Winston finally pulled his mug toward himself and drank. He exhaled slowly.

"Now we'd like to know who Osfrid went to see the day he was killed," Winston said.

"That we don't know," Egbert said, speaking for the first time.

"That," Winston snapped, "is hard for me to believe."

"All the same, it's the truth," Tonild said, leaning forward with a sigh. "Don't you think we appreciate the importance of that? If I knew, my soldiers would have paid the person in question a visit a long time ago."

I had to give Tonild credit. She was every bit as willing to defend her family's honor as her brother was, or any other Saxon nobleman would be for that matter.

"Osfrid must have dropped some kind of hint about where he was going, even if he wasn't explicit," I said, keeping an eye on Tonild as I raised my mug and drank, but she just shook her head sadly.

"Who do you *think* he was going to see?" Winston asked, leaning forward in his chair.

Tonild shrugged and glanced at Egbert, who replied that he had no idea and that they had already puzzled over this question quite a bit themselves.

Winston made a sound that was like wind blowing through dry grass.

"Who was Osfrid closest to?" Winston asked.

"No one," Tonild said. "Osfrid always maintained that a nobleman should be true to his word, stand by his agreements, and maintain good relations with other noblemen, but he never let anyone get close to him, as he believed that would expose him to treachery and betrayal."

A good rule to live by, I thought, and one that other noblemen would do well to follow. But Tonild was wrong about one thing: Osfrid had let at least one person get close to him.

"Had anyone paid Osfrid a visit?" Winston asked, tugging at his nose so vigorously that it looked as though he were trying to pull it off.

Tonild shook her head.

"Had he left the camp before?" Winston asked.

"We'd only just arrived that day," Tonild said.

"Osfrid's son died as Cnut's hostage?" Winston asked, now merely rubbing at his snout.

Tonild nodded again.

"So Osfrid viewed the king as his enemy?" Winston asked.

"No," Tonild said. "Osfrid realized that no one could really be blamed for what happened aside from not keeping a good eye on the boy. Osfrid did demand that the king pay wergeld, of course. Osfrid was a law-abiding man, and that's what you do. The king wouldn't pay and Osfrid was certainly angry about it. But the king's enemy? No. Besides, Osfrid was smart enough to know that if he openly differed with the king, the king would emerge the winner."

"Openly, yes," Winston said. "But what about in secret? Would Osfrid have willingly gone along with a plot if the plotters were strong enough collectively to bring down the king?"

"My husband was an honest man. Didn't I say he believed in keeping his oaths?" Tonild said fervently.

That line of thinking is precisely why treachery always succeeds. It is committed by honest men who have taken oaths. I didn't say any of that out loud, though.

"Why did you warn Horik and send him away when I wanted to speak with him?" Winston asked.

Egbert swallowed at the bluntness of Winston's question, which was directed at him.

"I never did such a thing," Egbert said.

"No?" Winston said, raising his eyebrows in suspicion.

"No," Egbert said, his voice suddenly high-pitched in his eagerness to convince us. "I went to get Horik and told him you wanted to speak with him. He rudely told me to go to hell. I implored him to come since it would reflect poorly on Tonild if we didn't all cooperate, but he practically ran away from me and then disappeared."

"You didn't tell us that when you came back," Winston said, studying the priest carefully.

Egbert blushed. "No," he said.

I scowled at Winston from across the table, but he didn't appear to want to follow up on the fact that a man who had just emphasized the importance of cooperating had lied through omission. Instead, Winston eyed the priest attentively.

"You said Horik was rude to you. So, he was angry?" Winston asked.

"Ye . . ." Egbert began, but didn't finish the word. Then he continued in a firm voice, "No, not angry. Scared."

Winston just nodded, as if that were the answer he'd been expecting. Then he lapsed into silence again.

"This Horik, did he have a friend he was especially close to?" Winston inquired.

Tonild and Egbert looked at each other and then both shook their heads no.

"He wasn't particularly well liked," Tonild said. "He was in charge of all of Osfrid's bodyguards. No one likes being scolded for neglecting their duties or wasting time."

"Was there maybe a woman Horik was close to?" Winston asked.

Now they nodded.

"Hmmm, yes, and a child," Egbert said, obviously eager to demonstrate his good will. "Horik's woman is in the tent they shared out back."

Winston glanced at me and then stood up.

"Take us to her."

Chapter 31

orik's wife's was a woman named Rowena. The baby didn't have a name yet. She simply called him "the boy." A long gash in the tent flap, running from the top to six inches above the grass, had been mended with a patch made from a burlap sack. Luckily it wasn't raining.

Rowena wasn't even twenty yet. Although quite attractive, she looked somewhat careworn, which I assumed came from the uncertainty of being left alone in the world so suddenly. Her braids were coming undone, there was soot on her left cheek, and when she opened her mouth, I saw that she was missing her bottom middle teeth.

Egbert mumbled soothingly that she needn't be afraid, that we just had a few questions for her. "Which might help them find Horik's killer," he concluded.

She stared at us wide-eyed, took the child off her breast, and set him beside her on a pile of old clothes.

"Thank you, you can go," Winston told the priest, who hesitated, perhaps wanting to object.

Winston waited until the flap had fallen shut behind Egbert before squatting down and reaching a hand out to the boy, who grabbed his finger, babbling.

"What a fine boy," Winston said, sinking all the way down to his knees to tickle the baby's belly.

Rowena lit up and reached over. She put her hand on the little guy's forehead and caressed it with two fingers.

"I'm sorry you've been left on your own," Winston said.

I thought that was an odd thing to say. I would have expressed my condolences for her husband's death, but I guess Winston saw it differently. I suppose he was thinking about all the difficulties that lay ahead of her.

The corners of Rowena's mouth curled up ever so slightly. It looked as though she were thinking, *well, this is my life now.*

"The night Horik left with Osfrid, the night the thane went to his death," Winston began, looking at the girl to make sure she knew which night he was talking about. "Do you know who they were supposed to meet?"

She shook her head.

"Horik didn't say? Did he maybe mention that he was going to such and such a place, because the nobleman had to meet such and such a person?" Winston asked.

Another shake of her head.

"Maybe you didn't speak to each other a great deal?" Winston pried.

"Horik was a good man," Rowena said, her voice pleasant. Her lilting accent reminded me of the countryside in the summer.

"Of course he was. I didn't say otherwise. But he wasn't much of a talker?" Winston said, smiling fleetingly.

She shrugged.

"And after Osfrid died, did Horik say anything then?" Winston asked.

I noted Winston's attentive eyes on the girl.

"He said it wasn't his fault," Rowena said.

Winston and I exchanged glances.

"Of course not," Winston said soothingly. "How could it be? He wasn't with Osfrid when it happened, was he?"

Now Rowena seemed wary.

"There wasn't anything Horik could do."

"No. If there was, I'm sure Osfrid would still be alive," Winston said. "But where was Horik when your master was killed? They left here together, but then went their separate ways?"

Rowena mumbled something inaudible. We waited awhile, then Winston asked her to repeat herself a bit more loudly.

"He was drinking ale with someone," Rowena said. She sounded defiant when she continued: "But the master was the one who told him to do it."

Winston and I exchanged another glance.

"So that was fine, then. He was just following orders," Winston said with a reassuring smile. "But Osfrid wasn't drinking?"

"They met some people, some men," Rowena said. "And then Master Osfrid told Horik that he should sit down and have an ale with the soldiers while he had a word with their master."

I opened my mouth, but closed it quickly. It was probably best to leave the questioning to Winston. Rowena seemed to trust him. And then he asked the question that had been on the tip of my tongue.

"So it was a nobleman and some of his soldiers?"

Rowena nodded.

"And Horik drank with the soldiers while Osfrid left with the thane?" Winston continued.

Another nod. The baby mewled in his heap of rags and she reached out to him. She stroked his round belly to comfort him.

"This nobleman, was he Saxon?" Winston asked.

Rowena made a few soothing sounds to the little boy, and only looked up once he seemed mollified.

"Yes," she said.

"Are you sure of that?" I asked, unable to bite my tongue any longer.

"Horik would never have left the master alone with a Dane," she scoffed.

"But he told you it was a Saxon?" Winston asked, giving me a look meant to silence me.

"Maybe . . ." Rowena said, thinking about it. "He said . . . He said the master met someone he knew."

I forced myself to remain quiet, which wasn't difficult since Winston practically barked, "Someone he knew? Are you sure about that?"

She nodded enthusiastically.

"Someone he knew. Not a friend?" Winston said.

She shook her head no.

"Hm," Winston said, looking at me. I shook my head to indicate that I couldn't think of any other questions. But then suddenly I did have one.

"Did Osfrid go willingly with this person he knew? Did they seem like friends or like people who had some unspoken business with each other?" I asked.

Rowena considered this for a long time, confirming my impression that she was neither dumb nor particularly eager to please us.

"He said . . ." she began and then paused. Winston and I kept our mouths sensibly shut and watched her in anticipation. "He told me that Osfrid said, 'I suppose I'm going to have to talk to that bastard.'"

Interesting choice of words: not asshole, liar, or thief, but *bastard*. If he meant it in earnest, our killer was a disagreeable fellow. If he meant it in jest, it could conceivably have been a friend.

"You've been a real help to us, and I think we're getting closer to Horik's killer. Did Horik say anything about what Osfrid and this man he knew were going to talk about?" Winston said.

"Something about Osfrid having changed his mind," Rowena said, furrowing her brow.

"Changed his mind? About what?" Winston asked.

"That I don't know," Rowena said, shaking her head. "Horik thought it had something to do with a deal, but he had no idea what kind."

"When did you see him last yesterday?" Winston asked.

"He came to tell me he was going into town for a while," she said sadly.

"Did he say why?"

"He'd received a message that someone wanted to meet with him. Someone who wanted to reward him," she said.

And that was all. Of course she hadn't asked him who he was going to meet, but we could figure that out. Osfrid's murderer had been afraid that Horik would put two and two together.

But then suddenly I realized that wasn't right. Horik had exposed himself. When we showed up in the camp asking questions, Horik realized he had two choices: he could either talk to us, or let the murderer know that his silence could be bought.

He'd chosen the latter and, in doing so, his own death.

"Horik's loyalty to his master died the moment his master did," I said, indignant. Winston and I were sitting in the grass outside the camp.

"Did Horik have an obligation to avenge Osfrid's death?" Winston asked, then pursed his lips as he mulled things over. "Perhaps. Or to provide for his own wife and child? I think Horik saw the world as it is. It won't take long for a young widow like Tonild to be surrounded by new suitors. And when she remarries, what are the chances that her new husband would want to keep Horik on as his head of security? A murderer, however, would certainly be willing to pay a pretty penny to buy his silence, well enough that he could secure his family's future for a while."

"Well, aside from the fact that the murderer had no intention of actually paying him. The killer just wanted to cover up his tracks," I said.

"Which Horik couldn't have known," Winston said, stretching and looking up at the late spring sun, which was quite warm by now. "You know, a mug of ale would hit the spot right now. You don't think you could . . ." he nodded over toward the kitchen tents.

I found Frida with two other servant girls, who giggled when I snuck up behind her and entwined my arms around her waist. She swirled around, lowering the wooden spoon she had been about to strike me with when she realized it was me and reluctantly let me kiss her. I could tell her reluctance was feigned, however, because her lips were soft and opened willingly to mine.

"You sure are fresh," she said, twisting a loose lock of hair between her fingers.

"Oh, I'm sure they've seen worse," I said, winking at the other two girls.

"Fool!" she exclaimed and then thwacked my elbow with her wood spoon. "That's for earlier. You gave the lady cause to be angry at me!"

"But I smoothed things over, too," I said with a grin.

After another couple of kisses, I was on my way back to Winston with two foaming tankards. Frida said that when we were done I should just set them by the juniper bush over by where she saw Winston's silhouette in the grass.

"Or," I said, "I could bring them back myself and repay you for the drinks."

"I have to go down to the stream and wash the dishes," she said with a pout. "Just put them in the bush. I'll bring them back later."

After urging her to be careful down by the stream, I made an offhand remark about how I might stop by and see her later if I had the time.

"No," she said, shaking her head. "Not tonight. We'll be busy with the washing up."

I brought the ale over to Winston, who accepted his tankard with relish. We drank in silence, the only sound that of the ale being swallowed. We were probably both wondering the same thing, which was confirmed by Winston's question when he finally spoke.

"So, who was this Saxon Osfrid met?" he asked.

As if I hadn't been wracking my brain over the same question.

"Who the hell knows. At least it's something to go on," I replied.

"Well, there aren't actually all that many Saxon noblemen here," Winston said with a loud burp. "And we don't even have to consider anyone in the entire Witenagemot."

"You mean because Osfrid called him a bastard?" I asked.

"Exactly. You wouldn't call just anyone that," Winston said pensively.

We resumed our silence. I rolled my empty tankard around in the grass and stretched, shielding my eyes from the sun.

"So it was someone Osfrid knew, but might not have wanted to deal with," I suggested.

"The word *bastard* implies a degree of scorn, doesn't it? It suggests someone who's not necessarily a full-fledged criminal, but someone you look down on," Winston said.

"Maybe his brother-in-law?" I said.

"You mean Ranulf the Indignant? Yes, maybe. No one has said so explicitly, but I've gotten the impression that Osfrid didn't think very highly of Ranulf. And Ranulf's motive is as good as anyone's. He's the only person we've met who held a real grudge against Osfrid."

"Is it really so simple as that?" I said, nodding contemplatively.

"No conspiracy? No plot hatched by subjugated Englishmen and dissatisfied Danes?" Winston asked with a shrug. "It would be by far the simplest explanation."

"But the simplest explanation isn't always the one that's true, is it?" I pointed out.

"Well then, who do you think we should be looking for?" Winston asked, lying down flat on his back.

After a while I stood up, gathered the mugs, and carried them over to the juniper bush Frida had indicated. Winston was lying perfectly still, but when I tiptoed closer to check if he'd fallen asleep, I could see that he was staring at the sky. I cleared my throat to announce my return. As he sat up, something suddenly occurred to me.

"There's one thing that speaks against this Ranulf," I said.

"What?" Winston asked.

"He walks around alone. Does he even have a retinue?" I asked.

Winston didn't respond, but slapped his thigh and stood up.

"There's only one place we can learn the answer to that," Winston said.

So we headed back into town.

Chapter 32

y the time we found Ranulf, who was sitting outside an ale stand with a tankard in front of him, the sun had just about reached its zenith. He didn't appear especially happy to see us. Rather, he looked bored, as though he had been hoping for some sort of diversion, but was now facing the prospect of further boredom.

We hadn't come straight here. By the time we'd reached the edge of the camp, I had so many questions in my head that I stopped Winston with a hand on his arm. I'd been mulling over a great many different thoughts, and wanted to find out why Winston seemed so dead-set on Ranulf before we got any further.

It was true, of course, that Ranulf appeared to have the most obvious motive. Still, I had my doubts.

"Tell me," I said in response to Winston's puzzled look, "why you refused to question Ranulf yesterday about the run-in I overheard him having with the Vikings."

"It wasn't important," Winston said.

"It wasn't? Not even if he's the murderer?" I said. I couldn't have been more surprised.

"My God, man. I dare you to name one Saxon who can avoid getting into trouble with the Danes," Winston replied. "If we were to walk through town and the camp right now, we would see no end of arguments among Saxons, Angles, Danes, Vikings, and whoever else happens to be here. They bicker about land, money, slaves, women—all the things noblemen consider important in life. Yesterday, while I was sitting at the inn painting, a

Jute and an Angle were arguing heatedly about who had the right to hunt in the woods surrounding their land."

"But doesn't it seem more important today, now that he might be the murderer?" I prodded.

Winston shook his head. "If he did kill his brother-in-law, he did it himself. He's proud; his sister said so. And he would have wanted Osfrid to know who killed him—and why."

I didn't agree but left it at that. Instead, I pointed out that we seemed to have completely ruled out Osfrid's other two brothers-in-law, who had nonetheless nearly cost me my life.

"Ulfrid and Torold wouldn't have had me attacked unless they had something to hide," I said.

"It was the Dane they were meeting with who issued the order that you be killed," Winston said, shaking his head again. "I remember you saying that. And it was a Viking who followed that order, not a Saxon soldier."

"But Ulfrid and Torold are conspiring with the Danes. They met one in secret. And don't forget what I heard them saying through the wall," I said.

"They're definitely involved in shady business of some sort or another," Winston acknowledged. "And their partners are making the wrong moves. You said you heard them say 'that was stupid' and 'murdering a girl could.' Doesn't that suggest that *whomever they're conspiring with* gave the orders to attack you? I also remember the Dane you overheard said something about orders being misunderstood. If we add all that up, we have a pair of Saxons who, sure enough, are involved in a conspiracy with some Danes, who misunderstood something and gave orders to kill you. We'll let the king work out the details for himself. He charged us only with solving Osfrid's murder."

I wasn't going to accept defeat that easily.

"But don't you think it would be a good idea to have a chat with that Dane they met with?" I asked.

"But you said you don't remember what he looks like," Winston said, giving me a teasing look.

Damn him!

"True. I guess I'll have to work on simultaneously fighting for my life and taking note of men who scurry by me while I'm doing it," I grumbled.

Winston gave me an indulgent look.

I didn't ask any further questions. Maybe he was right, and Ranulf was our murderer. If that was the case, all we had to do was prove it.

Which turned out not to be possible. Once we'd caught up with him at the ale stand, Ranulf listened courteously but clearly disinterestedly to Winston, who began by asking when he had first learned of Osfrid's death.

"I guess it was . . ." Ranulf began, putting on a show of making an effort for the sake of politeness. "When was it you saw me visiting my sister?"

"The day before yesterday, in the evening," I said, peering around to see if he had any soldiers or servants with him. But no.

"Then it was that afternoon," Ranulf said.

"Of that same day?" Winston asked, his voice thick with suspicion. Which Ranulf noticed.

"Yes. Is that so strange?" Ranulf said.

"It took a whole day for you to hear about it?" Winston asked, disbelieving. "Yes, that strikes me as very strange indeed."

Ranulf looked from Winston to me, shaking his head.

"I needed to arrive first," Ranulf said.

"Arrive?" Winston's lower jaw was hanging slackly.

"Arrive. Yes," Ranulf said, sounding smug. "It's not like eager messengers went riding out into the countryside in search of me to notify me of Osfrid's death."

I stifled a grin at the look on Winston's face. He looked like someone who had been overly confident that he could jump across a stream and didn't realize until mid-jump that the stream was too wide.

"So you didn't arrive in Oxford until the day before yesterday?" Winston asked, crestfallen. "You didn't mention that when we spoke yesterday."

Ranulf shrugged. "Why should I have?"

"Did you arrive before or after the funeral?" Winston asked, now looking like a man who had no idea how to turn the battle to his advantage.

"Before. But as I said yesterday, I had my reasons for not attending it," Ranulf said.

Winston seemed to deflate before my eyes.

"Where did you say your land was?" I asked.

"I have many properties," Ranulf replied, sounding outright arrogant now.

"But where were you staying before coming to Oxford?" I asked.

"At my estate in Brictisworde," he said.

I thought about that. Located in the northern part of the Danelaw, the village was a good three or four days' ride from Oxford.

"Did you ride alone?" I asked.

Now he seemed to be enjoying himself.

"Are you wondering if I'm lying?" Ranulf asked, amused. "Did I sneak into town, murder my brother-in-law, and then sneak back out again, only to turn around and make a show of arriving innocently?"

"Just answer the question," Winston said, his shoulders slumped but his voice sharp.

"I was accompanied by two Vikings who came to see me at my estate last week with a message from the king," Ranulf said.

Two Vikings. I could see where this was going.

"A message that you should attend the meeting in Oxford?" I asked.

He shook his head.

"No, I have a seat on the Witenagemot, so I received the fiery cross like everyone else. No, this was a message that I should hand over four of the lesser estates within my manor to them," Ranulf said.

"A forced contribution?" I asked.

"Call it what you will," Ranulf said with a shrug. "The victors always get to name the price of their victory. And the price for me was four estates."

Which he could no doubt spare if his sister was right and he had been richly rewarded for his oath to Cnut. What didn't make sense was why Cnut would be taking land from someone he had just rewarded. No sooner had I had the thought than I realized the reason: Cnut didn't want his Saxon subjects to forget that he had given them things and that he could just as easily take them away again.

"And these two Vikings," I continued, figuring we might as well get to the heart of the matter, "were they the same ones I saw you arguing with the day before yesterday?"

The young man stared at me in surprise. Then he nodded.

"They thought I'd tricked them by giving them the wrong information about the size of the estates."

"And had you?" Winston straightened up.

"I told them they could go to the shire reeve and ask him to adjudicate between us. There are plenty of men in the meadow—Saxons and Danes alike—who are familiar with the estates."

A man of the law, this Ranulf. At least when he was sure it would be on his side. He definitely didn't seem like a murderer. He left us with a polite, if somewhat arrogant, farewell. Winston looked across the table at me. A wrinkle had appeared between his eyes, and he sounded testy.

"Well, you were right," he said.

"Unfortunately," I said with a slight shrug.

"Were you really hoping it would be him? Any particular reason?" Winston said.

"Then our job would have been done," I said. I looked around and eventually spotted a girl carrying tankards. When my upheld hand finally caught her attention, she walked over to us, slowly, like someone who'd been on her feet for far too long.

I asked for food, and Winston said he'd like some, too.

"Then you have to go inside," the wench said, her voice hoarse. She gestured toward the door with a dirty thumb.

We got up, exhausted, and pushed our way in the door just as two drunk Angles were trying to get out. Once inside, we found ourselves standing in a sad-looking establishment, somewhat smaller and much darker than Alfilda's tavern. Three Danish noblemen were sitting side by side at a long table up against the rear wall with a group of Saxons, and four craftsmen were seated at a round table up front. Between the two groups was a wobbly three-legged table with a stool next to it.

Winston headed toward it and left me to search for something to sit on. The girl showed no sign of wanting to help me, and it took me a while to track down a folding three-legged chair with a small leather seat, which I finagled into place. I had just enough room to sit down at our table with the long table behind me.

We were each handed a bowl of unseasoned stew and a mug of ale. My request for salt was met with a cranky retort that I should have brought it with me. So we dug into our bowls of stew, devouring what meat there was, which consisted primarily of cartilage with a few bits of mutton glistening with fat.

Two of the Danes behind us were conversing loudly; their companion's contributions were limited to occasional grumbling. The Saxons got up noisily just as the worst of our hunger was sated. We sat in silence over the surprisingly tasty ale, each lost in our own thoughts.

"Well, I'll bid you farewell for now," said the Dane, who to that point had not uttered a word, standing up. His voice made me listen carefully.

"Just so long as we know where we stand with each other," he said. His footsteps indicated that he was heading toward the door.

I leaned over the table, caught Winston's eye, and whispered, "That's him."

"Him?" Winston stared at me blankly.

"The Dane that Ulfrid and Torold met with."

"Nonsense," Winston said, shaking his head dismissively. "You just told me you couldn't remember what he looked like. It's as dark as a dog's behind in here and now you tell me that's him?"

"I don't need my eyes to recognize his voice," I hissed.

"His voice? Are you sure?" Winston asked, suddenly sounding excited.

I nodded.

"Follow him. I'm coming," Winston ordered, getting up so suddenly he tipped his stool over. When the girl came rushing over at the sound, Winston tossed her a couple of coins and followed me out the door.

I squinted in the sunlight, peered up and down the street, and held up my hand in irritation at Winston, who was standing a little too close, breathing down my neck, asking whether I saw him.

To the left there was nothing. A ways down the narrow street a couple of beefy-looking women were immersed in gossip, but the street was otherwise empty.

To the right was one man walking away. He didn't appear to be in any hurry, and it seemed safe to assume that he hadn't recognized my face in the dark tavern.

I tried to recall what that Danish nobleman had been wearing the day before, but I really had no idea. The man walking down the street was wearing leather breeches, neatly stitched shoes, and a bright red jerkin—I couldn't see his tunic or sweater from where I stood. A sword hung at his side.

It had to be him. So I set off after him. He was looking straight ahead and walked like he knew where he was going. I came up behind him just as he walked past a kitchen garden that was fenced in with man-height twigs. There was an opening in the fence about ten paces ahead of us and just as we reached it, I sped up and shoved him with my shoulder so that he tumbled into the garden. I followed him in and stuck out my foot, tripping him as he struggled to regain his balance. He fell to the ground.

I dropped down to straddle his chest, grabbed his sword and had it drawn before he had a chance to catch his breath, which my knee had knocked out of him, and tickled his neck with his own sword blade.

"Not so fast," I told him. "We have some unfinished business to discuss."

He grumbled angrily at me and tried to stand up, but was stopped by the steel blade at his throat.

"We don't know each other," he said.

I could tell he was lying and turned to Winston, who had just stepped through the hole in the fence.

"It's him," I confirmed.

"Good," Winston said, looking around. There was no one else in the garden aside from us. Perfectly straight rows of onions, leeks, and cabbages filled the garden, and a wooden bench sat under an elder bush in the far corner.

"Let's put him over there," Winston instructed.

The sword got the Dane moving, and he sat down on the bench, glaring at me. I smiled back at him. After all, I had two swords, and he had none.

"Now," Winston said amiably. "We have a few questions for you."

Chapter 33

his Danish nobleman was rather hostile toward us, an attitude that did not appear to be due exclusively to my hard-handed way of getting him to talk. Sitting there on the bench, he fumed indignantly. His thick eyebrows had knitted together, forming a deep groove between them, and his eyes darted continually from Winston to my sword hand, back to Winston and across my face back to the sword, which I held steadily in my right hand.

I stood still, making sure to keep a foot's distance between the blade and my prey so that I could throw my weight into my sword arm and skewer him if I had to. Winston was still gasping from running to catch up and didn't say anything as he waited to catch his breath.

The Dane looked older than I was, but not as old as Winston. His hair was tinged with gray, his chin pointy, and his lips narrow. I guessed that his eyes would ordinarily have been blue—if they hadn't been darkened with impotence and rage, as they were now.

I perked up my ears, listening for any sounds in the street on the other side of the fence, but all was quiet. No one else had been in the street when I shoved him into the garden, and I couldn't detect any voices or footsteps out there now.

The elder bush we found ourselves under was quite a ways from the entrance and tucked away in the far corner of the garden. Unless someone actually stepped into the garden itself, no one would spot us from the street. I hoped that the garden's owner would stay away for a while.

"Your name?" Winston asked, breathing calmly once again.

No response.

Winston sighed ever so faintly.

"I'm Winston, and my companion here is Halfdan."

Silence.

"We're here on behalf of the king. We are acting in his name," Winston continued.

An angry look.

Harding once told me that it's difficult to tell the difference between a scared man and an angry man. And yet it can be done: Threats will get a scared man's tongue moving, but will cause an angry man's to freeze up.

I didn't move; I simply held the sword calmly so that the blade glinted against his chest. I did, however, lower my voice a bit. Being too loud is a sign of weakness, Harding had taught me.

"Perhaps you would rather speak to the king's housecarls?" I asked him.

He hadn't moved, but a drop of sweat glistened on his neck.

"Or maybe to the king himself? I'm sure he would be very interested to hear about a conspiracy against him," I pointed out.

"Rubbish," the Dane replied, his voice rasping dryly. His neck was now covered in a thin sheen of sweat.

"Rubbish?" I asked, raising my eyebrows. "You don't think the king should be interested in plots and conspiracies against him?"

Strange. I hadn't thought about my brother in days, and now I was reminded of him for the third time in quick succession. I remembered him saying: "Once a scared man opens his mouth, he can rarely stop himself from talking."

"I am not part of any plot against the king," the Dane said, clearly making an effort to keep his voice calm.

"You're not? Well in that case you owe us an explanation for why you met with two Saxon noblemen in secret yesterday." I spoke so softly that he had to lean forward to hear me, and I smiled to myself when his chest almost touched the tip of the sword.

"We didn't meet in secret," the Dane said, also speaking softly. Then he cleared his throat and continued more loudly: "It wasn't a secret at all."

"Oh?" I asked, my voice laced with skepticism. "Then why did you try to have me killed?"

He did not respond, which was not to my liking, so I leaned forward, and, still holding the sword in my right hand at the ready, I grabbed his shoulder with my left and shook him. "I said, *why?*"

"I . . . I didn't try to have you killed," he said, his lie sticking in his throat.

"You didn't? I heard you yell to your partner that he should kill me," I pointed out.

The Dane shook his head. His mouth twitched and then he looked me in the eye.

"I heard a racket out in the street and when I came running out I saw you two fighting," the Dane responded. "I assumed you'd attacked him, and my guard was entitled to defend himself. That's why I told him to kill you."

He was lying. I was convinced he was lying.

Winston stepped in: "I asked you your name."

"Sven."

"Could you be any more specific, Sven?" I growled. Winston poked me in the side with his finger to rein me in.

"I'm the son of Toke," the Dane said.

"And you're a soldier in Cnut's army?" Winston started asking questions in rapid succession in case I hadn't understood his signal to stop talking.

The Dane nodded.

"What was your business with Saxon noblemen like Ulfrid and Torold?" Winston asked.

At that, Sven clammed up, causing Winston to lean forward slightly, menacingly.

"My partner asked if you'd rather talk to the king's housecarls. Would you?" Winston inquired.

"I . . . I've won a lot of plunder. My brother back home got the land and the farm, but now I can buy my own. Those Saxon brothers were selling a large estate," Sven said.

I gave Winston a look that proved to be unnecessary. He did have a brain after all.

"And you had to meet in secret about that?" Winston asked.

Earlier, Sven had denied that the meeting was secret, but it seemed that he'd had a chance to think about what it must look like when three men hold a meeting in a ramshackle shed. In most cases, it suggested a desire to avoid prying eyes.

"There are Saxons who do not look kindly on their fellow countrymen selling off their land and property to Danes," Sven admitted.

So he *had* had time to think. That lie was so believable it could even be true.

"And the man who tried to kill my companion. Who is he?" Winston asked.

Sven wet his lips with the tip of his tongue.

"I . . . I didn't know him," he said.

"You're full of lies!" I bellowed so loudly that Sven jumped. Then I continued in a more subdued tone: "I overheard you talking about what happened the day before yesterday. About the attack on me. You said someone hadn't understood an order. So, tell me the truth."

My left fist struck him right on the breastbone, and he flinched from the pain. He looked as though he were going to deny it again, but then reconsidered.

"Ulfrid and Torold were the ones talking about that. It seems that you had had some kind of run-in with a Viking who recognized you and wanted revenge," Sven said.

This time I hit him just above his right eye, so hard that his head jerked back, and my hand stung.

"You're lying!" I said.

"No," he said, his hands coming up into a defensive posture. "It's true. I didn't have anything to do with that."

"But Ulfrid and Torold did?" Winston asked. He elbowed me in the side as he asked this question. I got the message and bit my tongue.

"I don't know why you were attacked," Sven said.

"You are going to have to make up your mind now," Winston said angrily. "Who sicced that Viking on my companion yesterday? Did he attack because he wanted revenge, or were the Saxons pulling the strings?"

Sven sighed and looked around for a way out, but realized that we had him cornered like hounds on a fox. He licked his lips again.

"It was both. Ulfrid and Torold hired the Viking to keep an eye on you" he said, nodding at me. "But he was the one who decided to kill you when he saw his chance."

"And where do you come in?" Winston asked.

Sven mulled over Winston's question, then shrugged.

"Ulfrid and Torold wanted the person following your buddy there to be a Viking. I happened to know a few Vikings who were up for anything as long as they were paid," Sven said.

"So you put them in touch with each other?" Winston said, but continued before Sven had a chance to respond: "Ulfrid and Torold didn't want to hire Saxons to keep an eye on my companion here, because they wanted to cover their tracks? A Viking would be harder to trace back to them?"

Sven nodded.

"So why did you meet with Ulfrid and Torold yesterday?" Winston asked.

"They refused to pay since they didn't want anything to do with an attack. They had wanted someone to keep an eye on a man, not kill him," Sven explained.

"So you brought the Viking to the meeting?" Winston asked.

Sven nodded again. "I didn't trust them."

With good reason, probably. Only one question remained, and I asked it: "Why would anyone need to keep an eye on me?"

Sven's face went blank.

"I have no idea," he said. "I don't ask questions like that."

That sounded about right. Men like him aren't interested in anything other than being paid. And they know that some things are better left unknown.

We let Sven go. He was brazen enough to ask for his sword back, but left when I told him I'd stick it behind the elder when I left.

"And," I continued, "if I see you in the street out there when I come out, or if I ever run into you with your weapon drawn, you'd better be ready to use it."

"He's full of lies," I said.

"Of course," Winston said, nodding. "There's a plot. Why else would threatening to call in the housecarls work?"

I'd had the same thought. No one would bat an eye at a Dane who had hooked some noblemen up with a few warriors willing to do their dirty work for them. That's what men do. It's either self-defense, as when I killed the Viking, or they're avenging a relative. I couldn't imagine housecarls caring one way or the other about that sort of thing. However, they would not look very kindly on a plot against the king. Surely Cnut wouldn't either.

"Earlier you said the king could work out the details for himself. Isn't that our job?" I asked.

Winston shook his head.

"We're just supposed to solve the murder," he reminded me.

"But shouldn't we at least tell the king about the plot against him?" I asked.

"Cnut's not dumb. He may not be aware of it, but he knows this kind of thing is going on. And he may want to remain ignorant of the details," Winston said.

I didn't understand.

Winston explained: "It doesn't matter in the least if a couple of Saxon noblemen and a handful of Danes come up with some plot against Cnut. They don't have the power to back it up. And if people find out about it, Cnut will just call in his axmen again to wipe out the plotters. But that isn't what the king needs right now. He needs all the nobility to get along tomorrow. And even if Cnut can't make them do that, he needs to make the meeting appear harmonious.

"If we present him with information about a plot, he will be forced to take action and kill the conspirators, which will sow discord instead of unity. So, let's solve the murder and hope that whatever evidence of a plot we find isn't clear enough that we'll be forced to report it to the king. Believe me, he won't thank us if we have to do that."

"Now what?" I asked

Winston got up off the bench where we'd been sitting since Sven had left.

"Now it's about time we go catch up with those Saxon brothers-in-law," Winston said.

Chapter 34

f course the guards at the lodging house refused to let us in. Were we the only ones they were so enthusiastic about keeping out? They flatly rejected Winston's assertion that he was there on the king's business.

"Then I would like to ask that you pass on a message to two noblemen in there, Ulfrid and Torold, sons of Beorthold," Winston said with an angry glint in his eyes, though he managed to keep his voice calm.

The leader of the guards, a broad-chested soldier with the thick braid of a West Saxon hanging down his back, spat into the dirt and stated that he was not an errand boy, he was a guard, a comment that caused Winston to walk all the way up to him, stare him right in his scarred face, and, through clenched teeth, declare that he'd better listen up. The soldier blinked in surprise at Winston's cold fury.

"Now, please decide if you're going to do what I asked," Winston said, his voice like ice. "Do it, or prepare to take the matter up with a division of housecarls. Because I swear to you on the Resurrected One Himself"—this was the first time I'd heard him swear to any god—"that I am authorized to summon as many housecarls as it takes to crush you and your colleagues."

The guard stared wide-eyed at my partner, whose whole body radiated a cool rage far more frightening than the noisy swearing typical of soldiers.

"And," Winston continued, "perhaps you'd like to give some thought to what excuse you will give to everyone inside when their front door is battered down by the Viking warriors who constitute the king's elite house-carls, Vikings that your stupidity will have brought down upon them."

"Well fine. I suppose we all pick our battles," the guard said, puffing out his chest in an attempt to preserve some dignity. "What is your message?"

He kept us waiting. When the guard finally returned, he gruffly informed us that he had passed the requested message on to the two Saxon noblemen: "Meet with Winston and Halfdan, King Cnut's investigators, so that they can decide which of you is a murderer."

While we were waiting for the guard to return, I contemplated how Winston, who had so recently rejected the notion that Osfrid's brothers-in-law could be murderers, could suddenly be so sure that they *were*.

I asked Winston, of course, as soon as the door closed behind the soldier's braid, and he responded with only a smug smile. It was only when I angrily pointed out to him that his words might result in two sword-swinging noblemen storming out at us—and since I presumed he didn't want to face them on his own, I would darn well like to know why I should single-handedly defend us—that he nodded and pulled me out of earshot of the other guards.

"One of them killed Osfrid," Winston said quietly. "Although the murderer could certainly have been anyone involved in the plot, one of these two dealt the fatal blow. And whichever one it was, he did it with relish, for a reason that I now grasp, and which you, too, ought to be able to see."

That was all I could get out of him and, though I twisted my brain in knots trying to figure it out, I didn't get any closer to the answer.

When the door finally opened, it wasn't the guard but a short Saxon nobleman who stepped out. A faint smile played on his lips as he walked over to us.

"Winston the Illuminator and Halfdan . . . ." He hesitated.

"Halfdan will do." I was in no mood to get into my family's downfall.

"Fine," he said, his voice gentle. "I'm Botwolf, son of Cenwolf."

I'd heard of him. He had been the last of the Saxons to lay down his sword at the Battle of Assandun, where he'd wielded it well against the Danes who had been trying to drive him from the site where his father had fallen.

"You wish to speak to the sons of Beorthold," Botwolf said. "They are awaiting you."

We followed his broad frame into the hall. There were no women or servants in there today. Three benches had been positioned on the hearth in front of the fire, delineating a square space on the floor. In the middle of it stood Ulfrid and Torold, legs planted wide apart. The benches were lined with a dozen or so seated noblemen. Sven Tostesøn, whom we hadn't seen since our little garden interrogation, was among them. He was watching me with hate-filled eyes.

I surveyed the others, but Sven was the only Dane. The rest were all Saxon. I looked over at Ulfrid and Torold, whom I'd never studied carefully before. Though I had seen them in the church at Osfrid's funeral, it had been dark. And when I'd followed them the day before, I'd only seen them from behind except for the brief instant when they stepped out the door after their meeting with Sven, and—as I already pointed out—I was quite busy fighting for my life at that moment.

Gray hair and deep wrinkles indicated that Ulfrid was the older of the two. He wore a sword, and expensive but not ostentatious clothing. He was as tall as me, but had narrower shoulders.

His brother was stronger without being stocky. He had a broad chest and muscular arms, and his clothes were slightly flashier than Ulfrid's. Torold also wore a sword, and I noticed that both men's weapons had long, slender blades that would pierce a man without difficulty.

We were not introduced to the other noblemen, who were all regarding us coolly.

One of them, a corpulent old man with greasy hair and angry-looking lips turned up in a scornful sneer, said, "Well if it isn't the Danish king's hounds."

A flush of rage flared up my neck, but Winston was faster than me.

"Better the hunter than the hunted," he said. "Because, just like King Cnut's other hounds, once we've picked up the scent, we are tenacious to the end."

Winston's eyes challenged the noblemen, but no one spoke. All eyes were now on the two brothers, who stared at us placidly, their legs wide and their thumbs hooked under their sword belts.

"You're accusing us of murder," Ulfrid said, his voice deep and clear. A man who was sure of himself.

"No," Winston replied, his voice no less firm.

"You're not?" Torold asked, inhaling in surprise.

"I'm accusing one of you of murder," Winston clarified.

The men on the benches started muttering angrily, but they fell quiet as Ulfrid took a step forward.

"That accusation will cost you your life," Ulfrid barked.

"King Cnut is waiting for us to report back to him this evening," Winston said, with a degree of equanimity I did not entirely share. "If we don't show up, he'll turn this town upside down looking for us. You plotters and schemers in here might be able to cover for each other, *if* you're the kinds of men who approve of dishonorable killings. But what about your guards outside? Will they forget that we came in? I'm sure you can silence your women, too, but your servants? Can you really be sure that not a single one of them will admit that they were forced to leave the hall so that you could receive us?"

"Are you calling us plotters and schemers?" Botwolf's voice was less placid than before.

Winston nodded. "You were all complicit in Osfrid's death in the sense that your plot led to his death when he wanted out of it. If you had simply let him out of it, perhaps you could have simply heard about his murder without having any part in it."

"You talk big," Torold said, taking a step forward, "but have no evidence of murder or conspiracy."

"Don't I?" Winston said, his words hanging in the silence that followed.

Finally Botwolf cleared his throat. "Men discuss the things they wish would change. That does not make them conspirators."

"Unless they take up arms against the master they've pledged to serve," Winston said slowly. "Though of course that hasn't happened. Yet."

"The Witenagemot and the Thing meet tomorrow," Botwolf said, still speaking for everyone. "Big decisions will be made and it is both right and reasonable for men to discuss these matters thoroughly amongst themselves."

"Right and reasonable, yes," Winston said, nodding at him in approval.

Winston seemed to appreciate Botwolf's stance, and I had to admit that I, too, admired the Saxon nobleman for so dexterously explaining away the plot as the noblemen's recognized right to discuss the affairs of the country among themselves.

"I am not here to side with you or the king," Winston continued, "but—"

He was interrupted by a scornful snort from Torold.

"You wouldn't walk away from it, though," Torold growled. "There are bigger men than either you or us, who—"

"Silence!" Botwolf's voice slammed down like a sword. His face was suddenly flushed with anger.

Torold stopped talking. His face, too, had gone scarlet with fury.

". . . but to expose a murderer," Winston continued impassively. "I'll be the first to admit that I had my doubts, right up until I walked in here. But now I'm sure." He narrowed his eyes at Ulfrid and Torold. "Here we've seen anger and threats and a guilty man trying to demonstrate his innocence." Winston turned to me. "Come on. The king is expecting us."

I saw Ulfrid's hand drop to his sword hilt, and I tensed my muscles, prepared to do battle then and there.

"Wait!" Botwolf shouted. Winston gave him a look of encouragement. Botwolf continued: "You have accused two Saxon noblemen of murder. It is your right as well as your obligation to present the evidence to the king, but since you are a fellow Saxon, I ask that you tell us why you are so sure of your conclusion."

I hadn't taken my eyes off Ulfrid. Now I noticed Torold moving to the left. They were going to attack me from two sides. I kept my eyes on Ulfrid and said, "So that we can be killed as soon as my partner finishes speaking."

"I give you my word that you can leave here," Botwolf said, stepping between me and the two brothers. "If you can prove that one of us here is guilty of murder, it is up to that man to clear his own name before the king." Botwolf looked Winston in the eye. "You said it is the murderer you are looking for, is that correct?"

"Yes," Winston said, nodding. "None of the rest of it matters to me." He looked around at the assembled men. "Do you not understand that is why I'm here? If I had any desire to expose the plot, I would have gone straight to the king. But I have my reasons for not caring about the plots and ploys of the nobility."

"And those are?" Botwolf asked, sounding genuinely interested.

"I want peace in this land," Winston said. "Just as Cnut does—"

"As Cnut *says* he does," Torold interrupted.

"As I choose to believe he does," Winston said without raising his voice. "I believe he is honorable. Think about it! Eighty-three thousand pounds of silver are safely in his hands right now. In addition to that he is poised to rule over a rich country, which is his, justly conquered; a country that has bled silver for many years and yet still has not been bled dry. The king knows that peace will make him richer than any other prince in the world. War and conflict, however, will cause this land to continue bleeding, which will cost him dearly. Yes, I believe the king when he says he wants harmony and peace rather than conflict."

The gathered noblemen had listened in silence. Several of them nodded to each other.

"And if peace does prevail," Winston continued, "Saxons, Angles, Jutes, Danes, and Vikings will all thrive. This land and its many peoples have suffered decades of bloodshed. My wish is the same as the king's: peace and harmony. That is why the murderer is my only objective here. The rest of it doesn't matter to me."

Botwolf looked from Ulfrid and Torold to the men seated on the benches. "And you can do that? Provide a reason for the murder that doesn't involve blaming these noblemen for plotting against a harmonious agreement?"

"And I will do so even more happily with the knowledge that the plot faded away, like a wave into the sand," Winston said.

Now they were all staring at him.

"I'm right, aren't I?" Winston said, smiling at Botwolf. "Torold did not reveal any great secret when he claimed that there are more powerful men than us involved. I don't even want to guess at who they might be, but I'm sure that they are close to Cnut. They do not act out openly against the king, because they are confident of victory. Tomorrow all the noblemen in the land will meet, and by then it will be too late. The blow should have been struck while everything was still uncertain. Stepping forward openly to oppose Cnut tomorrow is a task for lunatics. And these 'more powerful men' Torold spoke of know that. Therefore my message, which you will have to accept, is that the power is and will remain in Cnut's hands."

I saw in their eyes that the men knew he was right. And I saw something else: fear. Fear that the revelation of the murderer would bring everything into the light of day. They knew how Cnut thirsted for revenge against those who betrayed or opposed him, and they did not possess Winston's insights into why it was not in the king's own interest for their plot to be revealed.

"That is why," Winston continued, "the murderer is my goal. And there he stands."

Everyone's eyes fell on the two brothers, who stared resolutely back at Winston.

"Osfrid told his guardsman that he was going to speak to a bastard—yes, that's how highly he esteemed you," Winston said, his eyes resting coolly on the two men, "because he'd changed his mind. The person who told me that thought it had to do with a business transaction, but they were mistaken. Osfrid wanted out of the plot."

I could tell from Botwolf's eyes that Winston was right.

"Maybe you all thought the killer would be too honorable to expose you, but you sent the wrong man to ensure Osfrid's silence. You sent a man who had reason to hate Osfrid, a man whose sister Osfrid had allowed to die. Because Osfrid valued an heir more highly than his own wife." Winston's eyes fell on Ulfrid, who was baring his teeth in a wolflike manner. "Ulfrid, you told me yourself that it was lucky for Osfrid that it was a son who had cost your sister her life. For you are a nobleman yourself, and you know that heirs are a nobleman's greatest joy.

"But your sister died in vain," Winston continued. "Osfrid's new wife, Tonild, didn't give him any sons and he gradually became an old man. Tonild said that he had considered the possibility that he might die without a son. A possibility you also considered likely.

"Which would mean that your sister Everild was sacrificed for no reason. Her son was dead, true, but she could have been saved and nothing would have turned out any different for Osfrid. He would have been without a son, but married. Married to your sister Everild, who would still be alive.

"I don't know whether you actually discussed it in such explicit terms," Winston continued, "but I'm quite sure that you're the ones Osfrid met with. You used Osfrid's withdrawal from the plot as an excuse to avenge the death of your sister."

Winston paused. There wasn't a sound in the hall. Not even the brothers' heavy breathing was audible.

"You guaranteed our lives," Winston said, turning to look at Botwolf.

"I gave you my word," Botwolf confirmed. "You may leave freely."

We had made it most of the way to the door when Botwolf's voice stopped us: "And what will you tell the king?"

"That Osfrid was killed as an act of revenge for a wife allowed to bleed to death in her childbed," Winston said.

"Killed by whom?" Botwolf asked.

"Only you know that," Winston said, his lip curling upward. "You were the ones who sent one of these two to speak to Osfrid."

Chapter 35

he king had listened to Winston and asked a few questions, and when the illuminator was done with his account, Cnut turned and nodded to Godskalk. The leader of his housecarls, who had been listening, promptly turned on his heels and disappeared out the door of the Hall. Though the king had not uttered a word, his order had been clear: fetch Ulfrid and Torold.

A silence fell over the room. In addition to Winston and myself were the usual men we were accustomed to seeing around the king: Wulfstan, Thorkell, and Godwin.

Wulfstan's head was bowed as though in prayer. There was no way to know whether his prayers were for the deceased or for his murderer. Godwin's forehead was damp beneath his curly hair. I, too, was sweating in the Hall's stifling heat. Thorkell was pulling his dragon hilt up in its sheath and letting it slide back down.

We waited.

Just as we had waited to see the king. When we had arrived at the Hall in midafternoon, we had been informed that Cnut was busy, so we would have to be patient.

I wasn't convinced that Botwolf's guarantee that we wouldn't be killed would still apply once we were outside the walls of the lodging house. I also had my doubts that everyone who had heard him make that promise felt bound by it. So I had insisted that we should wait in the public square in front of the Hall.

We sat down in the grass by the front wall of the Hall. I drew my sword and laid it over my knees, which caused the guard by the front door of the Hall to look askance at me. With housecarls all around us, my sword at the ready, and a steady stream of noblemen coming and going, I felt relatively safe.

I watched the other men waiting outside. Some were let into the Hall immediately, while others waited patiently. A few were pacing back and forth restlessly in the square. I didn't recognize any of them from the Saxon lodging house.

Baldwin was standing across the square in front of his treasury building with a wooden stave in his hand. Heavily laden carts groaned their way toward him, the oxen snorting as they came to a stop. Guards had formed two lines to create a protected path from the cart to the front door of the building, and sweating men carried heavy sacks, barrels bound with iron bands, and silver bullion down this walkway past Cnut's master of accounts, who tallied the payments and carved a new notch in his staff at regular intervals.

Winston sat next to me, his eyes half closed. I, too, became drowsy in the warm afternoon sun, and straightened up a few times to counteract my desire to take a nap.

"So, you looked beyond the details to see the big picture," I said, turning to him.

He smiled approvingly at me. "You have a good memory. Yes, I guessed at a few of them and took the risk of presenting my hunches as facts."

"I should have seen it, too," I said. I'd been wrestling with this.

"You were blinded by a detail that clouded your view," Winston pointed out. He continued when he saw the puzzled look on my face: "The attack on you. Naturally you were wondering why someone wanted you killed. And that's how it is: If one detail overshadows the others, it becomes hard to see the big picture."

He was right.

"I still don't get it," I admitted.

"No," Winston shook his head soberly. "And now that both assailants have been killed, we'll never get it cleared up. I'm sure those two bastards"—

I smiled despite myself—"will keep quiet. Who knows? Maybe they were trying to scare us off? Perhaps Ulfrid and Torold hired Toste to keep tabs on you and supply them with information about what we were up to, but maybe Toste was simply acting on his own once he recognized you as the man who'd mocked him in that hamlet? Then his companion, the Viking who attacked you while you were eavesdropping on the brothers and Sven, simply wanted to avenge Toste's death?

"We'll have to live with not knowing the truth," Winston said.

There was a loud noise, like that of an oak branch breaking in a strong gust of wind. We looked across the square at the treasury. A cart had collapsed in front of it. The load of silver had been too heavy for the axle. Greedy men rushed toward it, but the guards were faster and they formed a human wall around the cart.

"You know a good deal about the business dealings of kings and noblemen. Not to mention plots," I said circumspectly.

"As I told you earlier, I've spent a lot of time in monasteries and abbeys," Winston said, leaning forward and massaging the small of his back. "Places like that are cesspools of gossip, and nothing preoccupies their residents as much as world events. Abbots, priors, and other church leaders are all noblemen's sons, and they keep close tabs on what's transpiring outside their walls. You'd have to be deaf, blind, and exceedingly dimwitted not to pick up on it. They also drop plenty of hints on what the various noblemen are up to."

One thing had occurred to me.

"Do you think Torold was telling the truth when he claimed that there are more powerful men involved?" I asked.

"Oh yes," Winston replied, smiling wryly. "At least, he and Botwolf believe that to be the case. It's possible that a thane or ealdorman showed some interest in the plot or even that someone like that genuinely wanted to participate. After all, it's not in their best interest to have too strong a king in this country."

"Who do you think it was?" I asked, glancing instinctively over at the guards by the door.

"Who the hell knows?" Winston said. "The way Botwolf got all worked up makes me think it's someone very close to the king."

"Godwin?" I whispered.

"Hardly," Winston shook his head. "Godwin sees Cnut as the ladder he needs to climb."

I leaned over close to Winston's ear and whispered, "Thorkell?"

"He's more likely. As I said before, the good jarl remembers a time when he was the most powerful Viking in England. And he *has* switched sides before, as easily as you change shirts. Not that that happens very often," Winston grinned and pinched his nose.

I was hungry, but didn't dare leave the safety of the open square. So I called over a girl who was walking by and she agreed to go to a tavern and get us some ale and bread. I gave her a quarter of a coin for her troubles when she returned with our fare, and Winston and I dug in.

My full belly and the ale made me even sleepier than before, and I must have nodded off for a bit, because I didn't see or hear the guard approaching. His foot in my side made me sit up with a start. Reaching for my sword, I instinctively rolled to my right to avoid the blow I figured was headed my way.

"Calm down," said the guard. I squinted at him. "The king is waiting for you."

When we stepped into the Hall, only the king's permanent three-man retinue was sitting with him, but Baldwin stood before him with his staff in hand.

"So the heregeld has been paid?" Cnut asked, sprawling in his chair.

"Fifty-five thousand pounds are in safe storage over yonder," Baldwin confirmed. He noted our arrival, but continued impassively: "I've had a message from London that their ten and a half thousand pounds are being stored by the reeve you put in charge of the town. The bishop in Winchester wrote that he has eleven thousand pounds. And finally, I have received letters from Lombardian, French, and English merchants that they will guarantee the last seven thousand pounds."

"Good," the king said, leaning back, satisfied. "The heregeld is paid. Now I can fulfill my end of the deal and meet with the Witenagemot and the Thing." Cnut looked over at us. "Do you have news that will secure you my mercy?"

Winston stepped up to the king and I followed.

Torold and Ulfrid's clothes displayed their rank as well as their wealth as they stood before the king, and their swords hung from their heavy, silver-inlaid belts. Only the four housecarls behind them suggested that they were at risk of not leaving the Hall as free Saxon noblemen.

"My man Winston has presented evidence against you," the king said, his voice stern. "He speaks convincingly of the indications he has found that one of you is a murderer."

I saw Torold eyeing Winston and clutching at his sword hilt. Though he remained calm, his voice was shrill when he spoke. "He's lying."

"He is?" The king looked from Torold to Ulfrid, who both nodded.

"I find him very convincing," Cnut said.

Ulfrid moistened his lips and peered behind the king. I looked to see what he was looking at. Thorkell's face was blank.

"You wanted to avenge your sister," Cnut said, making it sound as though this were the most natural thing in the world.

The brothers exchanged looks and I saw them exhale with relief. But I could have told them that: Winston was a man of his word.

"It is a man's right and obligation to avenge his kin," Ulfrid said and then slid his tongue over his lips again. "But we are not guilty of the charge that has been raised against us."

"You're not?" Cnut said, appearing almost puzzled.

"We evoke the wager of law. We will swear our innocence and find the required number of men to support us," Torold said, speaking so quickly that his words tripped over each other.

The king was obviously going to refuse Torold's request. The evidence against them was so strong that no one would blame him if he declared them guilty on the spot.

I was wrong.

Cnut looked at Wulfstan, who nodded and stated, "Such is the law."

"I know the law," the king's voice cut through the air. His eyes were on the brothers. "Tomorrow you will stand before the Witenagemot and the Thing and swear to your innocence in this case."

Ulfrid and Torold moistened their lips.

Cnut snapped at Godskalk, and he led the accused out of the room.

Cnut looked at Winston and me. "I will see that you two are rewarded tomorrow."

The late spring twilight had settled over the square by the time we stepped outside.

"So that was all for naught," I said. Winston turned and looked at me.

"What do you mean?" he asked.

"The murderer is going to go free," I said. "I bet the noblemen in that lodging house spent the entire afternoon deciding which of them would swear to Torold and Ulfrid's innocence."

Winston nodded. "The murderer will go free, yes. But for naught? At least we won the king's favor." Winston stretched. "And now, Alfilda awaits me."

I stared at his back in astonishment as he walked off toward the inn. Halfway across the square, he turned around and called to me, "Would you do me a favor and check on Atheling?"

Frida had said she was busy, but I thought I would surprise her anyway. She was bound to be free at some point, and I was in no mood to spend the evening in the tavern watching Winston and our hostess cast sheep's eyes at each other. I was not ready to see Alfilda in this new light.

I walked slowly through the camp. Though there was a buzz of activity in and right around the tents, the mood was relatively calm. It was as though the camp itself shared the anticipation of its inhabitants for the next day.

The guard in front of Tonild's tent recognized me and nodded back to me, but shook his head at my inquiry. He had no idea where Frida was.

"Where is she staying?" I asked.

He scratched his scalp and, after thinking about it for a while, decided she was sharing a tent with two other girls over behind the kitchen area.

I headed over there. I heard low voices and laughter coming from a cluster of small, patched tents that were competing for space by the cooking fires, and had to ask four different girls before one finally pointed to a ramshackle tent at the edge of the camp.

When I got there, I heard Frida's voice inside. She was speaking quietly and slowly and I understood that she wasn't alone, but I had no qualms about allowing a coin to buy us some privacy from her tentmates.

I cleared my throat, but nothing happened. So I called her name. It went quiet inside, so I repeated, "Frida!"

"Who is it?" she called.

"Me, Halfdan."

I heard an exclamation of surprise, then the tent flap was flung aside and a broad-shouldered male farmhand stepped out. "What do you want?"

"I have business with Frida," I said, staring at him in surprise.

"Oh you do?" he said, glancing nonchalantly at my sword. "And who are you?"

"Halfdan. And you?"

"Frida's boyfriend," he said.

Over his shoulder I saw Frida's head sticking out from beneath a blanket she had wrapped around herself.

"Do you know him?" the guy asked, turning to her.

"That's him, the guy who save my life yesterday," she said, and then looked at me and shrugged her shoulders apologetically.

"Then I owe him a thank you," he said, sticking out his fist.

I turned around and left. I might as well go check on Atheling.

Chapter 36

've never seen so many people at one time as were gathered that morning in the meadow by the river. The meadow was flat and dry, though presumably it was a mud pit in the winter. A platform had been erected at the edge of the meadow by a grove of trees and was now surrounded by about twenty grim-looking housecarls. Two chairs sat in the middle of the platform, one taller than the other, and another two were positioned off to one side behind them.

A wide area had been cleared around the platform. Beyond that, rows of men radiated outward like the spokes of a wheel. To the left, Englishmen, to the right, Danes and Vikings. Housecarls stood everywhere, evenly spaced five paces apart, and the meadow itself was surrounded by soldiers, whose eyes never lost their focus and whose limbs remained tensed in a state of readiness.

Behind them was row upon row of farmers, servants, peasants, craftsmen, merchants, conmen, and street performers—in short, anyone curious to see how the noblemen of England would get along that day.

Winston and I had been instructed to stand behind the platform. From there we watched as Wulfstan led in a procession of a dozen singing clergymen. Then came Cnut, dressed in bright red and blue and wearing a massive gold crown over his dark blond hair. The sword at his loins gleamed silver, and his belt was heavy with gold. Ealdorman Godwin and Jarl Thorkell followed behind him.

The king sat down. After the song had finished resounding over the meadow, the aging archbishop led a prayer in his high, slightly trembling voice. Then he, Ealdorman Godwin, and Jarl Thorkell stepped over to the king. The archbishop sat down next to him, and Godwin and Thorkell behind him. Then the king looked out over the gathering, which fell silent, like a flock of chickens who've spotted a hawk.

Cnut let the conspicuous silence go on for six heartbeats, then he stood up and began: "Men—Englishmen, Danes, and Vikings—all different peoples, but of the same origin. All compatriots from this day forward. Today we create one country together. Today we forge a unity that will prevail everywhere my power reigns.

"But before that we have an important matter to resolve. A man was murdered recently here in Oxford, a Saxon. Everyone immediately started eyeing each other with suspicion. The Saxons claimed the Danes killed him. The Danes and Vikings thought the Saxons must have done it themselves. And yes, some even dared to say he was murdered on my orders."

The eyes above his hooked nose surveyed the gathering sharply before he continued: "But, men! The law will prevail in this country. That is why I asked knowledgeable men"—he gestured at us with his hand—"to investigate the death, and their labors have borne fruit. They have presented me with compelling evidence that Osfrid the Saxon was murdered as an act of revenge for a woman's death.

"But the law will prevail here," Cnut said, glancing over at Wulfstan. "And the law says that no man is guilty if he is willing to swear to his own innocence along with twelve compurgators, who agree to swear that they believe the defendant. If that occurs, the evidence will be deemed invalid and dead. Step forward, Ulfrid and Torold sons of Beorthold."

It was so quiet as the two brothers stepped forward that a lark could be heard darting over the meadow on the far side of the river. They were dressed as they had been the night before and still carried their swords.

The king eyed them sharply. "You have heard the charge that has been made against you?"

They nodded.

"And what is your response?" the king asked.

Ulfrid answered for both of them: "We bear no guilt in this case, my lord."

"And you will swear to that?" the king asked.

"We will," Ulfrid said.

The king nodded and Torold stepped forward. Whereas Ulfrid had appeared calm as he answered the king's questions, Torold cast an angry glance our way, rocked impatiently on his feet, and fingered the hilt of his sword. It was wise to let him swear first.

Torold turned toward the crowd, raised his right hand to shoulder height, and swore in a loud voice: "To the charge of murder, which has been raised against me, I swear to my innocence."

"Are there men who will swear with Torold Beortholdsøn?" Cnut asked, looking over Torold's shoulder.

Twelve Saxon noblemen stepped forward willingly, all of whom I recognized from the day before. I saw the pride in their faces, but also discerned in their eyes their insecurity over whether Winston had kept his word.

Botwolf took the lead and was the first to swear his oath to Torold's innocence. The others each swore in turn after him.

"Good, Torold," Cnut's voice boomed over the meadow. "You're free and clear of this charge. Take your place among my noblemen."

When Torold had assumed his place with the noblemen, the king looked at Ulfrid, who stepped forward and swore the same oath as his brother.

The king looked briefly at Winston and me, then his voice boomed over the gathering: "Are there men who will swear with Ulfrid Beortholdsøn?"

Not one stepped forward.

I saw profound despair in Ulfrid as he scanned the ranks of his coconspirators.

No one moved. Ulfrid's eyes darted from one to the next in disbelief.

"Ulfrid Beortholdsøn," Cnut's voice cut through the air like a knife through tallow. "Your own people have judged you. Is it true," Cnut turned to Wulfstan, "that Saxon law says that he who commits murder in the king's presence is sentenced to death?"

The archbishop cleared his throat. "It does not please the Lord that we kill each other. A dead man cannot repent his sin."

"Answer my question." Cnut's face was dark with rage.

"Yes," Wulfstan admitted, deflating a little.

"Your life is mine to take, as you heard," Cnut said, causing Ulfrid to cringe. "And this would atone for your earthly guilt. But as the archbishop states, a dead man cannot repent his sin, and it is the Lord's will that sinners should be given the right to repent. Therefore I do not pronounce the sentence that I could." He turned to Wulfstan. "What is the wergeld for a thane?"

"Twelve hundred silver shillings," Wulfstan answered succinctly.

"That is the sum you must pay to Tonild, Osfrid's widow," Cnut announced, his eyes wandering over the rows of Saxon noblemen. "Another man was also killed by you or at your orders, a Saxon soldier. The wergeld for him is two hundred silver shillings."

I noticed that the king didn't need to ask the wergeld price for a soldier.

"You must pay that fine to his wife, who has been left with a child to care for," Cnut announced. The men of the Witenagemot nodded in acknowledgment.

"Surely there are men who will assist you if you cannot raise these sums alone. Thus there is no reason for you not to pay and close this case," the king said. A deathly silence fell upon the crowd as he sat down.

Epilogue

he king was gray from fatigue when he received us that evening. Still, he was smiling. And I understood why.

Cnut had proved that morning not only that he knew how to issue a ruling that was both fair and in accordance with the law, but also that he was willing not to act on knowledge that he had. As a result, the noblemen had willingly agreed that he was the king, one who would reign in accordance with those laws that had been in force up to that point. Wulfstan had been charged with writing a draft of a new set of laws, drawing its provisions from the best of all the preceding laws, but until such time as that was ready, all the noblemen—Danes, Angles, Saxons, and Vikings—had sworn to live under the old laws, which they were familiar with from the time of King Edgar.

Willingly, yes. But it had been a long day, with many words spoken.

"You fulfilled your task and have thoroughly earned my grace," the king said, smiling at us despite his exhaustion.

We bowed.

"But," he continued while the earls fawned, "you can't live off my grace. I promised you a reward. What would you like?"

Winston and I looked at each other. Winston cleared his throat.

"It is not our place to choose our price, my lord."

"If I ask you to, it is," Cnut said, staring at me now.

I knew my answer and wasn't as humble as Winston, as I'd learned that humility never pays.

"I lost my family's estate, my lord."

"You want an estate? To be a nobleman again?" Cnut asked me, his brow furrowed.

I nodded.

"I have enough noblemen," Cnut said, rubbing his chin. "Men who can think and act for me are in much shorter supply." He paused. "No," he finally said, "I am not going to make you a nobleman. I might require your services again. You shall receive a pound of silver each, in addition to my good graces."

Modesty isn't rewarded. Neither, it seems, is an honest request.

About the Author

Bestselling Danish novelist Martin Jensen was born in 1946 into a working class family and worked as teacher and headmaster in Sweden and Denmark before becoming a full-time author in 1996. He and his wife collect mushrooms and fungi, enjoy bird watching, and are botanical enthusiasts. Martin Jensen is the author of twenty-one novels. *The King's Hounds* is his first title to be published in English.

About the Translator

© 2006 by Libby Lewis

Tara Chace has translated more than twenty novels from Norwegian, Swedish, and Danish. Her most recent translations include Martin Jensen's *The King's Hounds*, Camilla Grebe and Åsa Träff's *More Bitter Than Death*, Lene Kaaberbøl and Agnete Friis's *Invisible Murder*, Jo Nesbø's *Doctor Proctor's Fart Powder* series, and Johan Harstad's *172 Hours on the Moon*.

An avid reader and language learner, Chace earned her PhD in Scandinavian Languages and Literature from the University of Washington in 2003. She enjoys translating books for adults and children and lives in Seattle with her family and black lab, Zephyr.